My Big Fat Witch Wedding

WICKED WITCHES OF THE MIDWEST BOOK NINETEEN

AMANDA M. LEE

WINCHESTERSHAW PUBLICATIONS

Copyright © 2021 by Amanda M. Lee

All rights reserved.

No part of this book may be reproduced in any form or by any electronic or mechanical means, including information storage and retrieval systems, without written permission from the author, except for the use of brief quotations in a book review.

❦ Created with Vellum

Prologue

18 YEARS AGO

"It should be outlawed."

My cousin Clove looked up from the book we'd placed on the floor in the center of the room, her eyes shining with unshed tears. She was the sensitive one. Our great-aunt called her a kvetch, but I was starting to think that word could be used for a variety of different insults. The truth revealed to us in the book had clearly shaken Clove.

"Maybe the book is wrong," my other cousin Thistle suggested. She was playing with her blond hair, pulling it up and then dropping it as she regarded her features in the mirror. She'd been making noise of late about cutting it all off. Her mother had so far denied the requests. Knowing my aunt Twila, though, Thistle would wear her down. My cousin was far too edgy for a blunt cut and mousy color. She would eventually get her way.

"I don't think the book is wrong," I countered. It was an old biology textbook we'd found while searching through the boxes of books our mothers designated for donation to an upcoming library sale. They'd told us to load the boxes into the truck. Instead, we'd hunkered down in the storage shed to look through them in an effort to avoid manual labor. Nobody had come looking for us, so it appeared to be working. Still, I was worried. That was normal for me.

As the oldest member of our group, I couldn't stop myself from worrying most days.

"The book could be wrong," Thistle argued. I once heard my mother explain that my youngest cousin was difficult just to be difficult. She was right. Thistle enjoyed being the contrarian in our little group. In fact, that's when she was happiest. This time I couldn't let it go.

"No." I vehemently shook my head, my blond hair flying. Mine was a honey blond compared to Thistle's dark blond, so it was glossy and bright despite the dimness of the shed. "It's a textbook. It even says Walkerville High School on it." I pointed for emphasis. "That means it was taught in high school."

"Bay's right," Clove said, a sniffle escaping. She cried far too much for my tastes, and she used that to manipulate people. But not today. She was legitimately upset today.

"I'm always right," I agreed. "But what am I right about today?"

"You can't teach something in school that isn't true."

"Oh, right." I nodded in agreement. "That is the rule."

"Oh, please." Thistle was having none of it. "We were taught in kindergarten that the Pilgrims and Native Americans had a nice dinner over maize and turkey for Thanksgiving. They conveniently left out the genocide that followed."

I opened my mouth to argue and then shut it. Loath as I was to admit it, she'd brought up a good point.

"But this is biology," I insisted finally. "I mean ... I don't think how babies are made can be fudged."

"I don't care how babies are made," Clove shot back. "I care how they come out. Our mothers told us it was like a miracle. One second the baby was inside and the next it was out."

The look Thistle shot Clove was disdainful. "And you fell for that because …?"

Clove glared at her. "Why would our mothers lie?"

"They always lie when they think something is going to frighten us," Thistle replied, matter-of-fact. "Do you remember when they told us that getting a tooth yanked at the dentist didn't hurt? That was a big, fat lie."

"I've never had a tooth yanked," I replied, not realizing how haughty I sounded until Thistle turned her ire on me. "What? I brush twice a day and I don't eat anywhere near as much candy as you do."

"Thank you, Miss Priss," Thistle drawled. "I can't tell you how much I appreciate when you're the good one and I'm the bad one."

"It's not about being good or bad. I care about my oral health."

"Oh, shut up." Thistle flicked my ear. Hard. "Let's get back to this baby thing." She snagged the textbook from me and held it up. There was a very disturbing drawing on the page. "Now, we all knew the bat story they floated when we were little was bunk. There's no way a magically-trained bat can lift a baby. It's like Santa Claus. That's one of the stories they tell just to shut little kids up."

"Oh, Santa Claus." Clove was mournful as she slapped her hands over her face. "Did you have to bring that up? I'm still sad about Santa Claus. And don't forget the Easter Bunny. I mean ... he was so cute when I saw him at the mall."

Thistle slapped Clove's arm. "Get real. A six-foot-tall bunny? How is that not frightening?" Her gaze was dark when she turned it back to the book. "What's even worse is the Tooth Fairy. How did nobody throughout history put it together that a winged woman coming into your room to steal teeth wasn't freaky?"

She had a way of breaking things down that made me uncomfortable. "Let's stop freaking Clove out," I said. "I want to talk about that." I jabbed my finger at the illustration. "There's no way a baby coming out of that ... location ... doesn't hurt."

"Of course, it hurts." Thistle was incredulous. "Don't you watch television? Whenever there's a birth on television, women are doing that huffing thing. They're all sweaty and screaming they're never going to have sex again. How can you have missed that?"

"Mom said it was a joyous occasion." My response came out shriller than I'd intended. "Why would I assume she was lying?"

"Because they're mothers." Thistle's forehead wrinkled as she glared at the book. "Mothers always lie. Remember when they told us that starting our periods was a monumental day in our lives and we should rejoice? Lying, lying, liars."

Before I could respond, the door to the shed burst open and the relative darkness we'd settled in — one naked bulb hanging down from the ceiling offering illumination — was eradicated by the blinding sun. The silhouette in the doorway was small, not even five feet tall, and even though I couldn't make out her face I knew Aunt Tillie had come to find us.

"Speaking of lying liars," Thistle growled.

"Hello, Mouth," Aunt Tillie drawled as she glanced between our guilty faces. "Your mothers are looking for you."

"Then why didn't they come to find us?" Thistle demanded. "Why did they send you? Oh, I know, they wanted to make sure you were busy and not bothering them."

"Or they wanted the job done right," Aunt Tillie fired back. "I'm an expert at finding misbehaving children. I could do it professionally."

"And here I thought you were going for beauty queen by day and alien hunter at night," I said. "What do you want?" I reached for the book — we didn't need Aunt Tillie knowing what we were up to.

"What do we have here?" Aunt Tillie grabbed the book before I could close it, her eyes going wide when she realized what we were looking at. "Why can't you guys just read dirty romance novels like other girls your age? I know your mothers have a whole box of bodice rippers out here. Read those."

"Oh, no." Thistle grabbed the book back and glared at Aunt Tillie with everything she had. "You're not taking that from us. We know the truth now."

"What's the truth?"

"Babies are not delivered by bats," Clove replied, her lower lip trembling. "They come from ... down there." She pointed to her crotch. "And it hurts. That book talks about stuff ripping ... and blood."

"There's also apparently something called the afterbirth, and it's gross," Thistle added.

"Don't forget the mucous plug," I volunteered, my nose wrinkling.

"Yes, we can't forget the mucous plug," Thistle agreed. "It's like a big ball of snot that accompanies babies into the world."

Rather than deny the charge, Aunt Tillie shook her head. "Why are you fixating on this? You're not even teenagers. You shouldn't worry about this until you're at least sixteen."

"Who says?"

"The law."

"Right." Thistle's eye rolls were the stuff of legends, and this one was not to be missed. "Maybe I'll call Officer Terry and ask him if that's true."

I couldn't stop myself from laughing when I pictured that conversation. Officer Terry Davenport was something of a father figure to us. He helped us build treehouses and listened to us rant about our mothers. He was a wonderful listener and friend. He was not, however, comfortable talking about "female stuff." That's what he called it when running away and telling us to ask our mothers.

"I'm serious." Aunt Tillie's gaze was heavy enough to level buildings, as if she was the Godzilla of witches, and it dragged down my shoulders when it landed on me. "None of you had better be pregnant."

I was horrified at the thought. "You just said we were kids," I reminded her.

"Yes, but you're getting to that age." She worked her jaw. "Do you want to know where babies come from?"

The shift in topic threw me. "Um ... no. Not from you."

"Besides, we already know where babies come from," Thistle snapped. "We're not morons."

"Oh, really, wiseass?" Aunt Tillie and Thistle had a unique relationship. They argued more than anybody else in the house we shared with our mothers. My mother said it was because they were the most alike. Aunt Tillie and Thistle both denied that.

"Really," Thistle confirmed.

"Okay, I'll bite. Where do babies come from?"

"Well, when a mommy and daddy love each other very much," Thistle drawled suggestively.

"They don't have to love each other," I argued. "They just have to do it. People who hate each other can make babies, too."

Aunt Tillie made a face. "What have you been watching on television? I'm appalled."

"Don't worry about it," Thistle fired back. "We don't need a lecture on where babies come from. We've got that covered."

"What do you need a lecture on?"

"We want to know about this." Clove retrieved the textbook from Thistle and held it up. "Our mothers told us that childbirth was a blessed event. They said the Goddess made it so all we know is joy when giving birth. Does this look joyful to you?"

Aunt Tillie took the book again and studied it. "I've never had children," she said. "I can't answer your questions on this."

"You mean you're too afraid to answer our questions," Thistle countered.

Aunt Tillie's narrow-eyed glare would've frozen someone else in place and possibly caused them to pee their pants. Thistle wasn't just anybody.

"I'm not afraid of anything."

"You're afraid to talk to us about this." Thistle was triumphant in her victory. "Oh, I can't wait to tell everybody in town that you're a big wuss who won't talk about childbirth with us."

I caught on to Thistle's ploy. "Yes, and how she told us it was dirty to talk about."

Aunt Tillie shifted her focus between us and let loose a heavy sigh. "Do you really want me to tell you about childbirth?"

It sounded like a challenge coming, but I nodded.

"We do," Thistle agreed. "Because if it's too gross, we've all decided not to have children."

"Not me." Clove was affronted. "I want three girls. I want that magical bat they told us about to bring them. I do not want to go through that." She pointed a shaky finger at the horrifying illustration. The longer the book was open, the more disgusting the illustration seemed to grow.

"Fine." Aunt Tillie planted her hands on her hips. "Here's what you need to know about childbirth. You have to squeeze something the size of a watermelon out of something the size of a lemon. You'll be sweaty. You'll likely poop on the table when pushing. You'll scream and hate your life. And, when all of that is done, you'll get a seven-pound screaming poop factory to take care of as your reward."

Clove's mouth dropped open. "That doesn't sound like a miracle."

"It's not," Aunt Tillie said. "It's horrible, and only two of you will be able to survive giving birth."

I jerked up my head. Aunt Tillie was a powerful witch. I'd never known her to be able to see the future, but she sounded sure of what she was saying. "One of us is going to die in childbirth?"

"No, I said only two of you will be able to survive the scenario I've just laid out. I'll leave you three to fight it out as to who won't be able to survive." She shut the book and added it to the pile. "You are too young to worry about this. I'm serious about the bodice rippers. They're much more fun to read."

"We're truth seekers," Thistle replied. "We like to have all the facts."

"You're out here hiding from your mothers because you don't want to get sweaty moving the boxes to the truck." Aunt Tillie smirked. "I like your ingenuity. This, however, is not what you should be focusing on. You're young. Stop freaking each other out with horror stories."

"Zombies would be cooler than babies," Thistle muttered.

Aunt Tillie bobbed her head in agreement. "Totally. I'm prepared for the zombie apocalypse. I am not prepared for you guys to have kids. You're a long way from that."

"It'll happen eventually," Clove pressed.

"Don't be so sure about that." Thistle was paler than normal. "That whole pooping thing has put me off kids forever."

Aunt Tillie snorted. "I'll give you one more truth about childbirth." She leaned forward, as if she was imparting some great secret monumental in scope. "When it comes time, it's going to hurt. But you'll forget that.

"You'll forget the tears and threats," she continued. "You'll forget the pooping."

"I'll never forget the pooping," Thistle said darkly. "No kid is worth that."

Aunt Tillie ignored her. "Childbirth is designed to put you through hell. But you'll forget because you'll get a little witch out of it."

"You just told us that little witches scream and yell," Thistle reminded her. "They're poop factories, too. There's a lot of poop in this supposed miracle."

Aunt Tillie laughed. "There is, but baby witches turn into toddler witches. They're very annoying. Toddler witches turn into little girl witches, and they can be fun. Then they keep growing and growing until they're actual little people. And then do you know what happens?"

"You can use the little witches to torture your enemies," I answered, thinking of Mrs. Little and the yellow snow we made for her yard every winter.

Aunt Tillie snapped her finger and jabbed it at me. "Exactly. Women have gone through this for centuries. They don't stop. There's a reason. You guys will figure that out on your own."

"What if we don't?" Thistle demanded. "What if we decide little witches are too much work?"

"Then you'll be just like me." Aunt Tillie's smile was benign.

"Oh, that's a horrible threat," Thistle complained. "Either we poop in front of people or end up like you. How is that a choice?"

Aunt Tillie shrugged. "You'll figure it out eventually. It's not something to worry about today."

"I guess that means you want us to carry the boxes out to the truck," I said, resigned.

"Or I was thinking we could go into town for ice cream. On the way, we could stop by Margaret's house. I have a new spell I want to try out."

"Is it mean?" Thistle asked.

Aunt Tillie nodded.

"I'm in." Thistle pushed the discarded books away and stood. "I'm with Clove. Babies are crazy. The whole process should be outlawed."

"Definitely," I agreed.

Aunt Tillie chuckled. "Something tells me you guys will change your minds eventually."

"Not me." Clove was adamant. "I'm holding out for the bat."

"Bold words." Tillie patted her shoulder. "I look forward to reminding you of this conversation when it's baby time."

"I won't change my mind." Clove stubbornly jutted out her lower lip. "There's only so much a person can take."

CHAPTER
One

PRESENT DAY

"This is the worst thing that has ever happened to anyone ever in the history of our world," Clove announced as she watched her husband Sam Cornell carry suitcases into our mothers' inn. "The absolute worst."

"I'm pretty sure Holocaust survivors would disagree," Thistle countered from her spot on top of the check-in desk. She'd planted herself there with a pint of Phish Food ice cream to watch the show.

"Shut up." Clove, normally the amiable one of our little trio, glared so hard at Thistle I thought her eyes might pop out. "I will kill you if you don't shut up."

Thistle's response was to take another heaping spoonful of ice cream and shove it in her mouth. Her hair was a pretty lavender this week — she said she wanted it to match her bridesmaid dress — and I found the color appropriate to her features. The blues she often chose were too icy. The lavender, however, made her face sparkle.

"I think the witches persecuted in Salem might have something to say about it too," my mother added as she watched Sam struggle with the suitcases. "Do you need help?"

Sam shook his head. "I've got it." Even as he said it, he almost tripped. Four suitcases — two on rollers — was too much for one man to handle, especially one as frazzled as Sam. "I've totally got it."

"Right." Mom let loose her patented sigh, the one that said, "I'm surrounded by idiots," and opened her mouth to yell. I was already cringing before she let it loose. "Landon! Terry!" Her voice carried under normal circumstances. When she wanted it to echo throughout the inn, however, it was like something straight out of a horror movie. One with dolls that come to life to kill people.

In a matter of seconds, my fiancé Landon Michaels arrived with my mother's boyfriend Terry Davenport. They'd been in the dining room, presumably reviewing files, even though I knew they were really stuffing their faces with pastries. They guiltily glanced around the lobby.

"What did we do now?" Landon asked.

Mom glared at him. "You have powdered sugar on your face."

Landon automatically swiped.

"Sam needs help getting the suitcases upstairs."

"I guess that means we're helping." Landon moved toward the suitcases without further prodding, his eyebrows drawing together when he saw how much luggage Sam grappled with. "Are you guys moving in?"

Clove, wider than she was tall these days, rested both of her hands on her huge baby belly and glared at him. "Where have you been?" Her tones hadn't been dulcet in months, and I swore she was becoming shriller with each passing day. "That's why we're all here. Our mothers are making me move in. They refuse to let me stay at my own home. They're making us move in here until the baby is born."

Clove's opinion on the subject was obvious.

"I knew that." Landon feigned patience. He didn't like being yelled at. "I thought it was a temporary move."

"It is," Clove snapped. "The second the baby arrives we're going back to the Dandridge, where I can do what I want when I want, and nobody can tell me differently." Her eyes were slits of hate when they landed on my mother.

Winnie Winchester was many things, including graceful under pressure and sympathetic when need be. None of that was on display today. No, my mother had decided she was in charge. She didn't care that Clove was past her due date and uncomfortable. She cared only that arrangements be carried out her way. "Would you like me to explain it to you again?" she gritted out.

Clove sniffed and looked away. "Everybody is so mean to me. I'm about to bring forth human life — I mean, if this baby ever decides to make an appearance — and everybody who is supposed to love me is being mean." She threw herself on the antique settee against the far wall. "Nobody has suffered like me."

I pressed my lips together in an effort not to laugh and turned my eyes to the grandfather clock. This day already felt way too long, but we were barely past breakfast.

Mom pretended she hadn't heard the outburst. "You're here because you're about to give birth to a baby that will be magical in origin. Not only are you a witch, Sam has witch in his blood. Your baby could be born under ... *different* ... circumstances."

"She means it could come out looking like a demon," Thistle offered helpfully.

Mom pinned Thistle with a look so dark I was surprised to find the sun was still shining. "I'll choke you with that spoon," she warned.

I decided to play peacemaker, but only because Clove's midwife was due to arrive at any moment and I figured a knock-down fight would make us look bad. "Everybody needs to take a breath," I started.

Mom's eyes were lasers. "That spoon can be used to choke more than one person."

Landon cleared his throat as he grabbed one of the suitcases from Sam. "Bay, sweetie, why don't you help me with the suitcases?"

I wasn't fond of manual labor, but the temperature in the room bordered on boiling and I needed a break from my mother ... and Clove's mother ... and Thistle's mother. Heck, I needed a break from Clove, too. The only one making sense today was Thistle, and that was always a bad realization. It's like identifying with the Joker instead of Batman.

"Sure." I smiled and skirted around my mother. I hadn't taken two steps before Mom's hand shot out and grabbed the collar of my shirt. She hauled me back without uttering a single sound.

"I assigned that task to Landon and Terry," she reminded me.

Chief Terry, who had known us for decades but had only recently started staying at the inn when he and my mother decided to give dating a shot, blinked several times in rapid succession. "And we're looking forward to helping," he said.

"Totally," Landon agreed. He was less fearful of my mother, which only proved his survival instincts were poor. That wasn't a good trait for an FBI agent, as far as I was concerned. "I just want to warn you that I want my bride in one piece for the wedding, which is in a few days." His tone was pointed. "I also want her happy, so as much as everybody is worried about Clove and her baby, this is Bay's week too."

His vehemence caught me off guard and I immediately started shaking my head. "It's okay, Landon," I reassured him. He worried constantly these days. He was convinced something terrible would derail our wedding. "Everything is going to be okay."

"I don't want things to just be okay," he insisted. "I want your week to be perfect. I want you to be the center of attention. You've earned it."

"What about me?" Clove asked pathetically. "I'm about to create human life out of thin air."

Landon glared at her. "You were due a week ago. You should've already had your day."

"Everybody is just so mean," Clove lamented, fat tears rolling down her cheeks. "I'm doing the best that I can."

When Mom spoke again, her tone was lighter. "Landon, Bay will have her moment in the sun. I promise you that. I won't let her be shoved to the side by Clove's theatrics."

Landon studied her face for a moment before nodding. "We'll take the suitcases upstairs."

"Thank you." Mom smiled at the men's retreating backs. When she returned her attention to Clove, an emotion I couldn't identify lurked in her eyes. "As for you ... ."

"Here we go," Thistle said gleefully as she shifted on the counter. "Let her have it, Aunt Winnie."

Mom pretended she hadn't heard Thistle and instead folded her arms across her chest as she regarded Clove. "You're not the first woman in history to give birth. You're not being tortured. You're not being mistreated. You're here because Sam is afraid to leave your side for five minutes in case you go into labor.

"Although lovely as a home, the Dandridge is on the outskirts of town and you have spotty cell reception," she continued. "We need you close so we can help when the baby decides to arrive. Your midwife will be here any moment. She will help us make sure you have a lovely environment for the birth.

"We're doting on you, fixing all your meals, and making sure you have someone to boss around twenty-four hours a day. We're doing all of this while planning Bay's wedding, something that she's allowed to treat as a big deal despite the fact that you think the world should revolve around you, Clove. So, I'm going to say it again, you're fine."

One look at Clove told me things were about to get ugly. Her eyes were glassy, her lower lip trembled and the hands gripping her huge stomach boasted white knuckles because she was holding on so tight. Sure enough, she burst into tears.

"My life is the worst," she wailed as the tears began rolling freely.

"Oh, good grief." Mom threw her hands in the air and stomped away from Clove. "Get it together, Clove. You're about to have a baby. You can no longer spend your life being a baby."

"Word," Thistle intoned, earning a harsh glare from me. "What? I've been dealing with this crap for months. I swear Clove has the gestation period of an elephant. I can't deal with another second of this crap. It's too freaking much."

Before I could explain how we were nowhere near done, the front door of the inn blew open with the force of a gale wind ... but there was nobody on the other side. When I was done pushing my hair out of my face, I stared at the empty threshold with open-eyed confusion ... and then a woman appeared.

She was small — Aunt Tillie small. If she managed to cross the five-foot mark it was only by a fraction of an inch. She wore a black ankle-length dress that fit her like a potato sack — no tapered waist — and her gray hair was pulled back in a severe bun. Her features were hardly pleasing. I'm not saying she was ugly, but her face was all hard angles and sharp planes, with a pair of glittering glasses perched on the end of a narrow-tipped nose. All I could think of was an evil governess from a children's story.

"You must be Minerva Prince." Mom abandoned her assault on Clove and focused on the newcomer, wiping her hands on her apron before extending one to the woman. "Holly with the Bay City coven said you come highly recommended."

Minerva stared at Mom's hand for a moment and then surveyed all the faces in the room. She lingered on Thistle the longest, her upper lip curving into a sneer. Finally, she focused her full attention on Clove. "I am your midwife." She said it like Darth Vader informing Luke that he was his father.

The tears Clove had been shedding moments before dried in an instant, replaced by a look of horror that she shared with me. I didn't blame her. Minerva was clearly not fun and frothy. Still, my survival instincts were fully intact. Better Clove than me. That's the mantra I kept repeating in my head.

"Suitcases are deposited," Landon announced as he returned with Chief Terry. "Sam is going to unpack them. He says it has to be done in a certain way or Clove will cry." He pulled up short when he saw Minerva. "Oh, I'm sorry. I didn't realize guests were checking in today." He looked more alarmed than apologetic.

"This is Minerva Prince," I explained. "She's Clove's midwife."

"And not an extra in a horror movie," Thistle added, shrinking back when my mother glared at her yet again. "What? You know, the people in this family used to have a sense of humor. I don't understand why that's no longer a thing."

"Probably because you're not funny." Mom made shooing motions to get Thistle to jump down from the counter. "Don't you have somewhere to be?"

"I'm with my family," Thistle replied. "I believe I was ordered to be here for Clove because she was fighting the big move. There are ten different places I would rather be."

She wasn't the only one. "We do have work to do," I said, avoiding Clove's accusatory gaze. It was clear she was going to have a long afternoon with Minerva. "We can get out of your way now that the midwife is here. I'm sure she wants to spend time with Clove."

"Actually, I would like to spend time with all of you." Minerva ignored her medium-sized rolling suitcase and pulled a clipboard from the side pocket of her crossbody bag. "I need to get a feeling for Clove's specific needs before the birth. Who is her birthing coach?" Minerva's eyes drifted over Chief Terry before landing on Landon. "I assume it's you."

Landon balked. "No way. I'm not being in the room when that baby comes."

Minerva's mouth flattened into a thin line of displeasure.

"He's not the baby's father," Mom explained. "Sam — that's Clove's husband — is upstairs getting their room in order. As I explained via email, Sam and Clove live in a lighthouse too far away for our comfort level, so they'll be staying in The Overlook until the baby is born. It just makes things easier. They arrived a few minutes before you."

"I see." Minerva had all the warmth of a snowman on a subzero day as she studied her clipboard. "So, you're the grandmother. That would make you Marnie."

Mom's lips quirked. She hated being mistaken for one of her sisters. "No, as I said when you came in, I'm Winnie. I'm Clove's aunt. Bay is my daughter." She gestured to me. "Landon is with Bay."

"Right. Right." Minerva bobbed her head. "You two are getting married." She jerked her index finger between the two of us.

"Yes, and I'm looking forward to it." Landon beamed at her, his notorious streak of charm on full display. "No man has ever loved a woman as much as I love Bay. I'm going to be the best husband."

Minerva blinked. "Perhaps you should have that embroidered on a pillow." She went back to looking at her clipboard as Landon's expression became a glare. "You would be Thistle, correct?" She focused on the witch in question.

"Yes," Thistle agreed. "But you don't want me hanging around. I have a bad attitude and will make Clove cry for reasons other than her stretching loins. The baby will be born with a sarcastic soul, and I've been told that's not a good thing."

I stared in open-mouthed wonder as Minerva nodded.

"At least you're aware of your limitations," the midwife said.

Thistle shot me a triumphant look. For once, her bad attitude was paying dividends. "I'm totally aware of my limitations. In fact, I need to head to town. I'm already late opening the store."

Sensing an opening, I stepped forward too. "I have to get to work as well. We'll leave you in the fine hands of our mothers, Minerva. We're certain they'll be able to cater to your every need. They are earth witches, after all." Minerva struck me as a stickler for rules, so I played a hunch, and it paid off.

"Yes, yes." She bobbed her head. "Earth witches are the nurturing sort. That will be fine."

I smiled at my mother, who glowered at me, and then gestured for Landon. "Do you want to follow me into town or ride together?"

Chief Terry answered before Landon could respond. "You two can drive together and I'll follow you. I'm expecting a quiet day, so Landon and I can suffer through sharing a vehicle."

"Awesome." I waved at Minerva, but her scowl had me dropping my hand. "Um ... good luck, Clove."

Pathetic as always, Clove glared at me. "So, so mean."

"Have fun." Thistle's parting shot was bright. "I can't wait to see how Aunt Tillie gets along with our new guest. That's going to be the dinner theater to end all dinner theater."

Mom's expression changed in an instant. "Where is Aunt Tillie?"

I shrugged. "I have no idea. She's an adult. She can take care of herself."

"Yes, I'm sure she won't cause trouble so close to the wedding and the birth," Thistle drawled. "She's a caring soul. She would never start something we have to finish when we have so much else to deal with."

I let loose a glare. "Let's not go borrowing trouble."

"Yeah, I'll leave that to Aunt Tillie."

And just like that, we abandoned Clove to her fate and escaped through the front door. I waited until we were in the parking lot to speak again.

"That woman is going to traumatize the baby."

Thistle nodded. "And Clove. You realize we're never going to hear the end of this."

I'd already come to the same conclusion.

CHAPTER
Two

I parked in front of The Whistler and met Landon in front of my car.

"Just think, in a few days I won't be dropping off my fiancé to play with his law enforcement buddies any longer," I teased as I leaned in for a kiss. "I'll be dropping off my husband."

He wrapped his arms around me and held tight. "In a few days we're escaping from your family and going on our honeymoon. Two weeks, just you and me." He kissed me hard enough I was breathless when he pulled back.

"That's my favorite combination," I said on a whispery exhale.

He flicked his eyes to my empty newspaper office. "You know, it's a quiet morning. You don't have to put this week's edition to bed until the day before the wedding. How about we play hooky and hide in your office all day? Now that you've got that couch in there, we can be comfortable."

It was a tempting offer. "I ... ."

He pressed his finger to my lips. "Before you say no, just remember that we can lock the door and set the security system. We can be naked all day, sweetheart. We can lose ourselves in each other and forget your family."

That was a running theme in his commentary these days. "I know they're being difficult." Apologizing for my family taking over our lives shouldn't be necessary, but I couldn't help myself. "I'm sorry that you feel Clove is getting all the attention."

He let loose an exasperated sigh and dragged a hand through his hair. He'd gotten it cut two weeks ago because he insisted his hair looked its best two weeks out and he wanted to be at his best for the wedding photos. I found it adorable.

"Bay, I don't want you apologizing." He was firm. "This isn't your fault."

"It's not your fault either," I reminded him. "Nobody could've guessed when we set the date of the wedding that Clove would go so far past her due date. Our wedding will be great even if she goes into labor during the ceremony."

His eyes filled with horror. "You don't think that's going to happen?"

Two weeks earlier I would've said no. Now I wasn't so sure. "This is about you and me." I grabbed his hands and gave them a hard squeeze. "What happens with everybody else is secondary."

He didn't look thrilled with my answer. "I want you to be the center of attention ... and me by extension."

That made me smile. "It's going to be a beautiful wedding. I promise." I leaned in for another hug. "As for playing hooky, I really can't. I'm covering the opening of that new magic store and the sooner I get the story written and laid out on the page, the quicker I'll be done with work this week and be able to focus on you."

"Oh, see, you've hit me in the feels." He grinned as he lifted me off the ground for another kiss. He looked reluctant when he released me. "I get it. I have reports to file, too. Just ... be safe."

"Nothing is happening around town," I reminded him. "We have a clear window for the wedding."

"Now you've jinxed us. Whenever you say something like that, bad magic hits town and the next thing I know you're commanding ghosts and sending them into battle."

"We'll be fine," I said. "Nothing will ruin our day."

His fingers were light as they brushed my hair from my face.

"Nothing will ruin our lives," he promised. "I need you to know that I've never wanted anything as much as I want to make you happy."

"I am happy. Even if Minerva sucks all the fun out of Clove, you and I will still be happy."

"Now you're talking."

AFTER DROPPING MY PURSE AND COAT in my office and checking emails and voicemails, I grabbed a notebook and headed out. The new magic shop, called The Charmed Cornucopia, had gone up fast. The space had only been vacated by the local potions purveyor three weeks ago. In short order, a new shop owner took over the space and spent two weeks with sheets hanging over the windows so the setup could be completed in secrecy. Today was the big opening and I was curious ... and maybe a little nervous. Clove and Thistle owned the premier magic shop in town, Hypnotic, and the new location was only one block away.

"Isn't this exciting?" Mrs. Gunderson, the owner of the bakery, asked, her eyes sparkling as she handed me a takeout cup of coffee and inclined her head toward the line outside the new shop.

"It's always fun when we have a new shop," I replied. "It's good for the town."

Mrs. Gunderson snorted. "That was a very diplomatic answer."

"It's the truth." I meant it. "Hemlock Cove can sustain multiple magic shops."

"Yes, but this one is even bigger than Hypnotic. I'm dying to know what they've done with the space inside."

She wasn't the only one. "I'll take lots of photos."

"Good. I love when a new store opens in town. You can practically feel the buzz up and down Main Street."

She was right. "I'm heading over now. Wish me luck."

"Good luck. Oh, and Bay, congratulations on the wedding." Her smile was kind. "You two have been through a lot. It must feel like a miracle that the day is almost here."

"It does." I went warm all over at the thought of marrying Landon. "Now we just have to get through the ceremony without Clove going into labor. If she steals Landon's thunder on the wedding day, he really will never get over it."

Mrs. Gunderson's eyes widened. "There's still no baby?"

I shook my head. "No, and everybody is starting to get antsy. Honestly, if I could get the call that she's gone into labor this afternoon I'd be thrilled."

"I don't blame you. Good luck anyway."

"Thank you." I saluted her with the coffee and headed back out to the street. There was indeed a line in front of the store. I took a few minutes to get quotes from excited shoppers and then watched as the sheets were dropped in tandem. Applause rippled through the people who had gathered on the sidewalk and then the door was thrown open in dramatic fashion.

The woman who appeared in the opening was tall, a bright smile gracing her pretty face. She had one of those willowy bodies that would've been at home on a fashion runaway, and her dress showed off her impressive figure to perfection. It almost made me feel guilty for having two doughnuts along with my omelet at breakfast.

"My name is Kristen Donaldson." She beamed at those who had assembled outside her store. "I'm from Salem." She paused dramatically, as if expecting a reaction. "That's Salem, Massachusetts."

This time she garnered a smattering of applause, but nobody seemed all that excited. It clearly threw her off her game.

"Well, I have a lot of stories to tell," she said as she gestured toward the store. "Come in. Look around. I'm looking forward to meeting each and every one of you." Her eyes landed on me when she said the last word bit. "Welcome to the Charmed Cornucopia."

I stood back and allowed the excited shoppers entrance first. I didn't want to infringe on Kristen's retail buzz. I was the last through the door and smiled when the familiar scents of lavender and basil hit my nose.

"Isn't it nice?" a voice said at my left, causing me to jolt. I found Kristen standing next to me. She was watching me ... and she seemed curious.

"It is nice," I confirmed, pulling myself together. My nerves were shot thanks to the approaching wedding. Landon was so convinced something would derail the ceremony that he'd almost convinced me it was inevitable. "I love the smell of lavender."

"Me too." She looked me up and down. "Aren't you Bay Winchester?"

"Yes. Have we met?"

"Oh, no." She shook her head and let loose a gay little twitter. "Some of the other store owners pointed you out. They said I should run ads in your newspaper."

"That's a smart idea," I agreed. "The tourists like to buy multiple editions for souvenirs. You don't need to do it next week, though. I figured I would do a story on your place and that will serve as free advertising."

Untethered pleasure washed over Kristen's features. "That sounds lovely. Will you run photos too?"

"Definitely." I nodded. "I'll take some today but I'll also send a photographer later in the week so he can get multiple shots. I'd like to say my photos are as good as his, but I don't have quite the eye he does."

"Send him anytime. I'll be here."

"Awesome." I turned my attention to the bookshelf on the east wall of the store. Some of the books were of the mass market variety. Llewelyn was stamped on half of them. Others looked like antiques. I withdrew one for a better look. "This looks ... old." Initially I was going to say "authentic," but caught myself at the last moment.

"It came from Salem." Kristen's smile never left her face. It seemed to be stuck there. I told myself that wasn't suspicious — the last new store owner in town had turned out to be an evil witch bent on murder — but I'd never found myself comfortable around overly cheerful individuals.

"Were you born in Salem?" I kept my expression neutral as I flipped through the book.

"I was. My mother is a seer. She owns one of the oldest magic shops in Salem."

"A seer, huh?" It was hard to wrap my head around the word. Kristen said all the right things, positioned herself as an expert, and yet she didn't feel like the real deal. She was running a hard sell on me, and that always felt like good business rather than responsible magic.

"Yes, she could divine the truth of a life with one touch."

"Palmistry work."

Kristen's eyes sparkled. "You know your craft."

"I know a thing or two about witches," I agreed. "The town is full of them."

"The town is delightful," Kristen said. "It's ... magical. I could feel the veil of power the moment I crossed the town line and slipped under it."

What a crock of crap. It took everything I had not to burst out laughing. Kristen might've been enthusiastic, but she didn't understand about real magic. Despite the books, I was almost certain she wasn't the real deal. That was a relief, and not just because the wedding was so close. If she turned out to be a danger, even a month down the road, we would have to deal with her. If she was just a store owner lying about her craft knowledge, we could ignore her.

"I love the veil," I agreed, returning the book to the shelf. It was the real deal. If someone with actual magic at their disposal attempted to cast a spell, it would work. Thankfully, most of the town's residents only played at being witches. My family knew better than to dabble with old books we didn't know the origins of.

"I hear you're getting married." Kristen threw out the statement as if expecting me to go giddy and weak at the knees. "How exciting!"

"I'm excited." I was, but not nearly as excited about the ceremony as Landon. I wanted the marriage. I wanted him. The wedding was just a fancy party. "In a few days we'll be on our honeymoon. I'll have your story placed on the page for the newspaper long before we leave. Nothing to worry about."

"Oh, I'm not worried." Kristen had yet to let her smile slip, and I found it disturbing. Even clowns didn't smile as much as she did. "I hear you snagged the last eligible bachelor in town who has good job prospects."

I hesitated. That was a weird thing to say. "Um ... ."

She laughed at my discomfort. "Margaret Little gave me an earful about you."

Why wasn't I surprised? "I'm sure she did. Don't worry, no matter what she said, I'm not evil."

"You don't seem evil."

"I'm not. Mrs. Little, on the other hand ... ."

"Oh, I think she's lovely." Kristen gushed. "She's the reason I have my store. If she hadn't started that grant program for new businesses, I would still be toiling away in my mother's store in Salem.

"I mean ... I love my mother," she continued, barely taking a breath, "but I want something of my own. When I heard what Mrs. Little was doing in Hemlock Cove, I jumped at the chance."

My heart skipped. "Mrs. Little owns your store?"

"She leased me the space in the building," Kristen said. "I'm basically renting to own. She made me quite the deal to come to town. She said she wanted the real deal. Only authentic witches from Salem could apply. The opportunity fell into my lap at the right time, because I was finally coming to the conclusion that my mother was never going to retire. If I wanted to do something on my own, I needed to leave Salem."

I pressed my lips together and forced a smile I didn't feel. "Well, that's ... great." It sounded anything but great. Mrs. Little was up to something. Still, I reminded myself that Kristen couldn't possibly be privy to Mrs. Little's true motivations. "So, how about you give me a tour? I'll ask you questions as we go and then call you later in the week when I'm putting together the story if I need more information."

"Great. I'm looking forward to the interview."

I smiled, but the only thing I was looking forward to getting was the skinny on Mrs. Little's involvement. I had no doubt she was trying to stir up trouble. What had she planned this time?

I SPENT AN HOUR WITH KRISTEN. I felt her out about a multitude of things. There was nothing suspicious about her. She was open, seemed honest, and was so excited about being in the newspaper it bordered on adorable.

I was still annoyed when I left. That anger wasn't directed at her. No, it was for Mrs. Little.

I wasn't surprised when I left the store and found the woman in question — she of the porcelain unicorn glory — standing on the street corner with one of her gossipy cohorts. They had their heads bent together, talking. That didn't stop me from marching over and interrupting them.

"I didn't realize you were running a grant program." I managed a smile, but it was more feral than friendly. "That's so altruistic of you."

Mrs. Little's smile was predatory. "I wondered if you would find out about that before your honeymoon. I figured there was a chance you would shirk your duties this week — a wedding is a big deal, after all — but I guess you're being diligent until the end."

"You don't sound happy about that," I replied.

"I'm always happy when someone does their job." She flipped a smile toward her friend. "I'll see you later, Bernice." It was a dismissal, flat and simple. She waited until we were alone to speak again. "I thought Hemlock Cove could use some new storefronts. I believe Hypnotic has been allowed to garner a foothold that might not be deserved."

She wasn't sly. She wanted to be, but she wasn't. Her motivations were all over her face. "You brought in Kristen Donaldson because you want to put Hypnotic out of business," I said. "Do you really think that's going to work?"

"Who said I wanted to put Hypnotic out of business?" She was the picture of innocence. Someone who didn't know her might actually fall for it, but I knew better.

"People go to Hypnotic because they like the ambiance," I said. "Clove and Thistle are good at their jobs. You're not going to force them out of business simply because you brought in another store."

"I brought in a store owner from Salem."

I waited for her to continue. When she didn't, I held out my hands. "So?"

"She's an authentic witch."

That's when things clicked into place, and I couldn't hold back my laugh. "Oh, you poor, deluded soul." I made a tsking sound with my tongue. "Not all the witches living in Salem are the real deal. Some are just really good actresses."

"Not my witch," Mrs. Little insisted. "I talked to her and know her mother is a seer."

"Okay, well, good luck with that." I patted her shoulder and then frowned as I stepped away, the wail of a siren filling my ears. I saw a fire truck tearing down the main drag. In a town the size of Hemlock Cove, fires were rare. The truck hardly left the garage that served as a fire station. "What's going on?"

Mrs. Gunderson, who had raced out of the bakery at the sound, said, "Somebody says there's something going on at the high school." Her face was ashen. "It's bad. Somebody might have a gun."

My heart dropped to my stomach. There were more important things than sparring with Mrs. Little, and apparently one of them was playing out at the high school. "Are you sure?"

Mrs. Gunderson continued staring after the fire truck. "That's what somebody said."

I would get the proof myself. "Thanks for the tip." I shot one more glare at Mrs. Little. "You should know that this won't work. The fact that you think it will makes you the saddest person in town."

"I know exactly what I'm doing."

"Yeah, you keep telling yourself that."

CHAPTER
Three

I walked – speed walked is more accurate — to the high school. When I arrived, I found absolute chaos.

"What the ...?"

My heart lodged in my throat when two girls raced through the front door, screaming as if they were extras in a monster movie. For a moment I stood frozen ... and then my instincts took over and I intercepted them. "What's wrong?" People were streaming from the building and heading for the cover of the trees.

"Let me go!"

I recognized the girl I'd corralled as Daisy Hawkins. Her parents had lived in Hemlock Cove for as long as I could remember. They were older than me by a good bit but younger than my mother. I knew them to be friendly at the various festivals we hosted in town, the sort who embraced Hemlock Cove's witch cover with gusto. Daisy seemed a normal teenager — cliquey with her friends and viewing anyone over the age of twenty as ancient.

"What's wrong?" I demanded, refusing to let Daisy escape my grip. The girl with her looked familiar, but I didn't know her name. She was the one who spoke.

"It's Granger. He's got a gun."

I thought my heart might explode. "What?" That couldn't be right.

I knew about school shootings, of course. They were all over the news. Whenever one happened, I thought my heart might break for the students, their parents, the teachers who would forever be scarred. This sort of thing didn't happen in Hemlock Cove. We were a small community, tight knit. She had to be mistaken.

"Granger who?" I searched my memory, forcing myself to remain calm even though I wanted to run screaming into the woods with everybody else.

"Granger Montgomery," the girl I couldn't place replied. "He's going to kill us all."

"Montgomery?" We had a few Montgomerys in town. "Caleb Montgomery's son?" Caleb worked at the lumberyard between Hemlock Cove and Shadow Hills. I knew him, though not well.

The look Daisy shot me was incredulous. "Does it matter?" This time when she pulled away she cocked her hand, as if to slap me. "You can't keep us here."

I held up my hands. "Run," I instructed, moving away from her. I glanced over my shoulder, searching for someone to take charge of the scene. The fire truck had set up shop at the end of the parking lot and some of the students had grouped around it. Otherwise, there was nobody to be found.

My hand shook as I pulled my phone from my pocket. Landon was the first name on my contact list. He picked up on the first ring.

"Have you rethought my hooky idea?" he asked by way of greeting.

"There's a boy with a gun at the high school." My voice was wooden. "The kids are escaping, but he's inside. One of the girls I talked to said his name is Granger Montgomery."

All mirth escaped Landon's tone. "Don't go in that school, Bay. We're on our way." I could hear Landon — and likely Chief Terry — scrambling in the background.

I understood his fear. "He could be shooting kids."

"Do you hear gunshots?"

"No, but ... ."

"Don't you dare go into that school!" His voice was a roar.

"I have to. But I won't go alone."

"Bay!"

"I can't do nothing." I pulled the phone away from my face to end the call and then thought better of it. "I love you," I said. "I know we're going to have a big fight when I see you again, but ... I can't do nothing."

"Bay, please don't." His voice cracked. "It's our job to deal with this."

"I love you."

His voice was a tinny echo when I moved to disconnect but I heard his words clearly. "I love you but I'm going to kill you, Bay!"

I had the foresight to turn my phone to silent before shoving it in my pocket. Landon would call — and call and call and call — until I picked up. I couldn't risk the phone dinging and alerting a gunman to my presence. I started across the lawn. The stream of students out of the building had slowed.

"Come." My voice was a commanding demand. I didn't look up when I felt the ghosts flood in to flank me. Viola, The Whistler's resident ghost, was one of them.

"What's happening?" she asked, confused. She hated when I summoned her but seemed to understand that something big was happening. Perhaps she could pick up on my emotions. She hadn't been overly observant in life. It was possible she was growing in death. I didn't have time to think about that too much. I had bigger problems.

"There's a boy with a gun in the school," I replied in a low voice. "I don't know if anybody is shot. I don't know if he plans to hurt others or himself. I only know he's in there and I need you to find him."

Viola opened her jaw, as if to question the order, and then nodded. "We'll find him."

"Report back to me as soon as you do."

The other two ghosts, neither of whom I recognized, raced off to do my bidding. Viola remained with me as I reached the door.

"Let me." Her smile was wan. "I can't die twice, right?" She poked her head inside, scanned the hallway, and then shook her head. "Nobody."

"Thank you." I couldn't muster a smile. "Do as I ask. I'll be fine."

Viola didn't look convinced but nodded. "Be careful, Bay. This isn't the sort of monster you're used to dealing with."

She wasn't wrong. "He might not even be a monster. Just find him."

She was gone in an instant, leaving me alone to walk the halls of the high school I'd attended more than a decade ago.

The first classroom I approached was empty, chairs scattered, backpacks left behind in obvious panic. I searched the corners in case anybody was lurking or needed to escape. There was nobody.

All the classrooms along the main hallway were the same. I turned down the other hallway. Hemlock Cove High School was laid out like a giant T. There was also a vocational building at the back of the property, across the parking lot.

My footsteps echoed as I traversed the hallway, and when I got to the art room, I found the first sight that would haunt my nightmares for a long time to come. The classroom was packed, the students crowded in the rear corner of the room, some weeping.

Andy Schultz, one of my former classmates, stepped in front of the students. He looked terrified.

"There are just students here," he said. "You can't hurt them."

I raised an eyebrow. Then he recognized me. "Bay?"

"Take them out through the front door," I instructed. "I've already walked that hallway. It's empty."

He was taken aback. "Did you really run into a building with an active shooter?" He looked amazed ... and maybe a little perplexed.

I said the same thing to him that I did to Landon. "I couldn't do nothing. Get them out. There's a fire truck at the end of the parking lot. Take them there."

Andy hesitated. "What are you going to do?"

"Keep going. Just get them out."

"Bay ... ." He shook his head. "You should come with us." He motioned for the students to follow him. "I'm going first, guys. You stick close together when we're in the hallway. No noise." He was firm, together, and he made me smile despite the circumstances.

"You're doing really well," I said. "Don't worry about me. I'll be fine."

"Bay, you shouldn't do this."

"It'll be okay." I hoped that was true. "Get them out. I have to keep going."

"You can't be in here alone."

I couldn't tell him I wasn't alone. "I'm fine. Worry about them." With one more heavy glance I exited back into the hallway and continued my trek. I could hear Andy and his class when they emerged and headed in the opposite direction. I didn't risk looking over my shoulder.

The next room belonged to the guidance counselor Jeff Bingham. It was empty. The room after that was the history classroom. It was half full. Jeff was with them.

"Bay?" He was flabbergasted when he detached from the wall and headed toward me. "What are you doing here?"

"Clearing the way," I said. "The hallway that leads back to the main door is clear. I've already sent Andy Schultz and a classroom full of kids out. You need to go. There's a fire truck at the end of the parking lot. Chief Terry and his men are on the way."

Jeff gripped the shoulder of the nearest student, a strapping teenager who looked ready to fight someone to the death to protect his classmates. "Come with us."

He was a good man who came onto the scene as I was leaving high school. He helped me fill out my college applications and steered me in the right direction when it came to listing extracurriculars. He could be creative when he wanted to and turned the work I did for the local newspaper owner at the time into a glorious exaggeration of my qualifications.

"There are only two more rooms on this hallway." I knew from memory. "If I clear them, Chief Terry can start searching the woods."

Jeff hesitated. "Bay ... ."

"It's fine." I refused to let the fear overtake me. "Your job is to get these guys out."

"What's your job?"

"To do something helpful. Go."

I walked back into the hallway, my heart rate increasing. If I was going to find trouble, I was running out of places to find it. My next stop was the principal's office. I expected it to be empty — Art Bishop was the principal, and he would've been in the thick of things when it came to getting the students out — but instead I found a teacher and a student standing in the middle of the room staring at one another.

The boy — he looked vaguely familiar, Granger Montgomery? — held a gun on Will Compton. There was nobody else present, just a disheveled student who looked so sweaty I thought he might pass out and a terrified teacher I'd interviewed a year ago. He was obviously terrified.

"Hello." It was the only thing I could think to say.

Will, his eyes wide and filled with fear, seemed dumbfounded by my appearance. I couldn't blame him. "Bay Winchester?"

I nodded, my lips a thin line, and focused on the boy. "Granger?"

"He's a good student," Will said. "I don't understand."

I briefly focused on the pistol Granger gripped in his hand. I wasn't an expert on guns, but the student seemed to be holding it at an odd angle, as if he was unfamiliar with the weapon. He aimed the gun at Will, but Granger's eyes darted between us so fast I wondered if he was even registering what was happening.

"I'm sure he's a great student," I said, drawing Granger's eyes back to me. "You don't have to do this." I kept my tone soft. I hadn't seen any bodies in the hallway, no blood. It was possible this was a cry for attention. While still bad, things could be a whole lot worse. "Tell me what you need, and I'll make it happen," I offered. "Just ... tell me what we can do to end this."

Granger's expression twisted into something grotesque. "He won't tell me where she is."

I waited for him to expand, but he didn't.

"She? Is this about a girl?" It seemed ridiculous on the face of it, but teenage hormones were known to get out of control from time to time. If he was melting down over a girl, perhaps I could talk him out of whatever path he'd decided upon.

"I need her," Granger insisted, his voice cracking. "She doesn't understand how much I need her. Why isn't she here?"

I decided to treat it as an interview. "Who is she? I can try to find her, bring her here." I had no intention of doing anything of the sort, but we needed time. "Just tell me her name."

"Why doesn't she come?" Granger sounded anguished. "I need her."

I hurt for him, but I had to get the gun out of his hand. "Granger ... ." I licked my lips, my eyes darting to the right when Viola appeared. Granger and Will didn't react, telling me they couldn't see her. That was good ... at least I thought it was good.

"I found him," Viola announced triumphantly and gestured to the teenager.

I shot her an incredulous look but said nothing.

"He looks sick," she noted, her gaze on Granger. "Like ... maybe he's on drugs or something. I bet that's it. Drugs are a scourge on this country."

I couldn't disagree. I'd also wondered if Granger was on something, but it was possible Granger was hopped up on adrenaline.

"Do you know who he's talking about?" I asked Will.

Will shook his head. "I ... don't ... know. I've never seen him like this before. He's the last person I would've expected to do something like this."

"I need her," Granger whined. "I just ... she can't leave me. It's not okay."

I nodded because it was the only thing I could think to do. "It's hard being alone, but Mr. Compton and I are with you." I gestured to Will. "We want to help you. Just tell us how we can."

"Make her come here!" Granger demanded. "I can't wait any longer. I'll die without her."

This was so out of my realm. "I ... ."

Viola moved without me ordering her to do so. She floated closer to the boy, studying the side of his face with the sort of intensity that made me feel uncomfortable. Then she did the unthinkable and karate chopped his arm.

My mouth dropped open when she made contact. There was an audible slap. Granger jerked up his head. Viola karate chopped again. This time Granger jerked back hard enough, fear flooding his eyes, that he dropped the gun.

I braced myself for an accidental discharge. The gun clattered to the ground without firing, however, and there was a moment of heart-stopping silence.

Granger looked to me, then to Will, and then toward the gun. I threw myself at him, tackling him into the receptionist's desk with enough force to rattle my bones.

Granger wrestled with me, and I fought with everything I had. I knew if he touched that gun again that there would be a tragedy.

"She's here," Granger crowed. "She came. I knew she would."

I continued to fight with him.

Behind us, Will grabbed the gun.

"Empty it," I ordered, hoping that was in his wheelhouse. I wouldn't properly know how to unload a gun, but Will hunted. "Make sure he can't use it against us."

Granger suddenly stopped struggling and looked over my shoulder. The expression on his face could only be described as awe. "She's here!"

I looked over my shoulder, expecting to find a tearful teenager, maybe even a female teacher. Instead, I found Will. He held the gun in his hand for a long moment, as if trying to ascertain exactly what he was holding. Then, as if in slow motion, he lifted the gun to his temple.

"I need her," he said to me, his eyes suddenly vacant. "Why isn't she here?"

I opened my mouth to bellow at him, to do anything I could to stop him. He pulled the trigger and the roar drowned out the scream that was on my lips.

CHAPTER
Four

I couldn't open my eyes because I didn't want to see. Underneath me, Granger had gone limp. It was as if all the life had gone out of him when Will pulled the trigger. All I could hear was the blood rushing through my ear canal. All I could feel was the pounding of my heart ... and then there was something else.

"Bay!"

I felt Landon's hands on me. He had me in his arms, rocking me back and forth when I finally managed to open my eyes. I saw his hair. He'd buried my face in the crook between his neck and shoulder.

"Baby." His voice cracked as his hands plastered across my back. "Look at me," he said. "Look at me," he repeated when I didn't respond.

Slowly, I tracked my eyes to him.

"Are you okay?"

I nodded dumbly.

"Are you sure?"

I nodded again.

"Okay, good." He hugged me against him a second time, his chest rattling as he sucked in a calming breath. "I can't believe you did this," he muttered. "I just ... can't believe you did this."

He wasn't the only one. Now, in hindsight, I felt like a bit of an idiot.

"He's dead," another voice said from my left. Chief Terry. Of course, he was with Landon. I didn't look in that direction because I didn't want to see.

"He shot himself," I volunteered on a broken breath.

"I thought it was a student," Chief Terry said as he moved closer to us, blocking my view of Will. "That's what the people outside said."

"It was a student." I gestured to Granger, who was still and staring at the ceiling. He showed no signs of life. "He had the gun."

"What?" Baffled concern etched across Landon's face as he moved me from my spot on top of the teenager. "I don't understand."

That made two of us. There was so much about this situation I didn't understand I had no idea where to start explaining.

"Bay." Landon gave me a little shake as he stared into my eyes. "We need to know what happened."

"She's in shock," Chief Terry said as he carefully removed Landon's fingers from my shoulders. I didn't realize how tightly he'd been holding me until the pressure lessened. "She can tell us what happened when she gets her bearings."

Landon brushed his hand over my forehead and stared into my eyes. "I need you to know something," he whispered as he leaned close. "I love you more than anything."

I waited for him to explode and tell me, despite his soft words, that he was angry. He had a right to be. I would have to take it when he started unloading. "And?" I prodded when he didn't say anything more.

He managed an odd half smile that didn't really fit the situation. "You're my whole life. The fear I felt coming here was ... profound. I think I'm going to need a lot of cake to make myself feel better later."

A tear slid down my cheek. I didn't even know I was going to start crying until it happened. "Aren't you going to yell at me for coming into the school?" I was bewildered.

"No."

"Yes," Chief Terry corrected.

"I'm not yelling at her," Landon countered, shooting a glare at Chief Terry. "She's been through enough."

"You're yelling at her." Chief Terry insisted. "She could've been killed."

"She wasn't." Landon used his practical voice. "She took care of the situation, like she always does, and I'm not yelling at her."

"I'll have Winnie withhold your bacon," Chief Terry threatened. "Just because she's a hero doesn't mean she's not an idiot. This was not okay."

Under different circumstances, the threat might've been funny. Nothing was funny today, however.

"Then I'll go without bacon." It was a bold pronouncement coming from Landon, and when he turned his eyes back to me there was a soft smile curving the corners of his mouth. "Or I'll order a pizza loaded with sausage and bacon and we'll eat in bed tonight, away from everybody else. How does that sound?"

It sounded glorious. I doubted he would be able to pull it off once word spread about what had happened. "I just need some air ... and maybe some water." I felt hollowed out, as if somebody had slipped inside and whittled out my guts. "Can I go outside?"

Chief Terry hesitated and then nodded. "Don't talk to the people out there. Go to the ambulance and have them check you over. We'll join you in a few minutes. Don't tell anyone what happened in here."

I couldn't even if I wanted to. "I don't even know what happened."

Landon cupped the back of my head and pressed a kiss to my forehead. "We'll figure it out. You're okay. That's the most important thing."

I DID AS INSTRUCTED. CHIEF Terry was angry enough that I didn't want to risk his wrath twice. Oddly enough, even though he wasn't my biological father, I folded under his disapproval much more easily than under my father's watchful glare. Chief Terry had helped teach us right and wrong, especially when Aunt Tillie was our babysitter. I hated to see him angry.

I sat on the lip of the ambulance rear doors and let Ginny Baker check me over. She'd graduated with Thistle, so was younger than me, and I didn't know her well. She looked concerned when I emerged from the high school and ordered everyone to give me some space. After checking my blood pressure and handing me a bottle of water, the concern in her eyes dissipated some. She was curious but didn't question me. Instead, she sat next to me, serving as a barrier when others looked as if they might approach. The only one who didn't seem leery of her was Mrs. Little. Nothing was going to stop her from getting answers.

"What happened?" she demanded as she stood in front of me, hands on hips. "Someone said you were in the high school. Are you the one who fired the gun?"

Rather than answer, I stared at my water bottle and remained mute.

"Did you hear me?" Mrs. Little demanded, moving closer. "I asked you a question."

"Give her some space," Ginny said in a low voice. "She's obviously been through something."

"Thank you so much for sharing your opinion, *Jennifer*." Mrs. Little dragged out the name. "I wasn't talking to you; I was talking to Bay."

"Well, she obviously doesn't want to talk to you."

"She has no choice. This is my town." Mrs. Little's fingers were like tiny blunt knives when she dug them into my arms. "Did you hear me?"

I reacted without thinking, anger coursing through me. The magic I summoned wasn't enough to hurt her, but I heard a small sizzle when I burned her with my rage.

"Ow!" She pulled her hands back and began waving them, as if trying to put out flames. Her eyes were full of consternation and accusation when I finally met her gaze. "What did you do?"

Thankfully I didn't get a chance to answer — it wouldn't have been pleasant anyway — because Landon and Chief Terry picked that moment to make their way to the ambulance.

"Don't get in her face," Landon warned as he slid in front of Mrs. Little and looked me over. "Are you okay?"

"I'm fine." My voice was stronger than I expected. "I already told you I wasn't hurt."

"That's not what I meant." He pinned Mrs. Little with an accusatory glare before turning back to me. "You didn't say anything, did you?"

"I said I wouldn't. I meant it."

"I know. It's just ... you're in shock." He kissed my forehead again. There was nothing romantic about the gesture, but it was filled with love. I wanted to let him hold me, wipe away the images that kept invading my head.

"I'm fine." I squared my shoulders, unwilling to look weak in front of Mrs. Little. I was still angry with her because of the new magic shop. What happened inside the high school was obviously more important. Her payback would be swift when it was time. I would let Aunt Tillie off her leash and watch the show with glee.

"Mrs. Little, we need you to back away," Landon said, using his most officious voice.

"Excuse me?" Mrs. Little was incredulous.

"We need to question Bay," Chief Terry explained.

Mrs. Little's face was blank. "So?"

"So, you're not part of the investigation." Chief Terry was firm. "We need to question Bay in private."

"I'm on the council."

"That doesn't give you a say in our investigation." Chief Terry's voice took on an edge I was all too familiar with. He was a patient man, loving to a fault, but he would turn into an angry daddy bear when he felt one of his cubs was threatened. Apparently I was the endangered cub today, and he wasn't going to put up with any crap. "Get away from Bay."

Mrs. Little worked her jaw as she glanced between faces. She was used to getting her way. Her victories far outweighed her defeats. However, almost all her defeats came at the hands of the Winchester witches.

"You won't be present when we question Bay," Landon insisted.

"I'm on the council," she repeated. "I have a say in Chief Terry's job status. He cannot hide information from the town council."

Temper I thought I couldn't muster flared to life. "Don't threaten him."

Landon raised a hand before I could get up a full head of steam and go after her. There was a warning in his eyes. He wanted to protect me, coddle me, and shut me away from the world so I wouldn't hurt. He also wanted me to shut my mouth and let him handle this situation.

"Chief Terry is not in charge of this investigation," Landon said. "The FBI is taking control."

I glanced at Chief Terry, horrified. Had Landon usurped his control without discussion?

"A shooting on school grounds means the FBI takes charge," Chief Terry confirmed. "I can't share information with you until they clear me to share it."

I glanced between them, my mind racing, and then bit back a grin. However inappropriate given the situation, I wanted to laugh. They were working together to play Mrs. Little. The FBI might very well be in charge, but Chief Terry would always have a place at the head of the pack when it came to his town. This was simply a way to close her out of the information loop. They were smart men, and they were taking control. I wanted to applaud them.

"This isn't over," Mrs. Little warned, her finger flying between them. "It's nowhere near over."

"We're terrified of your wrath," Landon drawled as he linked his fingers with mine and drew me to my feet. "Come on, Bay. We'll move to the shade and ask the questions we need to ask."

Mrs. Little's glare was aimed directly at me when I fell into step with Landon. "Is it appropriate for the FBI agent in charge to hold hands with a suspect?"

I went stiff all over. "I'm not a suspect."

"She's not," Landon agreed. "Stop being ... you."

"She was in a building where an individual was reportedly holding a gun on someone," Mrs. Little persisted. "She had no business being in that building. Of course, she's a suspect."

"She's not," Landon countered. "The suspect is in custody."

Mrs. Little's gaze was keen. "So ... nobody died."

Landon shook his head. "I wouldn't go that far. You'll learn more after notifications have been made and a news release has been approved. Until then, get off my turf and give me some space. This has nothing to do with you."

"I'll find out what happened," she growled.

"Not from us you won't." Landon released my hand and slid his arm around my back, reaching over to grab my hand again from the other side once there was distance between Mrs. Little and us. "Ignore her, Bay. She can't do anything to you. She's just trying to drum up attention because she's a pain."

"I'm well aware." I shot him a rueful smile. "Remember, I've known her longer than you. She's a ... well, you know." When he didn't say anything, I used a word I almost never uttered, a word my mother warned would result in my tongue falling out. It caused Landon's eyebrows to merge with his hairline. "I'm just saying."

Landon shook his head and darted a look at Chief Terry. "I'd say that's strong for my soft little witch, but I don't think any of us disagree with the word choice."

"I don't, but I don't want my sweetheart saying it," Chief Terry said, waiting until I was seated on a shaded bench between Landon and him to lean in and rest his cheek against my temple. "So, you did a stupid thing running into the school."

I was expecting the admonishment. "I wasn't alone. I took ghosts in with me. I used them as scouts."

"Well, I guess that's something." Chief Terry said. "It was still stupid, Bay. Ghosts can't stop you from getting shot."

"Actually, in this case, that's exactly what happened." I gave them a rundown of my activities inside the building. Landon grew tense when I told him about finding the classrooms of frightened children. When I got to the part about entering the principal's office, he sat straighter and listened intently.

In halting terms, I explained about Granger asking for "her" and how Will seemed frightened for his life. When I told them about Viola karate chopping Granger's wrist, Landon managed a weak smile. Then I explained how I threw myself at Granger to keep him from retrieving the gun.

"I don't know what happened," I said weakly as I rubbed my forehead. "I thought Will was picking up the gun to unload it. Granger was fighting like crazy to get the gun ... right up until Will picked it up. Then he stopped."

"Did Will say anything?" Chief Terry prodded gently. "Did he act as if being held at gunpoint broke him or something?"

"He said he needed her, wanted to know why *she* wasn't there. Then he put the gun to his head and ... ."

Landon pulled me tight against him and buried his face in my hair. "Sweetie, I'm so sorry." He stroked his hands over my head and shoulders. "I can't believe that happened."

"I can't either." I'd thought about it a lot when sitting next to Ginny. She didn't pepper me with questions. Instead, she let me settle with my thoughts. "Who is she?"

"Hmm?" Landon stirred, his gaze intense. "What?"

"She," I replied. "They were both talking about a woman ... or a girl, I guess. They both said they needed her. They were upset *she* wasn't there."

"I guess I hadn't really thought about that enough." Landon turned to Chief Terry. "Was Will Compton dating anyone?"

"Not that I know of. We're going to have to dig. We need to figure out where Granger got the gun. We need to know if he was dating anyone. We need to talk to his parents. We also need to make notification on Will. He's not a local so I don't think he has any family in town."

"I was trying to think of where he was from," I admitted. "I couldn't quite remember."

"He didn't grow up in Walkerville, but I think he has family in surrounding towns. I'm almost positive he told me he has an aunt in Shadow Hills. There might be a cousin or something in Hawthorne Hollow."

I rolled my neck. "I'm guessing you don't want to include me in that digging?"

Landon shook his head. "I'd rather you weren't involved ... at least until you've had time to settle. You've been through enough today."

"What's weird is that I thought we were going to get a happy ending when Viola intervened. At least as happy as possible under the circumstances. I can't believe how wrong I was."

"Bay, this is not on you." Landon was earnest. "You saved those kids. We don't know what would've happened if you hadn't gone in there."

"But we're still angry about that, though," Chief Terry stressed. "There will be a lecture later."

I tried to smile but my lips quivered as a fresh bout of tears threatened to overtake me. "I guess I've earned it."

Chief Terry sighed. "I guess the lecture could be implied. We don't really need to go through the motions or anything."

Landon snorted and the sound warmed me. "And you say I'm a softie where she's concerned."

"You are. You should be giving the lecture."

"Not going to happen." Landon's fingers were light as they traced over my cheek. "Go spend some time with Thistle. Just ... get off the street. Take some time to regroup."

I nodded. "Will you at least keep me updated?"

"I promise. As soon as we know something, I'll call. Just take care of yourself." He leaned in and kissed me. "I'm kind of fond of you."

"I'm kind of fond of you too."

"I know. Who else would be willing to swear off bacon for life because he's so devoted?"

That earned a laugh. "I love you." I wrapped myself around him.

He sighed as he held me tight. "You will never understand how much I love you."

CHAPTER Five

Landon and Chief Terry were interviewing students when I left. Part of me wanted to stick around to learn what they dug up, but the strange looks coming my way and the whispers starting to bubble up told me it was a bad idea. I raised my hand to wave my goodbyes and left.

Landon returned the wave. Even from across the lawn I could see the concern. There was a very serious conversation in my future.

I scuffed my feet as I made my way downtown, being sure to avoid the stares of the townsfolk who had gathered to gossip about the incident at the high school. I kept my eyes down until I reached Hypnotic and then took refuge inside.

"Are you stupid or something?" Thistle demanded as I threw myself on the couch in the center of the store. She didn't say hello or ask how I was doing. She launched directly into her diatribe. "What were you thinking? Are you a moron or something? Look what I'm saying. Of course, you're a moron. Only a moron would do what you did."

I slid my gaze to her as I propped my feet on one of the accent pillows. "How did you even hear about it?"

"The whole town is talking." She moved out from behind the

counter and sat in the chair next to the couch. "Did you really go into that school knowing there was an armed gunman on the loose?"

"What else was I supposed to do?"

"Um ... wait outside. It's not your job to deal with something like that."

"It shouldn't be anybody's job."

"I get that, but ... Bay, you had no idea what you were going to find inside of that building. What if there was more than one shooter? What if a bunch of kids had died? You would've been scarred for life."

I wasn't certain I wasn't scarred for life now. "I couldn't do nothing, Thistle."

"So, you decided to serve yourself up as bait?"

"I decided to clear the hallways, get the students out and send in ghosts to find the gunman."

She was taken aback. "That was smart."

"I found the gunman before they did." I gave her a rundown of what happened. When I got to the part about Viola karate chopping Granger's arm she smiled. But that mirth fled when she heard what had happened to Will.

"I don't understand."

"I don't either."

"But ... was Granger going after Will because they were interested in the same girl or something?"

That hadn't even occurred to me. "I don't know."

"Could Will have been dating a student?"

The possibility gave me an icky feeling in my stomach. I rested my forearm over my eyes. "Now I'm definitely going to have nightmares."

"You're going to have the sound of five witches screaming at you for being an idiot echoing in your nightmares. Clove is freaking loud. Your mother is going to be angry ... and Clove is going to cry ... and my mother is going to say something stupid."

"That is the story of our lives," I confirmed.

"Aunt Tillie is going to be angry she missed out on the fun."

"It was not fun."

Thistle's expression softened. "I'm sure it wasn't. Honestly, things could've been way worse. I mean … no students died. Was anybody else even wounded?"

I shook my head. "I can't figure out why this happened. Granger kept whining that *she* wasn't there. He wanted to see her. Up until the point he picked up the gun, Will seemed relatively normal."

"Did he seem surprised to see you?"

"Everybody in that building thought I was a blooming idiot. The teachers I ran into were grateful I managed to get them out, but you could tell they all thought I was a moron."

"Rightfully so. You are a moron."

When I peered under my forearm, I found her grinning. "It's not funny."

She sobered quickly. "It's not funny at all and I'm sorry you had to go through it. I was afraid when I heard. It was bad enough when word started spreading that shots had been fired at the high school. Everybody wanted to head over there."

"It's good you didn't. That would've only added to the chaos."

"I was on the street. Everybody was staring at that side of town even though we couldn't see anything. Mrs. Gunderson felt guilty for telling you what was happening. She told me she never expected you to race off the way you did."

"It's not her fault. I would've gone regardless. I am a reporter."

"You mean you're a moron."

"Keep it up, Thistle." There was warning in my voice.

"It was a stupid thing to do," she insisted. "Like … a really stupid thing to do." She paused. "But I'm really proud of you."

My heart pinged at the emotion in her voice. I couldn't make myself look at her because I didn't want to start crying. "Thank you."

"It was still stupid."

"So you've said."

When she exhaled, I knew she was going to change the topic. "I don't get Will killing himself. He always seemed like a nice guy, upbeat and happy. Why would he do that?"

"I was in that room with him, and I can't answer the question." I aimed for a smile and fell flat. "It was as if I was caught in a movie or something. I stepped outside of myself. I saw what he was going to do but couldn't stop him."

"How would you have stopped him?"

"I'm a witch."

"That doesn't make you omnipotent. Maybe you should stop channeling Aunt Tillie and realize you saved a bunch of lives."

"Or I cost Will his life somehow. Maybe if I hadn't gone in ... ."

"Oh, don't do that." Thistle made a face. "You can't second-guess yourself, Bay. If you hadn't gone in, how do you know that Granger wouldn't have shot Will and then gone hunting through the school? Those students only got out because you told the teachers the way was clear."

"We don't know that would've happened," I argued.

"And we don't know that Will wouldn't have died anyway. All we do know right now is that Granger isn't dead. He didn't kill anybody. If he was having some sort of mental breakdown there's still a chance he can be helped. What happened to him?"

"He was arrested. I'm sure he's in a cell right now ... or maybe they hospitalized him. After Will shot himself, Granger just lay on the ground like a big lump. It was as if watching Will commit suicide took all the wind out of his sails."

"Maybe that's what he wanted. Maybe he somehow forced Will to commit suicide."

"I was there, that's not what happened."

"You weren't there for the conversation before you walked into the office. Maybe there was some big argument beforehand. Maybe Will ... did something ... to Granger and that's why this happened. Maybe Will realized that word was going to spread and that's why he killed himself. It could be the best possible outcome."

I studied her face. Did she really believe that? "Then who is 'she?'" I asked. "Why did they both sound like they were broken-hearted over a woman? We've interacted with Will. I wrote a piece on him when he first moved to town. He didn't strike me as a predator."

"I hate to point out the obvious, but most predators get away with what they're doing for so long because they're adept at hiding who they are. We didn't know him well enough to judge him."

"But I've met evil people before. Sometimes what they are is obvious."

"And sometimes it's not. There's no hard and fast rule for this sort of thing. You can't blame yourself for what happened. You were a hero today."

My cheeks colored under the praise. That was so unlike Thistle. "I thought you said I was a moron," I reminded her.

"You're totally a moronic hero."

The chimes over the store door jangled to announce somebody was entering and I had to bite back a sigh. I was convinced it was a busybody store owner, or perhaps Mrs. Little had decided to chase me down for answers. Instead, I found two familiar faces – both smiling — studying me.

"Hi." The greeting escaped as I rolled to a sitting position. Scout Randall and Gunner Stratton were two of my favorite people these days. "I didn't realize you guys were in town."

Scout's smile was bright, sunny even, but there was an emotion I couldn't identify in her eyes. "We promised to help with your Hollow Creek problem, remember?"

How could I forget? The Hollow Creek problem was getting out of control. Magic shards from former battles were taking on a life of their own. So far, a group of teenagers had absorbed the shards and wreaked havoc on the area, resulting in multiple deaths.

"Do you have something?" I was hopeful. If I could focus on something else, maybe sleep wouldn't be as elusive as I was anticipating later this evening.

"No. Sorry." Scout held out her hands. "I was here checking on Evan. I thought I'd stop by, just to see if you'd come across anything we might be able to use to suck the magic out of that area."

I shook my head. "I haven't been focusing on that much."

"You're getting married." Scout moved to the couch, sliding her hand underneath my legs and shifting them to clear room so she could sit. Gunner grabbed a chair across from Thistle. "It's okay if you're distracted. A wedding is a big deal."

"I haven't been focused on the wedding," I said. "I wish I could say my biggest problem was making sure I don't stress eat my way straight out of my dress."

"What's wrong?" Scout was part witch, part pixie, and all mouth. I liked her a great deal, mostly because she was unflappable. A week before, she'd been in town searching for her former partner, a vampire she'd managed to partially heal. We'd bonded, and I was glad to learn she lived only twenty minutes away.

"Clove still hasn't given birth," I offered. "They moved her into the inn this morning and brought in a coven member as midwife. She might be evil."

"She totally looks evil," Thistle agreed. "Her name is Minerva, and she has the personality of a skin tag in an armpit."

Scout burst out laughing. "Have I mentioned I love your attitude?"

"I am a delight," Thistle readily agreed. "The midwife is going to be a pain. I can already tell. Bay and I slid out right after she arrived but I'm telling you that Aunt Tillie is going to have a problem with another witch gliding in and claiming dominion over her turf."

"Aunt Tillie is a gem," Scout said. "I love her."

"You can have her if you want," Thistle offered. "We've kept her to ourselves for long enough. We should share her joy and light with the world."

"I would take her, but I don't think the other Spells Angels would appreciate it."

The Spells Angels were a group of paranormal monster hunters who rode motorcycles and threw around enough power to level a mountain. Scout was with the Detroit bureau before moving to the Hawthorne Hollow region several months ago. She'd fallen in love with Gunner and settled in nicely in her rural environment, despite being a self-proclaimed city girl. I had a feeling I would miss her if she decided to relocate.

"You can still have her," Thistle pressed. "I feel selfish keeping her to myself this long. She should be shared with the world."

"I might borrow her for day trips," Scout said. "That's as far as I'm willing to go."

"I'll take what I can get," Thistle muttered, clearly disappointed. "The offer stands."

"I'll keep it in mind." Scout's eyes were searching when they landed on my face. "There's more than that going on. Spill."

I hesitated and then exhaled. There was no sense keeping them out of the loop. They would find out eventually. "It's a long story," I said.

"A kid went into the high school with a gun and Bay followed him to make sure he didn't kill people," Thistle interjected. "Instead of the kid killing people, a teacher picked up the gun and shot himself right in front of her. She's traumatized."

My eyebrows hopped. "Apparently it's not that long of a story."

Rather than laugh, Scout grabbed my hand. "I'm sorry. That's awful."

"There's more." I told her about Granger's pleas for 'she' to come to him. I explained what Will said before he killed himself. "The whole thing has me rattled."

"I don't blame you." Scout's expression was pensive as she absorbed the information. "I don't understand how this could happen."

"I'm more interested in the fact that the kid didn't kill anyone," Gunner said. "From the scene you described, he sounds as if he was despondent. Why take the teacher hostage if he was looking for a girl?"

I shrugged. "I can't answer that. Maybe Granger had a girlfriend and found out Will was having a relationship with her."

"In that case, I'm glad he's dead," Gunner said, tucking a strand of his long hair behind his ear. He was a striking man — the leather jacket gave him a rough-and-tumble look even though he had a kind heart — but his looks were hidden by sorrow now.

"We don't know that's the case," I stressed. "Maybe ... maybe Will was somehow shaken by what happened with Granger. He told me Granger was a good kid, that he never would've expected this from him. I thought he was picking up the gun to unload it. I never thought ... ." I didn't finish it.

"Bay, it sounds as if you went above and beyond today," Scout said as she squeezed my hand. "You ran into a building to save a bunch of kids."

"I think what you did today was more terrifying than that,"

Gunner offered. "When you run into a burning building, there are ways to escape. You can control your fate. When someone has a gun and you're unarmed, it's different. You put yourself on the line for a bunch of kids today. That makes you a hero."

"And a moron," Thistle added.

Gunner chuckled. "She might be a bit of a moron. Bravery before brains isn't always a winning combination. Things could've been so much worse if she hadn't intervened."

I frowned. "We don't know that either."

"Oh, here we go." Thistle threw up her hands. "Are you trying to force me to slap you? I'll do it. I've been itching for a fight all day and the only one willing to play is your mother. I think she could take me, so I decided to keep my mouth shut for a change."

"I could take you," I argued.

"No way. I'm the queen of the Winchester witches."

"I would love to be present when you tell Aunt Tillie that," I said dryly. "As for what happened at the school today, I'm going to have to live with it."

"You're a hero." Scout was firm. "I'm also curious who this 'she' is that both of them mentioned. That girl, if she's a student, is about to have her life upended."

I absently scratched my cheek. "I want to know who she is too. Landon said that he would call as soon as he knows something. He figured it was best I didn't hang with them today. Apparently, I'm the talk of the town."

"A local celebrity." Gunner winked at me in his amiable way. "How about I take the local hero to lunch? The local hero, her mouthy cousin, and my girlfriend. We want to run some ideas about Hollow Creek by you."

Despite what had happened and the fact that I thought I would never be hungry again, my stomach growled in response.

"I guess some soup might not hurt," I hedged.

"And doughnuts," Thistle said as she pulled me to a standing position. "Come on, hero, let's start figuring things out. You can't solve the Granger problem, but you can help figure out a way to cleanse Hollow Creek."

She had a point. There was no sense feeling sorry for myself. "Soup and doughnuts it is."

CHAPTER Six

Scout wanted to see the school, so I took her and Gunner. My agitation returned with a vengeance as I stood there, curious eyes boring into me. I refused to look up, afraid of what I would find. Did people blame me for Will's death? Did they think I somehow caused this?

Landon, who was interviewing a group of students with Chief Terry, broke away from them when he saw who I'd brought.

"I thought we agreed you would take it easy?" There was no accusation in his tone, only concern, as he brushed my hair from my face. He offered an easy smile to Scout and Gunner, but I felt the unease rolling through him.

"That's our fault," Scout said. She'd been focused on the school since we arrived. "We stopped in at Hypnotic and found her and Thistle talking. I wanted to see this place."

"Why?" Landon pulled me to him and hugged me tight. It was as if he couldn't stop touching me. He kept his eyes on Scout, but his warmth was all for me.

Scout finally dragged her eyes from the school and shrugged. "Bay told us what happened. It's weird."

"It's definitely weird."

"I thought I might be able to sense something. I don't."

Landon's brow furrowed. "Sense something? Like what?"

Scout held out her hands. "The way that Granger kid went from being the one who was in charge to the teacher killing himself, I thought maybe it was some sort of magical contagion."

"Like a sickness?" Landon knew a lot about magic, more than an average person by a long shot, but he was still trailing behind in some respects. "Granger isn't going to turn into a zombie, is he?"

Scout snorted. "Oh, you're so cute." She grabbed his cheek and gave it a squeeze. "I love spending time with you because of the things you say."

Landon jerked his cheek away. "You love spending time with me because I'm hot. That's the standard with all the ladies."

"Hey now." Gunner shot him a warning look, although there was mirth there. "Let's not be annoying."

"Agreed," I said, blowing out a sigh as I glanced around. When I pulled back from Landon, I made sure there was a smile on my face. I didn't want him worrying. "Have you found anything?"

Landon shook his head. "They've called in a state shrink to talk to Granger. He's no longer speaking."

That didn't seem right. "He was talking right up until it happened."

"Did he see the teacher shoot himself?" Gunner asked. "Maybe he's in shock."

"Bay saw it too." Landon's expression was dark, as if he wanted to destroy planets in my honor. "She's managing to hold it together."

I patted his arm and forced a smile I didn't feel. "I didn't actually see it. I saw what he was going to do and wimped out. My eyes were closed."

He brushed his thumb over my cheek. "I guess that's a small consolation."

"Not much, though." Scout looked at him. "This must be horrible for you. You're an alpha dude who wants to protect his woman. Not only were you not present for this, but she was the alpha when it went down."

Landon glared at her. "I'm not an alpha."

Everybody snorted in unison.

"I'm not," he insisted. "I'm a man who loves my ... Bay." His smile was soft when it landed on me. "I can't wait to call you my wife." He was stern when he turned back to Scout. "Did she tell you she called me before she ran into the school with the active shooter?"

"No, but that really must've been torture for you." She was sympathetic as she slapped Landon's shoulder. "Suck it up. She had no choice. She couldn't just sit back and do nothing."

"I know that." Landon was surprisingly calm. "I haven't yelled at her despite my promise to on the phone."

"He hasn't," I confirmed. "He's been good."

"I'm the best." Landon cupped my chin and leaned forward to rest his forehead against mine. "The run to get to the high school was the longest of my life. It took three minutes and each minute felt like a year."

"Give him a break," Gunner ordered Scout. "He's doing the best that he can. I can't imagine being separated from you in those circumstances. Being proud that you have a powerful woman at your side doesn't mean you don't feel fear."

Landon nodded. "See. Gunner gets it. By the way, there's pot roast for dinner tonight if you guys want to join us. I called Winnie to check. I know you like carrying it around in your hand and stuff after the last time you were there."

Gunner glowered at him although there was a hint of a smile on his face. "Can we stay for dinner?" He wheedled Scout. "Pretty please with sprinkles on top."

Scout nodded without hesitation. "A good meal sounds good. Besides, I figured we'd run out to Hollow Creek and check the situation out."

"Yeah, speaking of that." Landon was careful as he glanced around to make sure nobody was eavesdropping. "How is your little emotionally-tortured vampire friend?" He'd been stoic when Scout and Gunner informed him they were leaving the taciturn Evan in town to recuperate. Evan took over his dead uncle's farm and had been closed off there ever since. Even though we hadn't heard a peep from the day-walking vampire, Landon still expected trouble.

"We just came from there," Gunner replied. "Evan is ... cleaning the house. He needs something to focus on and right now that's housework. He talks to Scout, but the conversations vacillate from anger to reminiscing instead of zeroing in on anything important. Basically, there's no change."

"He's not bothering anybody," Scout said hurriedly. "He's just hanging out at the house alone."

"I'm just curious what the plan is," Landon reassured her. "Are you going to leave him in there indefinitely?"

"We don't have a plan. It's not as if I thought my former partner, a guy I believed to be dead and then found out was turned into an ubervampire, was going to turn again." She was morose. "This is a new situation for us. Evan is ... different. It's like he's a third person now."

"I'm not accusing you of anything, Scout," Landon said. "I get why you're having trouble deciding what to do. It's just ... Bay and I will be leaving town for two weeks. We're going on our honeymoon after the wedding. If Evan gets out of control ... ."

Scout stared at him but didn't speak.

"We can move here for those two weeks," Gunner said. "We can stay at the inn ... or camp."

The look Scout shot Gunner would've been funny under different circumstances. "We're not camping. How many times do I have to tell you I'm a city girl? You don't camp in the city."

"Well, we camp in Hawthorne Hollow ... and you're going to suck it up. I like camping. If I'm going to help babysit your feral vampire friend, you're going to have sex with me under the stars."

I couldn't stop myself from laughing, and then I remembered where I was and choked on it. Landon immediately rested his hand on my shoulder.

"Bay, I don't think you should be here." His voice was low and calm. "There's nothing you can do. We're getting witness statements and then heading out. We're almost done." He leaned close, his mouth only an inch from my ear. "Go with Gunner and Scout. Get away from town. Get some air."

"We're outside," I pointed out. "I shouldn't have any problem getting air."

"You still look like you're suffocating under the weight of all these stares. Go with them." He rubbed his knuckles up and down my face. "I'll see you at dinner. Your mom is making red velvet cake too – with ice cream."

Landon was a foodie. I wasn't particularly hungry — a suicide in a high school will do that to you — but I knew he would make himself sick if he worried about me. "I'll take them to Hollow Creek," I promised. "We need to solve that situation."

"You can ride on my bike," Scout said

"She has a car," Landon said. "She doesn't need to ride a motorcycle."

"I'm a very good driver," Scout replied with a laugh. "Besides, she loves riding. You heard her. She needs air. What better way to get it?"

Landon hesitated and then acquiesced. "Don't drive like a maniac." He gave me another hug. "Have fun. Let them ... do whatever it is they do that makes you laugh."

"I'll be fine," I reassured him, attempting — and failing — to grace him with a smile. "Don't worry. I'll see you in a few hours."

"And I'll love you forever." He gave me a kiss before relinquishing me to Gunner and Scout. "Keep a close eye on my sweetie. I don't know what you meant by the contagion thing, but I don't want her turning into a zombie before the wedding."

Scout snorted out a laugh. "I think I can manage that."

"WHAT DID YOU MEAN BY THE

CONTAGION thing?" I asked when we parked at Hollow Creek. Even from a distance I could see the magical shards we'd been dealing with for months had almost tripled in size since the last time we'd visited the spot. "Geez. Will you look at that?"

"Even I can see them now," Gunner said as he dismounted his bike. "Before, Scout had to use her magic to show them to me. Now they're obvious from a distance."

"What are we going to do?" I was breathless as we reached the bank of the creek. The shards, which had been an inch or two wide before, were now half a foot in diameter as they floated above our heads. They looked like broken glass, but they shimmered in such a way there could be no question regarding their origin.

"I don't know." Scout blew out a sigh as she touched the nearest shard. "I can't believe the rate at which they're growing. Has anyone been throwing magic around here?"

"Absolutely not." I fervently shook my head. "We've been careful to avoid this place as much as possible because it seems to be feeding on us."

"And everybody is following that rule?" Scout's gaze was pointed enough that I knew who she was referring to.

"Aunt Tillie is a total pain," I acknowledged. "She wouldn't come out here and add to this problem no matter how bored she was. Besides, she's obsessed with spying on Evan. We barely see her. She managed to get kidnapped by a djinn for a night and named him her new arch nemesis for three days, but she's been focused on Evan otherwise."

"You had a djinn here?" Scout's eyes went wide. "I've never seen one. I've only heard about them."

"It was over in Shadow Hills. My friend Stormy came across one. It's gone now."

"She killed it?" Scout almost looked disappointed.

"She's new to the witch game. You'd like her, so I'll try to wedge an introduction in when we get back from our honeymoon. She's a fire witch. She burned the djinn and locked him away on another plane. She wasn't up to killing him. She has to adjust to her new reality first."

"Well, that's probably smart." Scout went back to staring at the shards. "I'm looking forward to meeting her. True fire witches are supposed to be really powerful."

"She's definitely powerful. She's cute, too. She just got back together with her high school boyfriend and they're adorable. Oh, and she has a talking cat that claims to be a gnome shifter from another plane and says he's supposed to serve as her familiar. He's obsessed with reality television."

Scout blinked several times in rapid succession and then shook her head. "Yeah, I definitely want to meet her."

"I'll arrange it." I poked one of the shards with my index finger and watched as it flew through the air in the opposite direction. "What did you mean about the contagion? You mentioned it in regard to Granger and Will."

"Just that it sounds like Granger's obsession somehow transferred to the teacher." Scout narrowed her eyes as she focused on one of the shards, her fingers lighting with purple fire after a second as she funneled magic into it. She quickly drew her hand back, hissing as the magic offered a mini explosion. "Okay, that hurt."

Gunner took her hand to study her fingertips. "How bad?" he asked.

"It's fine. I was just trying to see if I could destroy the shards individually. It would take forever to clean up this area that way but turns out that won't work. The shards are now protecting themselves."

I was taken aback. "How can that be? They're not sentient."

"No?" The way Scout's eyebrows hopped told me she felt differently. "Watch." She aimed her finger at another shard, bright fire erupting from the tip. This time when she got close the shard started moving in the opposite direction, as if trying to escape from her.

"Well, that's not good." Gunner planted his hands on his hips as he glanced around at the glittering magical remnants that were quickly starting to take over our lives. "The shards recognized your magic the second time and recoiled."

"It's almost as if they're learning," I mused.

"We have a big mess to deal with." Scout pressed her lips together, the tilt of her chin telling me she was thinking hard. "We might need your fire witch out here before it's all said and done. I need to do some brainstorming on how to get rid of these things. I don't think we can wait to tackle them until after your honeymoon. They'll be too big."

I nodded in agreement. "It will give me something to focus on. I'm all for getting rid of the shards."

"You mean other than the teacher killing himself." Her voice was soft. "You know you can't blame yourself for that."

I held out my hands. "I'll always wonder if entering the school changed the course of Will's life."

"That kid was going to kill him," Gunner argued. "If you hadn't gone inside, other kids might've been hurt. If you ask me, you're a hero."

I couldn't contain my chuckle. "Now you sound like Landon."

"He's not so bad." Gunner jabbed a playful elbow into my abdomen. "He loves you. He's shredded about this."

I swallowed hard in an effort to stave off the tears. "He's being consumed by 'what-ifs.' He doesn't handle stuff like that well."

"He'll have nightmares tonight." Gunner was matter-of-fact. "You probably will too. You guys should just lean on each other for a bit and ignore everybody else."

"You just want to steal my pot roast," I teased, wiping the back of hand across my cheeks.

"Your mother loves me now. She'll make me pot roast whenever I want it. I don't need your pot roast."

"That's true." I blew out a sigh. "You're right about us having to deal with this situation before the honeymoon. I don't even want to think about what this place will look like in another three weeks."

"We'll figure it out," Scout promised. "Let's head back to the inn. I want to look through some of your mother's books. There has to be an answer."

"Just remember that Clove is living at the inn now until she gives birth. She has the most unpleasant midwife imaginable. I expect war between her and Aunt Tillie."

"Oh, see, dinner theater." Scout beamed at me. "Now I'm definitely glad we're staying for a meal."

That made two of us. "So am I."

"It's going to be okay, Bay." Scout always seemed calm, whatever the circumstances. "We'll figure out how to cleanse Hollow Creek and watch the situation at the high school in case it spirals. We won't let things get out of hand."

"That would be a nice change of pace for my family."

"Hey, I'm a professional. I've got this under control."

I fervently hoped she was right.

CHAPTER SEVEN

The inn was raucous with activity, the noise level almost deafening.

"Eee eee eee."

I frowned at the sound.

"What is that?" Gunner asked, cringing. He was a shifter so his hearing was elevated beyond that of a normal person.

"I don't ... ." Before I could finish what I was going to say, the now familiar sound of small wheels on hardwood floors became apparent.

"Eee eee eee." Aunt Tillie appeared, combat helmet firmly in place as she zipped into the lobby on her electric scooter. "Eee eee eee."

"I should've known," I muttered.

Snort. Snort.

Peg, Aunt Tillie's teacup pig, appeared behind her. The pig's eyes looked as wild as Aunt Tillie's, which was frightening to think about because my great-aunt was a menace.

"What's going on?" I asked when Aunt Tillie took a breath.

"Eee eee ... ."

I slapped my hand over her mouth and pinned her with a warning look before she could continue. "Stop making that noise," I ordered.

Aunt Tillie's eyes were narrow slits of hate. "*Mmph mmph mmph.*" I couldn't understand her with my hand over her mouth.

"I love this place," Gunner said, grinning as he took in the scene. "Hey, Peg." He dropped to his knees and started petting the excited pig. "I see you're still hanging out with this bad influence."

The pig seemed to have a unique effect on men. Even though she wasn't dressed in her tutu this evening, Peg was still a doll, and men went gooey all over when they saw her.

"I'm a good influence," Aunt Tillie replied as she slapped my hand away. "What do you think you're doing? Do you want to lose that hand?"

"I'm trying to stop the noise," I replied.

"Is it the most annoying noise you've ever heard?"

"Pretty much."

"Then my job here is done." Aunt Tillie looked smug as she darted a dark look down the hallway. "Did you hear my house has been invaded?"

I pursed my lips. Her mood told me it was going to be a long night. Normally she had to work herself up to this level of obnoxiousness. "Are you talking about Minerva?" I'd recognized the moment I saw the severe midwife that Aunt Tillie wasn't going to be happy. She'd made enemies with coven members from almost every corner of the state. It made sense that Minerva might be one of those enemies.

"Do you mean Mousy McGillicutty?"

"I guess." I turned to find Scout and Gunner smiling. Aunt Tillie was always funny to people who didn't have to see her regularly. "I thought her name was Minerva."

Aunt Tillie leaned close. "She's the devil."

"Who is Minerva again?" Gunner asked as he continued to lavish love on Peg.

"Clove's midwife." I straightened. "She can't have the baby in a hospital in case there's some magical explosion, so she has to have it here. She's not happy. She wants drugs and witches are proponents of natural birth."

Scout made a face. "Screw that. What sort of barbarians are you hanging out with?"

"I know, right?" When I heard the rule, it had put me off children for a good, long while. "You just know it was a warlock who came up with that rule."

"Actually, it's because of you that rule was instituted," Aunt Tillie replied, haughty. "You were born in a big ball of swaddling light."

I glared at her. "You're making that up." Even as I said it, I wondered if she could be telling the truth. Thanks to a head injury more than a year ago, I'd taken a trip through Aunt Tillie's memories and visited my own birth. There were indeed lights involved.

"Why would I lie?" Aunt Tillie countered. "You were the first baby in three generations to be born in a halo of lights. Given the fact that Sam has witch in his blood too, it only makes sense for everybody to be nervous."

"I didn't realize Sam had witch in him," Gunner mused. "Does that mean the baby could be extra powerful?"

I held out my hands. "We have no idea what's going to happen." That was the truth. "It's just better if we tackle it here."

"It's freaky to think about." Scout said. "You'd think they would've come up with a better way to deliver babies by now."

I glanced over my shoulder when the door opened and smiled as Landon and Chief Terry made their way in. Landon immediately came to me for a hug. "Hey."

"Hey." He gave me a kiss. "Are you okay?"

His doting was starting to wear thin, and he'd barely started. Once we were alone in the guesthouse tonight, he would be all over me ... and not in the fun way he usually was. "I'm fine. Did you guys learn anything?"

"Not as of yet," Chief Terry replied. He looked tired. "It took a long time to take all the witness statements. Granger's parents have been informed and are at the hospital with him. He's still not speaking."

"What did they say?" I shifted when Landon dropped to the floor to greet Peg. I was starting to think he needed a dog. "Did Granger have a girlfriend? Do they know who he was talking about?"

"They don't. They said he was more interested in video games and playing on his computer than girls."

"Maybe he was interested in guys and the girl was a friend or something."

"Maybe. Right now, the parents are understandably shocked. The gun belonged to them. It was locked in a gun case in the house, something we verified. Granger knew where the key was and used it. They have no idea what triggered this. They're thankful he's alive, but he's still not speaking. I told them we would be back to question them tomorrow."

"And what about Will?" I asked.

"We have very little on him. Neighbors said he was quiet and kept to himself."

"That's it?"

"For now." He moved closer to me. "You know you're not to blame for what happened." He was deadly serious. "I'm pretty annoyed with you given the choices you made today, but you're not to blame."

"Of course, she's not." Aunt Tillie burned Chief Terry with a glare. "Who says she's to blame? Was it Margaret? She's due for an ass-whooping, Tillie style." She raised her hands into fists.

"Nobody is saying that, at least not to our faces," Chief Terry replied. "I can tell Bay is worried about it."

"Why?" Aunt Tillie switched her gaze to me. "You saved all those kids. You can't possibly think you made the wrong choice."

"She shouldn't have gone into the school knowing there was an active shooter inside," Chief Terry insisted. "She knows better than that."

"Oh, whatever." Aunt Tillie's eye roll was so pronounced I was surprised she didn't fall off her scooter. "Don't listen to him. You did good today, Bay. Because of you, nobody died."

"Will Compton died," I countered.

"He killed himself. That's on him. You saved the kids. I'm no fan of teenagers — they're mouthy little pains who whine like they breathe — but Hemlock Cove never would've recovered if there'd been a mass shooting. You did what needed to be done." She sent a pointed look at Chief Terry. "And anybody who says otherwise needs to shut their traps."

"I hate when you take her side," Chief Terry grumbled. "Why can't you ever be on my side?"

"Pick the right side one day and we'll see what happens." Aunt

Tillie shifted her gaze to Gunner and Scout, as if seeing them for the first time. "Why are you here? If you're worried about that vampire, don't. He's the most boring vampire in the history of vampires. He just sits around that house and sulks, kind of like a teenager."

"We stopped in to see him," Scout confirmed. "I like to touch base at least twice a week."

"He's not doing anything. I hide in the cornfield and spy when I'm bored."

"Do you think he knows you're out there?" Gunner asked. "Maybe he's on his best behavior because he knows he has an audience."

"Maybe, but I don't think so. He seems ... tortured." Aunt Tillie was blasé about the situation. "All he does is sit there and stare into nothing. He's boring. He won't stop being boring until he comes to terms with the things he did as a vampire."

"Will that happen?" Scout asked. She looked alarmed. "Do you think he'll kill himself?"

"I don't think so, but I'm hardly an expert on emo vampires."

"How do you know he's emo?" I asked. "I'm surprised you even know that word."

"I know everything." Aunt Tillie glanced down the hallway again. "*Everything*," she stressed. "That new witch needs to know that."

Ah, that explained the attitude. "Is Minerva giving you a hard time about Clove?"

"She acts as if she knows more about childbirth than me," Aunt Tillie muttered. "I was there for all your births. She said she's attended hundreds of births and I was wrong to tell Clove to embrace the Scientology way of giving birth."

"And just what's that?"

"Silent births. You can't scream because it traumatizes the baby for life. You have to suck it up and squeeze out the kid without panting and screaming like a moron."

I had no trouble picturing Aunt Tillie giving that suggestion to Clove. "You didn't call her a baby, did you? Clove, I mean. She's very anxious about giving birth as it is. Every day that goes by without her going into labor just makes it worse."

"Oh, I know." Aunt Tillie made a face. "She said that because she's a week overdue she has a one-week-old child inside of her. She's afraid it's going to be the size of a toddler when she finally squeezes it out. I told her a story about my friend Judith. She had a baby that was so overdue the baby could talk when it came out."

I glared at her. "Why are you making up stories to frighten her?"

Aunt Tillie was affronted. "Who says I made it up?"

"That's ridiculous."

"And we all know you don't have friends," Landon added as he stood. He was apparently more interested in hovering over me than doting on Peg this evening. It felt like a small miracle.

"Oh, stuff it." Aunt Tillie was having none of it. "I'm an expert when it comes to delivering babies. I could do it professionally."

"I love this place," Gunner reiterated with a laugh. "It's never boring. I believe someone promised me pot roast. Where is that?"

"Men and their stomachs," Scout said as she slung an arm around my shoulders. She was more clingy than normal, and it was throwing me off. "Come on. I want to meet this devil midwife."

"I'll introduce you," Aunt Tillie offered as she turned her scooter around. "Just don't look her in the eye or she'll steal your soul."

"Got it." Scout's grin was wide. "We'll take her down together if it comes to that."

Aunt Tillie kicked her scooter to get it going and then started down the hall. *"Eee eee eee."*

Landon's shoulders jerked. "What is that noise?"

"I have no idea." I slipped my hand into his simply because I enjoyed the tactile contact. "Maybe she thinks that noise will scare away the devil."

"She'd better not do that all through dinner," he grumbled. "It'll screw up my digestion."

"We can't have that."

The rest of the family — sans our mothers, who were likely putting the finishing touches on the meal in the kitchen — were in the dining room, where there appeared to be a standoff.

"I don't think I like your attitude," Thistle snapped from her spot at the end of the table with her boyfriend Marcus. She looked furious. "You don't get a say on whether or not I'm in the room with Clove for the delivery." Her glare was aimed at Minerva, who was sitting directly across the table from her. "You're not the boss of me."

"You tell her, Mouth," Aunt Tillie encouraged. "*Eee eee eee.*"

"Stop that!" Thistle roared, taking me by surprise with her vehemence. "I will choke you with your own tongue if you don't stop making that noise."

Aunt Tillie slowed enough to level a furious glare on my cousin. "You're on my list."

"What else is new?" Thistle flicked her eyes to me. "Can you do something to make her stop with that noise?"

Oh, if only. "Sure." I bobbed my head and did something I never thought I would. "Mom!"

My mother immediately poked her head out of the kitchen at my dulcet screech. "Hello, Bay." Her eyes were curious as they roamed my face. "I hear you were a hero today. We have pot roast, your favorite red velvet cake, and I'm sending Landon home with a bottle of Aunt Tillie's wine as your reward."

As far as greetings went, I'd heard worse. "Um ... thanks."

She stepped closer to me, her eyes grave. *Here it comes,* I told myself. She's going to unload the diatribe Chief Terry's been holding back all day.

"We're very proud of you." Mom's voice turned misty. "What you did today ... you were phenomenally brave. People have been calling all afternoon to tell us how amazed they are by what you did."

"This is crap," Chief Terry complained. "Somebody has to yell at her. She ran into a building where there was an active shooter. That is not something to be celebrated."

"Did you yell at her?" Mom's voice had an edge that had Chief Terry taking a step back.

"No," he replied after a beat. "I wanted to." Chief Terry was used to kowtowing to my mother. "She could've been hurt, Winnie."

"She wasn't."

"She could've have been." Chief Terry's frustration bubbled over. "I know she's strong ... and brave ... and powerful. None of that would've helped if Granger Montgomery was hiding in a corner when she walked into that school. He could've pulled the trigger without her even recognizing what was coming."

I slid my eyes to Landon, knowing that he'd been thinking the same. To my surprise, he shook his head.

"She thought it through despite how quickly she had to move," Landon argued. "She sent the ghosts in first to scout the place for her. She wasn't going in blind."

"Oh, look at you." Chief Terry made a face. "You were cursing her name for running in. You were furious. The second we got to her, you turned into a big pile of mush."

Landon held out his hands. "I don't know what you want me to say. I trust Bay to handle herself in situations like this. Was I worried? Yes, but she handled herself. She did everything right."

"Will Compton still died," I pointed out. "I didn't do everything right."

"Oh, stop flogging yourself, Bay." Landon's voice was firm. "You did what you could. There's no way you could've known that he was going to pick up that gun and shoot himself. You couldn't have stopped it. You did the right thing and I refuse to let you feel guilty about it."

I studied his face for several seconds and nodded. "I just never thought I would witness something like that."

"I'm sorry it happened." He pulled me close and kissed my temple. "Everyone is calling you a hero. I get you're uncomfortable with it, but you are a hero, so suck it up and take your props."

"Totally," Aunt Tillie agreed. "As an even bigger hero than Bay, I understand this life. You've heard of the thug life? This is the hero life. I've been living it a long time."

"The hero life?" Thistle asked darkly.

"Yes." Aunt Tillie bobbed her head. "It's a heavy mantle to wear but you'll get used to it, Bay. I'll teach you."

"Oh, well, great," Thistle muttered. "This freaking family is nuts. Can we go back to talking about me? That's where the conversation was heading before Bay came in and sucked up all my attention."

"Yes, let's talk about Thistle," I said as I sat in my usual seat,

Landon and Chief Terry flanking me. "Why is she upset?" Anything to get us off the hero topic was welcome.

"This .... *person* ... says I can't be in the room when Clove gives birth," Thistle groused, inclining her head toward Minerva. "I don't know that I want to be in there, but who is she to keep me out?"

"Why don't you want Thistle in the birthing suite?" Mom asked in her most diplomatic tone.

"Because she is full of negative energy," Minerva replied. "Clove will pick up on it, as will the baby. Do you want the baby to have a bad attitude?"

Mom blinked several times and shook her head. "Thistle, suck it up. If you want to be included in the birth, you need a better attitude." She headed back to the kitchen. "Dinner will be ready in five minutes. Scout and Gunner, we're happy to have you. There's no need to walk around with the pot roast in your hand this time, Gunner. We have forks, more than enough to go around."

Rather than be offended by the admonishment, Gunner smiled. "Have I mentioned I love this family?"

Thistle glared at him. "Do you want to take my spot? Apparently, I'm negative."

"You're totally negative," I confirmed. "You should embrace the hero life like Aunt Tillie and me. That would make you less negative."

Thistle's eyes flashed with rage. "You know what? I'm starting my own list, and you're all on it."

"Awesome." Gunner bobbed his head. "Can I help add names?"

I grinned as I briefly leaned into Landon. I was tired but spending time with my family was the best way to get me out of my doldrums.

"We'll sneak out early," Landon promised as he kissed my forehead. "We'll take the cake home and eat it in bed."

"Sounds like heaven."

"Of course, it does. You're a hero. Heroes are easy to please." He turned his attention to Aunt Tillie. "Heroes should also smell like bacon as a reward."

Aunt Tillie didn't shut him down. "That might be doable if you get that evil devil spawn out of my house." She glanced at Minerva. "And keep her out."

Landon swallowed hard as he regarded the icy midwife. "Or you could just do it out of the goodness of your heart."

"That sounds nothing like me."

CHAPTER
Eight

We left Landon's Explorer at the inn, figuring we could pick it up after breakfast the following morning, and walked to the guesthouse. Mom loaded us up with cake, cookies, and pie, so we had plenty of choices for snacks. Landon took the food into the kitchen, and I fumbled with the lock to make sure it latched properly. When Landon returned to the living room, I felt his eyes on me.

"I'm fine," I said as I forced myself to turn away from the door. "Don't worry about me."

His blue eyes were full of compassion when I finally found the courage to meet his gaze. "It's normal to be hyper-vigilant after going through a trauma like you did," he said. "You don't have to be apologetic about it."

"I'm not apologizing."

"Right." He let loose a sigh and then pointed to the couch. "It's cuddle time."

My lips inadvertently curved. "What?"

"It's cuddle time. Take your clothes off."

"In other words, it's romance time." I laughed. "I thought you wanted to take the cake in the bedroom for that."

"That's not what I'm doing." He pulled his shirt over his head and kicked off his shoes, leaving them in the center of the living room floor. Then he unzipped his jeans and stripped down to his boxer shorts. "Come on." He climbed onto the couch and lifted the blanket.

I studied him for a long time, confused, and then toed off my shoes. I removed my pants next, and then doffed my shirt. I expected him to start kissing me when I rolled under the blanket with him. Instead, he situated us so we were stretched out together.

"Closer," he instructed as he pulled the blanket over our heads, wrapping me tight.

We were skin to skin, and somehow the simple act of letting him hold me eased some of the anxiety I felt.

We were on our sides, and he tucked my head into the hollow beneath his neck. Then he buried his face in my hair and inhaled deeply. He did it over and over again.

"Are you waiting for the bacon curse to hit?" I asked. "I'm not sure Aunt Tillie will come through for you tonight. I think she's more worried about Minerva than making your bacon dreams come true."

"I don't care about the bacon curse."

That was a lie and we both knew it. "Landon ... ."

"I don't care about the curse," he reiterated. "Not tonight. You already have an intoxicating smell."

"I probably smell like sweat and Hollow Creek. By the way, those magical shards are out of control. Scout thinks we need to move soon. We can't wait until after the honeymoon."

"You'll figure it out." He sounded sure of himself as he inhaled again. "As for your scent, you smell like Bay."

"Oh, yeah?" He was being unbelievably sweet. "What does Bay smell like?"

"Bay smells like many different things. It changes daily, but there's always the overwhelming scent of love at your core."

"That is corny."

"I'm fine with it."

I laughed again, as I'm sure he intended. "What do I smell like tonight?" I wanted to drag this conversation out, this moment of just us, and forget about what happened earlier in the day.

"I can smell the pot roast you inhaled at dinner." He sounded as if he was reporting on a scientific story he'd read in the newspaper. "I was glad to see you had an appetite."

"Yes, well, I was sort of glad too."

"You smell like the wine you sipped." He pressed his lips to mine. "You taste like the wine, even though you only took three sips."

"Were you watching me?"

"I'm always watching you, Bay." His eyes were clear when they locked with mine. Even though the blanket was over our heads, I could make out his features in the limited light. "You're my everything."

My heart constricted. "Me too."

"You're your own everything?"

"Ha, ha. No, I mean you're my everything."

"I know." He went back to inhaling my skin like an addict. "Every day, Bay — ever single day — I think this is the moment where I hit my limit on how much I can love one person. I think there's no loving you more than I do. Then I wake up and love you even more the next day."

I thought I might cry. "If you're angry about the school ... ."

"Shh." He gave me another kiss. "I meant what I said. I'm proud of you."

"But you're afraid too."

"I am. I can't help myself. But the pride far outweighs the fear."

"Because you love me more than you've ever loved me before," I said.

"Until tomorrow," he agreed. "I'll love you even more then."

A sniffle escaped. "Don't. I'm going to cry."

"It's okay if you do. You've earned it. Nobody will judge you for it."

"I might judge myself."

He shook his head. The blanket had done a number on his hair and yet he was still the handsomest man I'd ever seen. "I won't let you do that. I know that what you saw today was horrific, that you're going to have nightmares, and you're going to second-guess yourself. You did more today than anybody else could have."

"I think you're unnaturally biased." I ran my finger down his cheek. "You love me more than bacon. You said as much today. I think that makes me the most loved woman in the world."

He grinned. "I've always loved you more than bacon. Thankfully, most days, I can have both. If it ever came to a choice, I would always choose you."

"Thankfully you don't have to choose." Something occurred to me, and I moved to roll away.

"Where are you going?" He grabbed for me. "I'm not done cuddling."

"Hold on." I went to the table by the front door, an old console table that had a locking drawer. I used my magic to open it rather than waste time going into the bedroom for the key and returned to the couch with a long, thin box in my hand. "Here."

"What's this?" He stared at the box, confused. "It's not time to exchange wedding gifts."

"I know. I saw this the other day and thought of you. It's not a big deal. In fact, I was going to wait to give it to you on our honeymoon, maybe make a game out of it. You can have it now."

He carefully untied the ribbon before removing the wrapping paper. When he saw what was inside, he began laughing. "Chocolate-covered bacon? This cannot be a real thing."

He studied the contents, inhaling deeply, and grinned. "This could be the coolest thing anybody has ever gotten me."

"They're two of your favorite things."

"You're my absolute favorite thing." He gave me a kiss, and then to my surprise, he closed the box and dropped it on the coffee table.

"Hey, you have to eat it."

"I will, just not now."

"Why not?" I was suddenly suspicious. "I bought that just for you. I'll make you eat it whether you want to or not, and you know exactly why."

"Yes, you're trying to prove a point. I told you that bacon could be paired with anything. You said that wasn't true. You're trying to force my hand. Don't worry, bacon chocolate sounds amazing."

"I can't believe you remember that." I was shocked. "We were halfway through one of Aunt Tillie's bottles of wine when I told you that."

"I remember everything you've ever told me." He brushed his thumb against my cheek. "Everything."

"What's your favorite thing I ever told you?"

"That you love me."

My heart skipped and my eyes burned with unshed tears. "That's my favorite thing you ever said too."

"I know." He graced me with another kiss. "What's your least favorite thing I ever said to you?"

"Oh, I'm not playing that game. We're supposed to be happy going into our wedding."

"I know the worst thing I ever said to you. It was right after I found out you were a witch and I said I needed time to think."

He was right. "We're together now. That's all that matters."

"If I could take that back, Bay, I would." He was solemn. "I love you so much — so, so much — and I hate myself for walking away that day."

"You had to be sure. I would rather you walk away then than tear my heart out a year later."

"I will never leave you." He pulled me tight against him. "I knew the second I left that it was a mistake. My heart ached for you from the moment I said it."

"You weren't gone long."

"I was still wrong. I need you to know that you're stuck with me forever."

"I know. You're stuck with me too."

"There's nobody I'd rather be stuck with."

We held each other for a long time, long after our hearts fell into rhythm together. I was drifting, close to sleep, when he spoke again.

"We still have cake, Bay."

I laughed. "I won't let you miss out on your cake."

"I also need to sleep in a bed. I'm too old to sleep on the couch."

"I guess that means you want to get up."

"I just want to move into the bedroom and add cake into the mix."

"Sounds like a good deal." I paused, considering. "Just one thing before we get up." I licked my lips and traced a finger down his chiseled cheek. "Do you think things will change once we're married? I mean ... are we still going to be able to do things like this once we get back from our honeymoon?"

"Why wouldn't we do?"

I shrugged. "Maybe we'll become disillusioned with romance."

"That'll never happen. I love you too much to ever lose interest in romance."

"Good. I kind of like it when we do schmaltzy things like this."

"So do I."

"I am going to start monitoring your bacon intake once we're married. You've been warned."

His eyes narrowed. "You really know how to suck the fun out of a quiet night at home."

"I want you around forever."

"Well, we'll argue about that after the honeymoon." He gave me a long kiss. "I need you to know one thing with absolute certainty: You're the love of my life, Bay. I didn't think that was a thing before I met you. I thought it was some ridiculous romance movie thing, but it's true.

"You are my match," he continued. "You fill me with so much love. I've never laughed as much with anybody else. I've never cried as much with anybody else. I know it's impossible to love anyone as much as I love you. You're it for me."

I slid my fingers between his and studied our joined hands. "It's you and me forever, right?"

"And well beyond that." One more soft kiss and then he tickled my ribs. "Now let's get that cake and have some fun."

I gasped I was laughing so hard. "I knew you wanted me to take my clothes off to make things easier for yourself."

"I am an excellent multi-tasker."

DESPITE LANDON'S BEST ATTEMPTS AT tiring me out so I wouldn't dream, it was inevitable.

I knew what was about to happen long before my eyes popped

open in the murky dreamscape. A quick glance at the sky told me there was no sun to be found. When I lifted my hand, I couldn't detect any air movement, no wind, no bird chatter. Everything was still, unmoving, and the Hollow Creek of the dream was vastly different from the one I'd visited in the real world a few hours before.

"*Witch*." The single word was a hiss.

I jerked my head to the left, focusing on the magical shards that had turned dark and were coalescing into the form of a woman.

"Hello." It was the only word I could form as the magic finished making the form. "Um ... who are you?"

"Who are you?" The form was decidedly female, as was the voice. There was no face to greet me with a sneer or a scowl, just darkness, but I knew I was dealing with a woman.

"It doesn't matter who I am." The figure floated rather than walked, giving me a wide berth as she circled. "What matters is what's to come."

"And what's that?" I refused to show fear despite my uncertainty. I'd expected to dream about what happened at the high school. I guess, in hindsight, I shouldn't have been surprised that Hollow Creek took top billing.

"This place, these people, you don't belong here or among them." The shadow sounded like a snake as she circled me.

"I was born here," I countered. "It's my home."

"And yet you don't belong here."

"Yeah, I'm thinking you're the one who doesn't belong here," I said. "What do you want?"

"To make sure you understand ... there's no taking it back."

I was caught off guard. "Taking what back?"

"Any of it. You can't take it back."

"What? What don't you want me to take back?" Only one thing came to mind. "If you're talking about Will Compton, no, I can't take back what happened to him. But I will find out why it happened."

"You can't take it back," she repeated. "I won't allow it."

"You won't allow what?" Frustration bubbled up. "I just told you that I know I can't take Will's death back. What are you saying?"

Eyes that I didn't realize were there flared to life, red and burning with outrage. "You can't take it back."

"You've said that already." My temper burned hot, like the creature's eyes. "What do you want from me?"

"You're no longer the power in this town. Too long you've coasted on an unearned reputation. This is my town now."

I studied her with fresh eyes, confused. "I think you're mistaken," I said. "This is my town."

"You've already lost it."

"Come see me in the bright light of day and we'll talk about it."

She hissed again, ceasing her circling to take up position directly in front of me. "Soon."

"Soon what?"

The shadow grew until she towered over me, embers of hatred glowing hot in her eyes as her mouth opened to reveal two rows of razor-sharp teeth. I took a step back and began to fall over a cliff that hadn't been there a second ago.

"Soon."

I FELL STRAIGHT INTO A SITTING position in my own bed, letting out an echoing gasp into the darkness of my bedroom.

"Bay." Landon stirred when he realized I'd woken and immediately reached for me. "Come here, baby."

"I'm okay," I reassured him as he tucked me in at his side. "There's nothing to worry about." He pulled me practically on top of him, settling my head on his chest and tucking the blankets in around me. His voice was thick with sleep. "Nothing can get you here."

That was true, but the thing from my dream still felt real. "I'm okay," I reassured him. He needed his sleep. "You don't have to worry."

"I can't help but worry." He moved his hand over my back, drawing light circles to lull me. "We'll figure out what happened. Don't drive yourself crazy trying to sort it all out. We'll do it together."

"I know." I pressed my eyes shut and willed myself to fall back asleep. "Landon?"

"Hmm?"

"I love you."

He sighed as he wrapped me even tighter. "I love you more."

"It's not a competition."

"Of course not. I've already won."

"Maybe I won."

He chuckled into my hair. "I definitely won. Now close your eyes. Morning will be here soon enough. You need your sleep."

I didn't think it was possible. The voice from the dream was chasing me in the real world. Within a few seconds, though, my eyes felt too heavy to keep open. Landon's rhythmic breathing soothed me as I began to slip away.

The last conscious thought I managed was that the form at Hollow Creek had been female. Was that the "she" Granger and Will had mentioned? I didn't have time to think it over, because the next second I was gone into a different dreamland, one much better than the previous.

The question would still be waiting for me the next morning — and it would have to be answered.

CHAPTER Nine

Landon was wrapped around me, spooned behind my back, when I woke the next morning. When I rolled to look at him, I found his eyes open and contemplative.

"You have to stop worrying." I tried not to sound exasperated. "I'm fine. Our wedding is going to be great. The honeymoon is going to be amazing. Everything is going to work out."

"I know." He brushed my hair from my face. "You had a nightmare last night."

There was no sense lying to him. "Not the sort of nightmare you think."

"No? What do I think it was?"

"You think I saw Will killing himself again."

"I guess that's not what you dreamt about? Were you in the school? Were you trying to find kids to save?"

"I was at Hollow Creek and the magic shards turned black and formed a woman."

He was taken aback. "What?"

I grinned. "Even my nightmares are weird. She warned me that I wasn't the power in the area any longer — like that's how I see myself — and that I didn't belong here."

His eyes narrowed in concentration. "That is weird." He kissed me. "Was it a real witchy dream or just your anxiety?"

"I don't know."

"Last night you said that something has to be done about Hollow Creek before we leave for our honeymoon."

"Yes. Those shards are growing every day. Scout tried using some magic on one and it bounced back at her, burned her fingers."

"What's the plan?"

"I don't know. Scout said she would help. We'll probably have to enlist Thistle and Aunt Tillie."

"What about Stormy?"

I smiled at mention of Shadow Hills' newest witch. "She doesn't even know what she's doing half the time."

"But she's powerful. You said so yourself. Her magic is different from yours."

"It is. I don't know that fire magic is going to help us. We'll have to figure out something. If we leave for two weeks, we'll return to one big magic shard. That won't be good for anybody."

"It doesn't sound like it."

"Also, Gunner couldn't see the shards the first time he visited. He could yesterday."

"He's paranormal."

"But the magic is growing. We have got to get it under control."

"Is that what you're focusing on today?"

"Probably."

"Probably?" He arched an eyebrow. "Please tell me you won't stick your nose into the Will Compton stuff when you're not researching the Hollow Creek stuff."

"I haven't decided."

He pulled back far enough to rub his face. "Just be careful, okay? I have no idea what we're dealing with, but your dream worries me."

"My dream worries you in conjunction with Will's death?" I couldn't hide my surprise. "Why?"

"Because you said the magic coalesced into a woman in your dream. *She*."

"Oh." I hadn't even put that together. "Maybe my dreams were connected to what happened yesterday after all."

"Just be careful. I can't believe I'm about to say this, but maybe you should keep Aunt Tillie close. She's powerful, and that way you won't be alone if something does happen."

"Plus, it would keep her away from Minerva."

"Actually, I'm looking forward to that blowing up." Landon's smile was easy. "I can't decide which of them will win in a war."

"Aunt Tillie will always win."

"That's what I'm counting on." He leaned in and gave me another kiss. "I don't know what we're doing today but I'll keep you updated."

That seemed too good to be true.

"I have come to the conclusion that trying to protect you is the wrong way to go. You're stronger than me."

I balked. "You're the strongest person I know."

"I do have a great personality to go along with my devastating good looks," he said. "But you're my super witch, Bay. You can do things nobody else can. Trying to keep you from doing them is wrong.

"I want you safe," he continued. "I never want you to hurt — not in your heart or anyplace else — but it's time to be realistic. The magical stuff in Hemlock Cove isn't going anywhere. You're a doer. We're just going to do all these things together."

I couldn't stop myself from smiling. "You're growing as a person."

He laughed. "I just want to be the partner you need me to be."

"You are. There can never be anybody else."

LANDON WAS IN GOOD SPIRITS WHEN we arrived at the inn. We entered through the back, cutting through the empty family living quarters, and followed the noise through the kitchen. The dining room was full of people — thankfully they were all in on the magical secret — and they were all arguing.

"I'm sick of you," Thistle snapped. For once, she wasn't arguing with Aunt Tillie. "You're not the boss of me. If I want to go upstairs to see Clove, I'm going to freaking go upstairs."

I glanced between her and Minerva, who was studying my violet-haired cousin with steely-eyed menace. My mother and aunts surrounded the two women, and everybody looked as if they were about to melt down. "What's going on?" I asked, hoping to head off a fight.

"Minerva just gave Clove an exam," Mom explained. "She's dilating."

"What does that mean?" Landon asked as he glanced at the empty dining room table. "Where's breakfast?" He might've been a giving individual, loyal to a fault, but his life revolved around set mealtimes.

"Breakfast is almost ready," Mom replied. "We need to handle this first. Clove could go into active labor at any time."

"Here's hoping for today," Aunt Tillie offered from her spot at the head of the table. "If that kid doesn't come soon, we're all going to die of boredom."

Marnie pinned Aunt Tillie with a dark look. "You're about to become a great-great-aunt. I would think you would be excited about that."

"Well, you think wrong. Babies are boring. Plus, Clove is a whiner on a good day. She's been intolerable for weeks."

"Knock that off," I warned, flicking Aunt Tillie's ear.

She yelped as she covered her ear and glared. "Do you want to smell like pickled pigs' feet on your wedding day?"

Snort. Snort.

Peg was under the table and apparently didn't like mention of pigs' feet as an edible delicacy.

"There's my girl." Landon dropped down to smile at her. "Don't listen to Aunt Tillie. She's all talk."

"Excuse me?" Aunt Tillie's eyebrows hopped toward her hairline. "You're supposed to fear me."

"I'll fear you after breakfast," Landon said. "I have priorities."

"Oh, whatever." Aunt Tillie shook her head. "We need that ... *person* ... out of our house. She's bossy, and you know how I feel about bossy people."

"Yes, only you are allowed to be bossy," I agreed.

"You're definitely on my list," Aunt Tillie muttered.

"I hate to say it, but I agree with Aunt Tillie." Thistle's eyes brimmed with defiance. "Minerva wouldn't let me up to see Clove this morning. She says Clove is going to have breakfast in bed and relax."

"I don't see anything wrong with that," Mom said. "I mean ... Clove is having trouble getting around these days. She's very big."

"I wasn't asking Clove to walk down the stairs and come to me," Thistle shot back. "I was trying to go up there and see her. Why isn't that allowed?"

"I've already told you." Minerva sat at the table, posture perfect, fingers entwined as she regarded Thistle with cold calculation. "You're nothing but a big ball of negative energy. You can't be around the baby."

"Since when is that the rule?" Thistle demanded. "Aunt Tillie is nothing but negative energy and she was our primary babysitter."

"And look how that turned out," Minerva drawled.

"Was that insult aimed at Aunt Tillie or me?" Thistle snarled.

"Take your pick."

I dragged a hand through my hair and focused on my mother. "You brought her here," I pointed out. "Don't you think you should be putting out these little fires?"

Mom shrugged. "Minerva is here to make sure Clove's labor goes off without a hitch. If she believes Thistle is a detriment to the process, who am I to argue?"

She had to be joking. "You always argue and take control."

"Yes, well, Minerva and I had a long talk last night." Mom's eyes were imploring, as if she was willing me to see her point of view. "Clove's baby is already affecting emotions. She has been for months. She can also pick up on our emotions. She'll be even more powerful when she's born. We have to be smart about this."

There was something she wasn't saying, and I was instantly suspicious. "What are you worried about?"

"We don't know what's going to happen. That's the point. We need help. That's why Minerva is here."

"Yeah, but we've been welcoming magical babies into this family for more than a century. Why are you so worked up now?"

Mom wrung her hands, her shoulders hopping. "There's more scrutiny now. Before, we were just the oddball family who enjoyed having home births. Now we're welcoming another baby, one who could be extremely powerful, and we're doing it in a branded town."

It was an extremely well thought out answer, but there was more she wasn't saying. Something told me that pressing her in front of Minerva wasn't a good idea, but I wasn't about to let the midwife bully us into keeping our distance from Clove when she was at her most vulnerable.

"The baby already knows us," I pointed out. "She's ... familiar with us. She's touched us all. There's no reason to believe that she's uncomfortable around Thistle. Keeping us from Clove will only ratchet up her anxiety."

"Clove must be kept calm," Minerva insisted. "She's not even five feet tall and she's going to be giving birth to a child that is already one week overdue. It will be a difficult labor no matter what."

"Is Clove in danger?" I asked, the thought making my stomach constrict. "Is there something we should know that you're keeping from us?"

"Women have been giving birth since the dawn of man, witches even longer," Minerva said.

"Is she saying that witches have been around longer than women?" Landon asked as he leaned closer to me. "That doesn't make much sense."

He wasn't wrong, but I waved off the question. Minerva was just digging her heels in now. "We're thankful that you're here to help us," I offered. "Truly thankful. But Clove is our family. This baby will be the new apple of the Winchester eye."

"We're not big on apples unless they're in pies," Thistle countered. "It's far more likely that she'll be the bottle of wine of the Winchester eye."

"It doesn't matter what food item she is," I insisted. "She's our family. We're going to love her just as much as we love Clove. You can't keep us from her."

Minerva flicked her eyes to Mom. "We talked about this."

"We did," Mom agreed. "I thought you brought up some good points. The thing is ... Bay is right. If you separate Clove from the rest of the family, it will put unnecessary stress on her. If she has to stay in bed from here on out, we'll go to her. We won't let you isolate her, even if you think it's for her own good."

Minerva stared at Mom a moment longer and then nodded. "Fine. If this one wants to go up, I'll allow it." She vaguely gestured at Thistle. "She and Clove work together, so they're used to one another. I draw the line at Tillie."

"I'll go up there if I want," Aunt Tillie snapped.

"You're too loud." Minerva insisted. "Clove needs a peaceful environment if she wants to give birth to a peaceful child."

I practically choked on a laugh. "Are you being willfully blind? We don't do peaceful in this family. Clove's kid is going to be spoiled rotten. She's also going to be mouthy and obnoxious. That's how we do things in this house."

"She's right," Aunt Tillie said. "Where's breakfast?"

Mom made a face and started for the kitchen. "We're thankful for your help, Minerva, but we're not cutting Clove off from the family. In fact, we'll be making regular trips upstairs to sit with her. If you think the baby is coming soon, we'll be there every step of the way."

"How lovely," Minerva pouted.

"Breakfast is in five," Mom announced before disappearing into the kitchen with Marnie and Twila.

That left Thistle, Landon, Aunt Tillie, Minerva, and me to make small talk.

"Where's Chief Terry?" I asked, looking at his empty chair.

"He was called out last night," Thistle replied. "That's what Winnie said."

Landon, reaching for the juice carafe, stilled. "Why wouldn't he call me if something came up? I'm only five minutes away."

"You were busy coddling Bay last night," Aunt Tillie replied. "There's nothing that would've compelled him to drag you away from her."

"But ... ." Landon's forehead creased. "Did it have something to do with what happened to Will Compton?"

"No idea." Aunt Tillie showed little interest in the conversation. She was too busy glaring at Minerva.

Thankfully, Chief Terry picked that moment to arrive in the dining room. His eyes were heavy, bags drooping beneath them. He looked as if he needed a nap rather than food.

"What happened?" Landon asked. "Why didn't you call me?"

"Bay needed you last night," he replied, dropping a kiss on top of my head as he sat in the open chair next to me. "Besides, I am capable of going out on a case without you. Believe it or not, I managed it for decades before I met you."

"Yes, but you're older and wiser now," Landon insisted. "You should've called."

"You needed to be with Bay." Chief Terry insisted. "There's nothing you could've done anyway."

The sadness in his eyes told me that something bad had happened. "What was it?" I asked in a low voice. "Someone we know?"

Chief Terry heaved out a sigh and rubbed his cheek. "You know Marlon Perkins?"

I nodded as Landon shook his head.

"He's a salesman," I explained. "He sells lawn mowers."

Chief Terry nodded. "Yeah. He handles the entire region."

"Is he dead? Did he kill himself?" My mind immediately went there.

"He's in custody."

"What happened?"

"Well, he shot his wife Clarice and then calmly called it in to the 911 dispatchers."

Stunned disbelief washed over me. "Why would he do that?"

"He seemed confused when I questioned him. "He just knew that 'she' made him do it."

I jerked my eyes to Landon, the images from my dream the previous evening momentarily taking over.

"Did he say who 'she' was?" Landon asked.

"No." Chief Terry smiled when Mom carried a huge platter of pancakes into the room. "He's in a cell. He has an attorney coming. We should be able to question him in an hour or so."

"Is Clarice really dead?" Mom asked. Obviously, she had inside information thanks to Chief Terry being called away in the middle of the night.

"She is. I'm sorry."

"That's horrible." Mom shook her head. "Clarice always entered those wonderful pies in the baking contest every year. She was a good woman."

"Yes, pies decide that," Thistle said dryly.

"We need to figure out what's going on here," Landon said. "That's two people who have done this now."

"Three," I corrected. "Granger Montgomery was the first who showed signs. When he no longer held the gun, he went silent and then Will was somehow infected."

"I don't know that I like that word," Chief Terry said. "That makes it sound like this is going to spread."

"Isn't it?" I turned back to Landon. "You have to take me with you. I might be able to ... *see* ... something on Marlon that you guys can't."

"You didn't see anything on Will," Landon argued.

"I didn't know to look. I was focused on Granger. Now I know to look. You need me."

Landon looked caught, but ultimately nodded. "It seems I always need you these days." He smiled. "You can head into town with us after breakfast. Your car is still there anyway."

"Okay." My hand shook a little when I reached for the syrup container.

Landon wrapped his hand around mine and helped me bring it back over my plate. "We'll figure it out, Bay. We're a team. We'll do it together."

I swallowed hard. "We're a team."

"Forever," he insisted.

"Forever and always."

CHAPTER
Ten

Chief Terry needed a shower before heading back to town. That allowed Landon and me to check on Clove. She was in bed, a tray propped over her huge belly, and she had syrup on her chin.

"What's up?" I couldn't contain my grin as I glanced at Sam, stretched out in bed next to her reading a book.

"My life sucks," Clove replied darkly. "That's what's up."

I grabbed the napkin from her tray and wiped her chin, earning a glare for my efforts. "Minerva says it will be soon."

"She said I'm dilating finally," Clove said. "Actually, she said I've been dilating for days but I'm now dilating enough to mean the baby is actually imminent. It could still be days, though."

"Well ... the finish line is in sight."

"It doesn't feel like it." She slapped Landon's hand when it encroached on the plate containing her sausage links. "I will kill you," she warned ominously.

"Wow." Landon smiled despite her fury. "They say pregnant women have a glow about them. I didn't realize it was a glow of rage."

"Totally," Sam agreed. He smiled despite his predicament. "We're both very excited to see our little girl."

"Have you thought of any names yet?" I asked, hoping to change the subject. "Last time we talked about it Clove was in the midst of her Disney princess phase. Jasmine. Aurora. Ariel."

"Those are stupid names," Clove groused, her lower lip jutting out. "I can't believe anyone even suggested them."

"I believe you suggested them."

"I did not."

I looked to Sam for help. "She had a whole list."

"I've decided that I'm going to go with whatever mood Clove is in at any given moment," Sam replied. "She didn't suggest the Disney princess names. I believe Thistle did."

There was no way Thistle suggested those names. "Um ... ."

"Everything is Thistle's fault right now," Sam added before I could say anything else. "She's responsible for global warming and that horrible movie about the stripper who is going to make it big. You know the one. That chick from *Saved By the Bell* was in it."

"*Showgirls*," Landon said.

I pinned him with a dark look. "How do you know?"

"Every boy of a certain age who wanted to watch porn but couldn't because of an overprotective mother saw that movie. It was the *Magic Mike* of its time, a movie I believe you've watched at least twenty times with your cousins."

He had me there. "What other names are you considering?" I asked, hoping to cajole a smile out of Clove.

"We're going to name her Never, as in never coming, and call it a day," Clove replied. "Sam, my pancakes are dry. I need more syrup."

My eyes went wide. Clove was never this demanding, but Sam didn't bat an eyelash. He rolled straight out of bed. "I'll get it."

After waving goodbye to Clove, Landon and I followed Sam into the hallway.

"Well, she's the Devil," Landon noted. "How are you dealing with her moods?"

Sam's shrug was noncommittal. "I just keep reminding myself that she's creating a human life. She's the one who has to push it out. She's the one who can no longer see her ankles, which is good because they're swollen and I've already heard an earful about how ugly swollen ankles are. I've had it relatively easy. She has to deal with this part of it. Once the baby is here, she'll be back to her old self."

He was likely deluding himself, but I didn't say anything. He needed to get through this, and so far he'd been Clove's rock. I didn't want that to change. Once the baby was born, we would better be able to help him. Until then, Clove was his personal monster to slay.

"Well, don't be afraid to take breaks," I said, giving him a firm hand squeeze. "She's being horrible but can't help herself. Mom and the aunts can give you a break when you need it."

"She seems to think they're annoying right now."

"Oh, they're always annoying, but they're still going to be your lifeline today. Make sure you call if she does go into labor."

Sam's smile was warm. When he first showed up in Hemlock Cove, I didn't trust him. Now I couldn't fathom how we ever got through a day without him. He was wonderful for Clove. "I will. You guys be safe doing whatever it is you're doing."

"Of course, we will."

Landon waited until we were in the lobby with Chief Terry to speak again. "It won't be that easy, will it? Getting the old Clove back, I mean."

I shook my head. "She's going to be full of hormones, overwhelmed and dealing with a new set of problems. She'll be in pain and will barely be able to move. She's just going to be a different sort of monster."

"Well, that's something to look forward to." His smile was bright. "Tell me you won't be that way when we have kids."

"What answer do you want to hear?"

"The one that allows me to sleep at night."

"I'll be an absolute angel. I won't be anything like Clove."

He slung an amiable arm around my shoulders. "That's exactly what I wanted to hear."

THE FRONT OF THE POLICE STATION buzzed with activity. Chief Terry immediately went to the front desk and whispered something to the secretary. Then he glanced at the people who had gathered for information. One of them was Mrs. Little.

"We still don't know what happened," he announced. "There's nothing any of you can do here."

"I'm friends with Clarice," Mrs. Little barked, elbowing her way to the front of the group. "I demand to know what happened."

"He just told you that they don't know what happened," I snapped.

Chief Terry shot me a warning look, which I defiantly ignored. I had no intention of putting up with Mrs. Little's nonsense. In years past, I might've kowtowed to her thanks to residual fear from my childhood. That was not the case now. I didn't fear her, or pity her, and there was no way I would force myself to tolerate her. She wasn't worth my time. She'd proven that over and over again.

"All we know is that Clarice was shot," Chief Terry said. "She was dead before we arrived at the scene."

"Did Marlon do it?" Mrs. Little demanded. "That's the rumor going around."

Chief Terry made a face. He hated when his men gossiped with the townspeople. He'd warned them repeatedly. Unfortunately, everybody knew Chief Terry was a big softie and would never actually fire someone for spreading information. "We're still trying to ascertain what's going on."

"What 'we' are you talking about?" Mrs. Little asked. "Is Bay Winchester part of this crack team that's going to solve your murder?"

I opened my mouth to tell her exactly what she could do with her interest, but Landon slapped his hand over my mouth before I could make things worse.

"Bay is here to help me with something," Landon replied. "It's unrelated to what happened at the Perkins house."

"Oh, really?" Mrs. Little's tone was withering. "Are we actually supposed to believe that? What could Bay possibly be helping you with?"

"She needs to sign her statement on what happened yesterday," Landon replied.

It was rare for Mrs. Little to be knocked off her game. "I see ... well ... then I guess you'd best get to it."

Landon moved his hand from my mouth to the small of my back. "Right this way, Ms. Winchester."

I glared at him the entire way through the door and down the hallway. I managed to keep quiet until we were out of earshot. "Ms. Winchester?"

He smirked. "I can't help it if I like saying your name. It makes me think of a naughty librarian."

"Let's not go there," Chief Terry warned. "She's still my little sweetheart."

"We've been over this." Landon didn't feign patience. "Wife trumps little sweetheart."

"No, it doesn't." Chief Terry shifted his eyes to me. "Where did you guys land on the last name?"

I'd thought it would be a sore spot. Landon was primal on things like that. I figured for sure he would want me to become Bay Michaels ... or even Bay Winchester-Michaels. Instead, he thought it best I keep the Winchester name because it sparked fear in the hearts of our enemies. I was still on the fence.

"She's staying Bay Winchester," Landon replied. "Those who fear the name will recognize it. I want her safe."

"It could be Winchester-Michaels," I countered. "The Winchester would still be in there."

"But it's a distraction," Landon countered. "I want people to fear you if it serves as a layer of protection."

"And when we have kids?" I prodded.

He hesitated.

"Our kids will have at least part of your name," I reminded him.

"I ... need to think about it." He blew out a sigh. "We'll talk about it after ... well, after." He inclined his head toward the holding cell area.

I nodded in understanding. "Do you want me to go back there with you, or are you going to put him in an interview room?"

"He's staying in the cell," Chief Terry replied. "He's dangerous. It's better this way."

"Okay." I gave Landon's hand a squeeze. "You can still call me Mrs. Michaels when we're in bed alone at night if that does it for you."

Landon's lips quirked. "Will you wear an apron and serve me bacon when we're playing that particular game?"

"I guess, but I really am going to start monitoring your bacon intake."

"Don't torture me so close to the wedding. Keep the diabolical stuff to yourself for now."

"Okay, Mr. Winchester."

He pinched my flank in playful fashion and then turned serious as we moved into the holding cell bay. Marlon sat on a bench, disheveled, and stared at nothing in particular.

"Marlon," Chief Terry said, drawing the man's attention. "Did you get in touch with your attorney?"

Marlon nodded. "I told him not to bother coming. I'm guilty and want to be locked away forever." His voice was distant and thick with tears. The remorse was obvious.

"Before we get to that, I need you to run through it for me." Chief Terry sat in one of the chairs scattered around the room. "Tell me what you did yesterday."

"I killed my wife." Marlon's voice cracked. "You already know that."

"I still need you to run through it." Chief Terry was calm. "You went to work, right?"

"I'm always at work." Marlon turned bitter. "Clarice wanted me to consider retiring in the next two years. She was keen to travel, but I kept brushing her off. I thought I would go crazy if I didn't have a job to go to five days a week. I guess I went crazy anyway."

"Just tell me what happened, Marlon," Chief Terry instructed. "We can't help you without the details."

"I don't want you to help me." Marlon was adamant. "I want to be punished."

"Then tell us the details and we'll punish you," Landon interjected.

"It was a normal day," Marlon insisted. "I went to work, signed off on shipping fifteen new lawnmowers to a place in Shadow Hills, and then went to the diner for lunch. I eat with a few guys there if I'm in the area."

"Frank and Tim?" Chief Terry prodded.

"Yes. After that, I had to run over to Hawthorne Hollow. That woman out in the woods, the one with the pet bear, needed a blade replacement. I couldn't get a worker to go, so I did it myself to shut her up."

"Mama Moon," I murmured, more to myself than anybody else.

Marlon nodded. "That's her name. She reads tarot cards or something. After I handled her stuff, I went to the office and checked up on the inventory I ordered for next week. Then I went home. It was a normal day."

"Was Clarice at the house when you got home?"

"She was in the kitchen."

"Cooking dinner?"

"She was baking. She made a pie. Apple. My favorite."

"Did you talk to her?"

"I ... said hello." Marlon's expression contorted. "I asked how long until dinner. She said it would be at least an hour. I went out to my shed to get some things to kill time."

"What things?" Chief Terry asked, his voice never rising or falling.

"I was going on a hunting trip next week, to the Upper Peninsula. I needed to check on my tent ... and ammunition." He choked off a sob. "That's where I got the gun. I have a gun safe. I got the gun out."

"Why?" Chief Terry prodded. "Why would you do that?"

"I ... don't know. She told me to."

My shoulders jerked. There it was. *She*.

"Who is she?" Chief Terry asked.

"I don't know. I didn't recognize her. She wasn't even real. She was there but not there. Do you know what I mean?"

Chief Terry slid his eyes to me before shaking his head. "I'm afraid I don't know what you mean."

"I could hear her. I could see her. She was a person, but not really. She floated in the black smoke, like a ghost, but wasn't really there." His voice was barely a whisper. "I think she was in my head."

"She told you to kill Clarice?" I blurted, earning a warning look from Chief Terry and a surprised gasp from Marlon. It was as if he was registering my presence for the first time.

"She said I had to do it for her," Marlon replied, his bloodshot eyes filling with tears. "It seemed like the most normal thing in the world. There was nothing inside of me saying it was a bad idea. I just ... did it."

"You did what?" Chief Terry's gentle voice was back. "Tell me exactly what you did."

"I loaded the gun in the shed and then marched straight into the house. Clarice didn't even look at me. She was washing potatoes in the sink. I ... raised the gun, pointed it at the back of her head, and then I pulled the trigger."

"You didn't hesitate?"

"No. It seemed like the only thing I could do until ... well ... until I'd done it."

I spoke again, not caring that Chief Terry wanted me to remain quiet. "What happened after you shot her? Did the woman congratulate you? Maybe she thanked you."

"She was gone. She wasn't there once I pulled the trigger."

There was one more thing I needed to know. "Did you feel bad about what you'd done when she was gone?"

Marlon's eyes flashed hot. "Of course, I did. Clarice was my wife. I loved her. I just ... don't understand how this happened." He buried his face in his hands. "How could I have done this?"

That was a question we still didn't have an answer for, but I was beginning to understand ... at least a little.

"WHAT DO YOU THINK?" CHIEF TERRY asked when we were in his office. "Is he telling the truth?"

"He's telling the truth as he knows it," I replied.

"The black smoke," Landon prodded. "That sounds like your dream last night."

Chief Terry looked pained. "What dream?"

He knew about our problem at Hollow Creek, so I didn't have to catch him up. I explained how the magical shards in the dream turned into a woman and threatened me.

"So, if we take care of the problem at Hollow Creek all of this will stop?" he asked hopefully.

I held out my hands. "I think the magic at Hollow Creek has grown out of control. It's not sentient, no matter what the dream said. We're dealing with someone else, likely a woman, who is directing the magic into a specific form."

"Who is that?" Chief Terry demanded.

"I don't know, but I'm going to find out, though. You have my word on that."

CHAPTER Eleven

Landon insisted on heading out to Hollow Creek with me. He knew I was going when we were finished with Marlon and simply jabbed a finger.

"I'm going."

I nodded, resigned. "Okay, but if I tell you to do something, you're going to do it."

"Maybe I really should become Mr. Winchester," he mused as we headed toward the parking lot.

"Would you do that?" It seemed like a ridiculous question, but he shrugged. "I don't know. Landon Winchester. It doesn't sound bad."

It also didn't sound like him. "I think hyphenating my name would be okay."

He didn't look convinced. "Bay, I want people to fear you. It's important given everything that happens around here."

I didn't disagree. Still, part of me wanted us to be joined on paper. "We'll talk about it later."

"Okay." He smiled. "Let's take out the magic shards." He was gung-ho, which I always appreciated, but it wasn't going to be as easy as he hoped.

There were two motorcycles parked in the field next to the creek. Landon's raised eyebrow was a question, so I nodded.

"Scout and Gunner." I hopped out of the car and gave the bikes a long once-over. "Have you ever considered getting a motorcycle?"

"I guess, when I was younger. Why?"

"I don't know. I think they're kind of sexy."

He slowed his pace. "Which one of them do you find sexy? Keep in mind, the only acceptable answer is Scout."

I laughed. "I didn't say I found *them* sexy. I just like riding on a motorcycle with Scout. It's somehow ... freeing."

"Have you ever been on Gunner's motorcycle?"

Of course, he would go there. "No. He's a gentleman. Also, in case you haven't noticed, he's completely devoted to Scout."

"I know." Landon grumbled as we hiked through the weeds. "I like him. It's just ... well ... ."

I waited, feigning patience.

"It's his hair," he said finally. "I'm the only one who should have sexy motorcycle hair."

I had to swallow my laugh. "You know, when I met you, there was a motorcycle involved. You were undercover with that gang."

"I'm well aware. That wasn't my motorcycle, though. It belonged to the bureau."

"Yeah. I wish we could've ridden on it."

He studied my profile for a long beat. "You're serious."

I shrugged. "I just like it. I don't know how to explain it."

"Well, I'll see if I can borrow one from impound when we get back from our honeymoon. There's no sense in not giving my wife a little thrill."

"See, now you're talking." I slipped my hand into his as we finished the walk to the creek, where we found Gunner and Scout surveying the water. Scout's hair was wet. "What's up, guys?"

"Hey." Scout greeted us without looking in our direction. "So ... did you know your magic shards talk?"

I pulled up short. "Excuse me?"

"It's true," Gunner confirmed. "I've heard them."

That couldn't be right. "What do they say?"

"They're snarky," Scout replied. "I'm pretty sure they're you."

"Me?" I could practically feel the color draining from my face. "Are you saying I caused this?"

"No." Scout shook her head. "Or, well, not just you. I meant your entire family. A lot of them are Tillie."

"One of them threw Scout into the water about twenty minutes ago," Gunner explained. "Then it laughed like a crazy person, and I swear it sounded just like Tillie."

How was that even possible? "I've never heard them talk."

"Well, just wait." Scout used her finger to tap a shard, causing it to fly. Sure enough, I heard a voice emanating from it as it floated away.

Just because you've never seen Bigfoot, that doesn't mean he's not real. He could just hate people. We hate people and we're still real. He's totally a real thing whether you believe in him or not.

"No way." Landon stepped forward, eyes wide. "Did you hear that? It was Clove."

I was flabbergasted. "You can see them?"

"I can't see them, but I heard that."

I let out a breath. "I ... don't ... know what to say."

"It's weird," Scout acknowledged as she tapped another shard. This one was easy to make out.

You're on my list.

I pressed my lips together, amused despite my apprehension. "Aunt Tillie."

"I've heard all of you since I've been here," Scout offered. "It's like a highlight reel of your lives. If I wasn't so worried what happens next, I'd suggest it's a fun walk down memory lane."

"Yeah, well ... there's more." I told her, in halting terms, about Marlon killing his wife. I also explained about my dream. "They have to be connected, right?"

"I'd say so," Scout said. "I just ... have never seen anything like this. These are fragments of your magic."

"I know. We've been down here hundreds of times. We've fought more than a few enemies here. Somehow we created this ... *mess* ... in the process."

"I think it's this place." Scout tapped another shard. This one sounded like me.

I'll make you eat a dirt sandwich with mustard.

My cheeks heated. "Thistle was probably irritating me."

She tapped another shard. This one my mother. She wasn't talking to me, though. She was talking to Landon. Then, almost immediately, his voice became apparent as it chased her question.

Because at first, I was afraid she would say no. I know now that was irrational, but I felt real fear. Then Clove got engaged and I didn't want her to think it was a reaction to that. I want Bay to be the center of attention like Clove has been since she announced her engagement.

"Holy ...!" Landon's eyes went wide. "That's when I asked your mother for permission to marry you."

"Which still seems weird," I groused. "I mean ... she's my mother, not my boss. What would've happened if she said no?"

"She wouldn't say no," Landon replied. "She knows I make you happy."

"I know, but ... she could've said no. She gets in bad moods."

"She never gets in a bad enough mood to deny you something you want ... and you wanted me more than anything."

"You're so full of yourself." I shook my head, although I couldn't hold back a laugh. "We're in big trouble here. Somehow these shards have taken a form, and someone is using that form to kill people."

"To what end?" Scout asked. She seemed addicted to touching the shards. When she hit another, it was Aunt Tillie's voice that came ringing through.

I'm coming for you, Floyd!

"Okay, I have to know what that one was about," Scout said with a hearty laugh. "Who's Floyd?"

"A dead man," I replied. "He beat his wife, cheated on her, and was a genuine menace. When he died — or was murdered — she helped hide the body in the yard of the inn. It was dug up when her greenhouse was constructed and finding him released his poltergeist. Floyd went on a rampage and Aunt Tillie went after him."

"Please tell me that Floyd got what was coming to him," Gunner said, his gaze dark.

"He did," Landon confirmed. "Bay and Aunt Tillie took care of him. I would like to point out that all of this happened when my parents were visiting for the first time. The poltergeist made quite the impression on them."

I was mortified at the memory. "Oh, geez. I forgot about that." Suddenly, I straightened. "Your parents are arriving tomorrow. They're supposed to be staying at the inn. Given what's happening... ."

"Calm down," Landon ordered as his hand landed on the back of my neck and began rubbing. "I talked to Winnie when you were in the bathroom this morning. We agreed it makes more sense for them to stay at the Dragonfly."

"Seriously?" This was news to me. "What if they don't have any open rooms?"

"They're helping with the food for the wedding," Landon reminded me. "They're only opening half the rooms this week. My parents and brothers won't be eating at the Dragonfly, so they said it was fine for them to stay there. Your father wants to get to know them."

"It does sound safer," Scout said. "Plus, that opens up a room at The Overlook for Gunner and me." Her smile was bright. "We think it best we hunker down here until this is settled."

"Scout thinks it's best," Gunner corrected. "I love the food, so I'm fine with it."

"You helped me," Scout insisted earnestly. "You didn't have to. You didn't know me. You still offered your help. You've also been keeping an eye on Evan. Now I want to help you."

"I appreciate the help." I meant it. "I have no idea what I'm doing." I touched one of the shards. To my utter surprise, the voice that came out belonged to Thistle, from when we were children.

"You just told us that little witches scream and yell. Then they're poop factories too. There's a lot of poop in this miracle you're telling us about."

"Wow." Landon chuckled. "I can't believe that."

"Aunt Tillie explained the miracle of birth to us when we were young," I said. "Thistle wasn't the only one to melt down about the crapping on the bed thing."

"Yes, well, nobody needs to dwell on that." Landon said. "What are we supposed to do with these shards?"

"That I can't answer." Scout said. "I've put some of our team members on research. Rooster thinks it's a good idea because if we don't contain this here it could spread to Hawthorne Hollow. By then it might be too big to contain."

"That's frightening," Landon muttered.

"Doc and Bonnie are doing research. I also sent a text to Mama Moon. We need help."

"What if we conduct a seance or something?" Landon suggested. "If Bay can control ghosts, can she command the ghosts to eliminate these shards?"

I tapped another shard and laughed when I heard Aunt Tillie remark on Landon's hair.

What sort of man has long hair like that? Does he want to be a girl? Is he hiding his true feelings?

Landon glowered. "Maybe this isn't as much fun as I thought. Still, it doesn't feel dangerous, not like the other stuff we've dealt with."

"But it is," I insisted. "This magic has turned into something dark. It's helping someone else kill people."

He continued rubbing the back of my neck. "So, what do we do?"

"I need to know more about the victims," Scout said. "What can you tell me about them?"

"Granger Montgomery is a seventeen-year-old kid who enjoys spending his time playing video games and screwing around on a computer," Landon rattled off. "His parents said he's never had a girlfriend. They don't know who 'she' is. He hasn't said a single word since the incident in the school.

"Will Compton was thirty-eight," he continued. "He was single and apparently had an online girlfriend. She lives in Arizona but was planning to visit Hemlock Cove over the Christmas break to meet him in person."

I hadn't yet heard that part. "Wait ... she was going to fly to another state to meet a man she only knew from the internet?" That didn't sound smart to me. "What if he was a pervert or something?"

Scout let loose a cackle. "That's exactly what I was thinking."

Landon shrugged. "I don't particularly feel that it's smart either but it's not going to happen now. We didn't find anything on Will's computer to suggest he was a pervert. Our techs are going over it but so far it's clean."

"Right." I rubbed my forehead. "We shouldn't speak ill of the dead. He's a victim in all this, and he lost his life."

"It's okay," Landon reassured me. "Sometimes you just need to decompress in situations like this, even if inappropriate humor helps."

"What about the guy last night?" Gunner asked. "What's his deal?"

"Marlon Perkins," I supplied. "He sells lawnmowers. He was pleasant but boring. His wife wasn't one of my favorite people because she was one of Mrs. Little's cronies, but she wasn't one of the really bad ones. She wasn't outright evil. She just liked to gossip."

"That's normal for a small town," Scout mused. She reached out and touched another shard. This one squeaked like Clove.

My eyes are leaking.

I laughed despite the serious conversation. "She always used to say that when she was trying to manipulate people. She was smaller than the rest of us and could cry on cue. Adults went gooey at their cores over the combination."

"That's always helpful," Scout said. "How is she doing?"

"They say it could be any time." I held out my hands. "Knowing there's an evil entity running around town doing the bidding of someone who wants to hurt people doesn't fill me with much faith this birth will go smoothly. We have no idea how the people infected have been chosen, or what the ultimate goal is."

"Sweetie, we'll figure it out," Landon promised. "Don't work yourself up. We have a few days to end this before the honeymoon."

"Unless you get infected and decide to shoot me," I argued. I didn't mean to say it. "You have a gun at the ready. Most of the people in this town do. What if this entity convinces you that I need to go?"

Landon immediately started shaking his head. "Won't happen. I will never hurt you." Even as he said it, he looked conflicted. "Of course, I'm sure that Marlon felt the same way about Clarice. You saw how wrecked he was after."

"I'm not saying you would ever purposely hurt me. In fact, if something does happen, I don't want you to blame yourself."

"We're not playing that game." Landon was firm. "We're going to be preemptive." He glanced down at the weapon on his hip. "Can you put a spell on me so I can't use my gun?"

"No."

"You can't?" He looked disappointed.

"I mean ... I probably could, but I won't. What if you run into trouble with someone else who is armed? You won't be able to protect yourself."

"I prefer me being shot to shooting you."

"Well, we'll have to come up with something else." I refused to back down. "Maybe we can lock all the guns in the inn in the greenhouse and put a spell on the building to keep people out. Then you can lock your gun in the Explorer at night and we can put a spell on it for the overnight hours."

"I guess that's better than nothing," he muttered.

"We need to get into the nitty-gritty of this before anybody freaks out," Scout said. "We still have no idea why someone is doing this, let alone how the victims are selected."

"It might be random," I suggested. "Maybe those affected are open to the infection through some means we're not aware of."

"That's possible," Scout said. She tapped another shard. This time the voice was mine, the words directed at Landon.

Not tonight. Maybe some other night. I've got some things to think about. I've got some things to do.

Landon cringed. "Of course, we'd have to hear that," he groused, his smile disappearing. "I just love being reminded of that time in our lives."

I gripped his hand. "It's part of our past. We're looking to the future."

"The answer is here," Scout said. "We just have to figure it out."

CHAPTER
Twelve

"Okay, so ... you're going to stick close to these guys, right?" Landon looked between Scout and me when we returned to where we had parked.

"I am," I confirmed. "At least for now."

"For now?" He cocked an eyebrow.

Of course, he would pick up on that clarifier. "For now," I agreed. "I can't give you an itinerary of how I plan to spend my day when I don't know what we'll find."

"I don't want an itinerary. I just ... want you to be careful." He ran his hands up and down my arms. "We're getting married in a few days. I would really like you to be at the ceremony."

"So would I. Otherwise you'll have to marry someone else and that would totally bum me out."

"There's nobody else for me." He gave me a quick kiss and slid his eyes to Gunner, who just happened to be stretching his arms over his head and showing off his muscles, the long hair that irritated Landon blowing in the soft breeze. "You're riding with Scout?"

Scout snickered. "Oh, how cute is he?" she taunted.

"Very cute."

Gunner had no problem figuring out what was annoying Landon. "I have my own witch. I don't need yours."

"My witch is the best witch," Landon argued.

"Those are fighting words." Despite the male posturing, Gunner grinned at him. "She can ride with Scout. You have nothing to worry about."

"Oh, if only." Landon moved to his Explorer, keys in hand. "Let me know if you find something. If we can figure out who this ... entity ... is going after next, we might be able to get ahead of it."

"We don't even know how the victims are selected," I reminded him.

"I know. I just ... don't like this." He glanced down at his own weapon. "Not being in control of yourself is terrifying. The thought of hurting the thing you love most, though ... ." He shook his head. "I don't like it."

"We'll figure it out," I promised. "We're smarter than we look."

He smirked. "You've got me thinking you're the smartest woman in the world. I believed that long before now."

I rolled up to the balls of my feet to kiss him. "I should get a button made that says that, and then you can get a button saying you're with the smartest woman in the world."

He stroked his hand over my hair. "I would wear it." He gave me another kiss. "Be careful. Don't do anything weird."

"Dude, you're marrying into her family," Gunner said. "You like weird."

"That's true." Landon fobbed his Explorer and then shot me a helpless look. "I don't know where to look."

He wasn't the only one. "We're going to hit the research hard today. Something has to shake loose."

"From your lips to the Goddess's ears. Be good, Bay. I love you too much to lose you."

"Because you need a bride at the wedding," I teased.

"Because I need you with me forever," he said. "Just ... watch your back. There's something evil out there. I don't want it coming for you."

. . .

THE RIDE INTO TOWN WASN'T LONG ENOUGH for my liking, and when Scout parked in front of Thistle's store, I was reluctant to take my helmet off.

"I'm going to try to talk Landon into getting a motorcycle," I said as I stashed the helmet on the seat.

"Is he against it?" Gunner asked. He was stretching again, and two women — tourists — clearly liked what they saw. One of them tripped over a seam in the sidewalk and almost went flying.

"When we met, he was undercover," I explained. "He was with a motorcycle gang. I thought he was a righteous jerk and yet I was still hot for him. At the time, I thought it said something about my taste in men."

Scout's laugh was warm and gregarious. "How did you figure out he was a cop?"

My smile faded at the memory, whispers of sound from my terrified race through a cornfield rushing to the forefront of my brain. "He took a bullet for Aunt Tillie."

"Seriously?" Gunner's surprise was evident. "That was ... nice ... of him."

I laughed. "When he was in the hospital we talked. I visited him when he was recovering. Then he was in town to fill out some reports and work on some other things. I really liked him."

"You told me that he left once he found out you were a witch," Scout noted. "Is that one of the snippets we heard earlier?"

I nodded. "He's still angry at himself over it."

"He shouldn't be angry. He needed to be sure. He left and then realized he couldn't live without you. That's true love in my book."

"He wasn't even gone that long," I acknowledged. "A couple weeks. I was sad and depressed when he was gone, a total mope. When he came back, it was like a switch had been flipped. He never made noise again about leaving."

"Because he knew," Gunner offered. "He knew that you were his match. My guess is that all he's wanted since then is to make you happy."

"And fatty dinners from my mother," I agreed with a grin. "It doesn't take much to make him happy."

"How did he take what you did yesterday?" Scout asked. "He seemed okay at dinner last night, but I wondered if he might fall apart when it was just the two of you."

"He was good. He insisted we hide under a blanket on the couch and say a bunch of schmaltzy things to one another, but that's not out of the norm for him. He likes to express his feelings."

"Aw, so sweet." Scout lightly punched my arm. "Now, come on." She inclined her head toward Hypnotic. "I didn't get nearly as much of Thistle's snarky mouth last night as I would've liked. I absolutely love her attitude."

"You're on a short list of people who can say that and mean it." I pulled open the door. "Truthfully, most of the time, I like it too."

Thistle was behind the counter, her forehead creased as she stared at a ledger. She seemed annoyed. Of course, that was her normal mood, so it didn't seem out of the ordinary.

"Problem?" I asked when she looked up.

"If I tell you that I miss Clove because she has more patience for doing the books, will you think less of me?" she asked.

A chuckle escaped before I could swallow it. "That's not why you miss Clove."

"Of course, it is."

"No, you miss being able to talk with her about random topics all day. She's been out of commission for months. It's not the same as it used to be."

Thistle's lips curved down. "And it'll never be the same again. Do you know she wants to set up a playpen in here so she can have the baby at work?"

I wasn't surprised. "Why is that a problem? It will save them money. That way they won't need a nanny or babysitter."

"She needs to drop that kid off with our mothers." Thistle was insistent. "Then things can at least go back to a semblance of how they used to be."

Thistle didn't like change. It was one of the most frustrating things about her. The only thing she liked to randomize was her hair color. Everything else needed to follow routine. She reminded me of Aunt Tillie that way.

"Clove won't want to be away from the baby at the start," I said. "That's natural. When things settle down, she'll drop the baby at the inn two or three days a week. Our mothers will insist on it."

"Why not five days a week?" Thistle's gaze was dark. "That would be easier for me."

"The world doesn't revolve around you." I moved to the desk and took the ledger from her. "I'll balance the books. Take a break. Something weird happened at Hollow Creek and we could use another opinion. As for the baby, you can talk as tough as you want, but I know darned well you're going to spoil the crap out of that kid."

"I am not." Thistle was affronted. "I don't even like babies."

"Neither did Aunt Tillie, but she spent the most time with us when we were little."

"Don't tell me you just compared me to Aunt Tillie." Thistle made a horrified face. "Am I the Aunt Tillie of our group? That's the meanest thing you've ever said to me."

I laughed as I carried the ledger to the couch. "You can't be surprised. You've always been the one most like her."

"Okay, *that's* the meanest thing you've ever said to me."

"I think it's cool," Gunner said as he watched me study the numbers. Math was never my strong suit, but I could balance the books at the newspaper easily enough. Given the inventory moving through Hypnotic, however, there were more numbers to deal with. "Oh, give me that." He took the ledger from me. "What is it with women and math?"

"That's a very sexist thing to say," Scout chided as she sat on the arm of his chair. "I'm going to punish you for it later."

"That's why I say sexist things. I like being punished."

"Pervert." She elbowed his side and then focused on me. "Do you want to tell her what's happening at Hollow Creek?"

"Right." I launched into the tale of the talking magic shards, keeping it brief. "It's a problem," I said as I wrapped things up. "Gunner can now see the shards and Landon could hear the voices."

"Well, crap." Thistle leaned back and studied the ceiling. "What do we do?"

"I don't know, but this is getting out of control. We should have done something months ago," I admitted. "We let it slide because we had other stuff going on, but now we're in trouble."

"Big trouble." Thistle blew out a sigh and then stood again. "I've been doing some research." She moved behind the counter and grabbed a book. "When the numbers get to be too much for me, I take a break and go through the books. I think I found something." She handed me a leatherbound book.

"What am I looking at?" I studied the page, which contained an illustration of a woman surrounded by what appeared to be bits of pollen. "I don't get it."

Thistle made a face. "It's not dandelion fluff. It's magic."

I looked at the drawing again and focused on the text. "It's in Latin."

"I'm working on translating it. If Gunner can focus on my books, then I can finish translating. I think there might be information on a ritual."

I handed the book back to her. "While you guys do that, I'm heading to the high school."

Thistle balked. "Why? Please tell me you're not going to torture yourself by trying to think of ways you could've done things differently and saved Will Compton."

I was beyond that. "I need to look around to see if there's anything magically funky. We believe this all started there."

"I'll go with you," Scout said. "Gunner can stay and help Thistle."

Rather than argue, as I expected, Gunner nodded. "If something happens, call."

"We can take care of ourselves," Scout reminded him.

"I know, but it makes me feel manly to swoop in and save my witch." He didn't bother looking up when he said it, but I could see the corners of his mouth twisting.

"Ha, ha." She pinched his flank hard enough he yelped. "It's best nobody is alone right now anyway. We won't be gone long."

"I'll miss you with every breath," he drawled.

"Keep it up and I really will punish you tonight," she warned.

"I keep telling you it's not a punishment if I want it."

"Wow." Thistle shook her head. "Now I really do wish Clove was back."

I pointed at the book. "Translate that thing. If there's a ritual, I want to do it soon."

"You mean before the baby is born," Thistle surmised.

I nodded. "The baby picks up on emotions. It's best we get this settled before she arrives."

"Then we'll get it done." Thistle's response was simple. "Don't get in trouble with Scout. I don't want to miss any more fun."

I grinned because I knew that was as close to a declaration of love as Thistle was capable of. "No promises."

WE WALKED TO THE HIGH SCHOOL BECAUSE it was easier than driving three blocks. It remained closed, police tape blocking off the location. It looked as if Chief Terry had some of his guys inside collecting evidence given the patrol cars parked in the lot.

"Can we get inside?" Scout asked, glancing around.

I was leery about crossing the tape because I saw several people — adults and teenagers — milling about on the far side of the property. "Maybe we should wait."

She followed my gaze and nodded, frowning when one of the teenagers glared in our direction. "I would think you guys would be popular with the teenage set — witchcraft never goes out of style with that age group — but I'm guessing not."

I shook my head as the girl continued to glare. "That's Amelia Hart."

"Do you have a relationship with her?" Scout asked when I didn't provide more information.

"You could say that." I licked my lips, debating, and then pushed forward. "We've been dealing with her and three of her friends for several months. The four of them went out to Hollow Creek and somehow managed to tap into the magic of the shards."

"Are you kidding me?" Scout's eyebrows hopped. "What did they do?"

"Nothing good." The memory still gave me chills. "Do you know how they say that teenagers can't be deemed sociopathic because their emotions are so volatile?"

"No, but I do now."

"Well, these kids decided they wanted to get money and move to California. They enticed one of our local vendors — a guy who apparently had no problem with the age difference — and had him help them 'kidnap' one of their friends." I used the appropriate air quotes.

"Thistle's boyfriend Marcus was seriously injured when this went down," I continued. "He was struck in the back of the head and spent a night in the hospital. Thistle was ... wrecked."

"Do you blame her?"

"No. That's why I don't get annoyed when Landon starts feeling protective. I get it. When you love someone, fear can render you useless."

"It really can."

"It's better to work with someone than constantly fight against them."

"I agree."

"Anyway, the girls purposely set up a kidnapping. Todd Lipscomb — he ran the kissing booth and is a total jerk — transported Amelia to a place she could hide. Then the other three girls made up a story about her being kidnapped."

Scout's face was blank. "Why?"

"They were going to ransom her and use the money to move to California. They managed to tap into the magic at Hollow Creek to carry this out."

"What did you do?"

"We figured things out, stopped the ransom exchange and modified their memories. We thought that was the end, but it turns out it wasn't. One of the girls was murdered a few weeks later. It's been an uphill battle ever since. The memory modification didn't take with Amelia. She's bitter ... and frustrated ... and impossible to control."

Scout pursed her lips as she regarded the girl. "Do you think she's involved in what's happening at Hollow Creek?"

"It's possible. She's not naturally magical. Everything she's managed to do is on borrowed magic. What's happening now seems as if it should be beyond her capabilities, even if the magic at Hollow Creek is growing."

"Never say never," Scout said. "Do you want to go talk to her?"

"I ... don't know." Amelia wasn't alone. I didn't recognize any of the girls with her. Her previous friendships had apparently fallen by the wayside. "It feels as if focusing too strongly on her is a mistake."

"Well, I don't think you have a choice in the matter." Scout was grim. "She's heading this way."

We remained in our spots as Amelia picked her way over to us. Her friends did not join her. She stopped when she was still a good ten feet away, and the glare she lobbed at me was full of teenage angst and hatred.

"Bay."

"Amelia." I said her name in the same derisive tone she used to utter mine. "Do you need something?"

"I was just coming over to say that I heard what you did yesterday. People are talking about it all over town."

"So I heard."

"People don't understand how Granger had the gun, but Mr. Compton is dead, supposedly because he shot himself."

"I'm guessing you don't believe that," I noted.

"There's very little I trust when it comes to your family," she said. "This doesn't seem like the sort of thing you would involve yourself in."

"Is it the sort of thing you would involve yourself in?" I asked pointedly.

Her eyes narrowed. "What does that mean?"

I could never tell if she was acting. She was that good. Today was no different.

"It was just a question," I replied. "As for what happened in the school yesterday, if you have questions you should talk to the school counselor. I understand there will be an assembly before students return to classes so you can talk things over."

"Yes, because an assembly will fix everything," she said dryly. "Is that all you have to say?"

"That's all I have to say," I confirmed. "If you need to talk to someone, the school will make counselors available."

Amelia rolled her eyes. "I should've known you would be as useless as ever."

"Hey!" Scout's voice snapped out, hard and strong. Her dislike for Amelia was evident. "Show some respect."

Amelia turned haughty. "Who are you?"

"Someone you don't want to mess with," Scout said. "I get that you're a teenager and that means people give you a pass for bad behavior, but I'm not like anyone else you've ever met. I won't give you a pass on anything."

"Should that frighten me?"

"Yes." Scout folded her arms over her chest and looked Amelia up and down, as if studying a bug she was about to stomp. "If you're involved in this, there will be no third chance given the other things you've done."

I was impressed with the threat, especially given the way Amelia backed up. Did she sense the power radiating off Scout? Was she afraid?

"You're not the boss of me," Amelia said finally.

"Keep telling yourself that. Until then, keep your nose clean. Nobody has time to deal with you on top of everything else."

Amelia's eyes darkened. "Just ... don't talk to me."

"You came over here," I reminded her.

"Yes, well, now I'm leaving." There was a bit of extra flounce in her step when Amelia turned and strode back to her friends.

"We definitely need to watch her," Scout said as she watched the girl go. "There's something wrong with her."

"Let's circle the property to see if we can find anything. Then I'll call Chief Terry and tell him we need to get on the grounds."

"Sounds like a plan."

CHAPTER Thirteen

Chief Terry and Landon insisted on going inside the high school with us. They figured it would look less suspicious to the outside world. Mrs. Little had showed up with her gaggle of gossips, something we discovered after completing our circle of the property, so I was glad for the entourage.

Unfortunately, we found nothing that could be considered helpful. When we emerged, Amelia and her friends had disappeared. I filled in Chief Terry and Landon about what had gone down with her. They said Amelia's attitude was hardly new. They didn't want to focus on her to the detriment of the case, and I couldn't blame them.

After that, we returned to Hypnotic. Scout and I ran the store so Thistle could translate the ritual. Gunner seemed perfectly happy with a calculator and the ledger book. When it was time to close the store, he proudly presented Thistle with a balanced ledger. She was so grateful she hugged him — out of the ordinary for her — and then we all left for the inn.

"We're going to see if your mother will let us rent a room," Scout explained when we reached the lot and she retrieved a bag from the storage bin. "We think it's best we stick close for a night or two."

"Thank you." I meant it. "I don't want to tear you guys away from your other duties."

"Oh, don't worry about that." Scout's smile was easy. "We don't have much going on. Rooster wants us to keep an eye on Evan. He's not convinced there won't be a reversion of some sort. Besides, you helped us, so it's only fair we help you."

"I like the idea of you guys being around," I said as we walked into the inn. "Another witch that I trust on the scene is always a benefit. In fact ... ." I forgot what I was going to say, and my mouth dropped open when a burst of magic hurtled in my direction.

Scout's reflexes were either more honed than mine or she was expecting trouble because she easily plucked the magic out of the air and squeezed it until it disintegrated.

"What was that?" Gunner demanded, fists at his sides.

Then I heard it, the sound of small wheels on the floor. Aunt Tillie appeared, and there was no doubt she was the source of the magic because she was dressed for battle.

"What in the world?" Gunner's aggressive stance faded as he took in Aunt Tillie's outfit. She was clad in camouflage fatigues — no leggings for a change — and had a matching coat tied around her neck. The helmet she wore was black and had what looked to be a fake grenade strapped to it. At least I hoped it was fake.

"What are you doing?" I demanded as I moved to intercept her.

She might've been in her eighties, but she was faster than she looked, and she easily zipped around me.

Snort. Snort.

Somebody had dressed Peg in a black leather tutu. The pig looked somehow dangerous in the get-up ... right until she wiggled her butt and raced for Gunner.

"Hey, pretty girl." Gunner dropped to the floor, his smile wide and welcoming. "You look like you should be in a sidecar on my motorcycle."

"She's preparing for war," Aunt Tillie declared. "We've already picked our enemy."

I was about to ask who that enemy was when another figure appeared at the bottom of the stairs. Minerva, dressed in a stark gray dress with one of those collars that buttoned all the way up to her chin, was furious when she glared at Aunt Tillie.

"I know what you've been up to," she warned, disdain dripping from her tongue. "I won't stand for it."

Minerva didn't radiate power like some of the other witches I'd encountered — Scout for example — but she still made me uneasy enough that my stomach constricted.

"What's she doing?" I asked.

Aunt Tillie clucked her tongue. "Hey! You're supposed to be on my side. I'm innocent here. She's the enemy."

Scout caught an errant energy blast from Aunt Tillie. "What are you trying to do?"

"She's trying to roil my atmosphere," Minerva snapped. "She wants to upset your cousin to the point that she's propelled into labor against her will. She's not fooling anybody."

"Is that true?" I demanded of Aunt Tillie, darting a look toward my mother as she appeared in the lobby.

"What now?" Mom hissed, her gaze bouncing from face to face. She had flour on the bridge of her nose and must have been in the middle of a project when the melee started. She hated being torn away from her dough.

"We just got here," I replied, straightening. Why I felt the need to explain myself to my mother was beyond me. I was an adult, for crying out loud.

"Thank you for the newsflash, Bay," Mom said dryly. "I love being up on current events."

"I don't think you're being heralded as a hero any longer," Gunner said in a low voice. "Tread carefully."

Mom shot him a glare, but her expression softened when he met it with a charming smile. Gunner had no problem making friends. Apparently, he could melt the hearts of women the world over just by being himself.

"Scout and Gunner would like a room." I took advantage of the momentary lull in the conversation and redirected it to what I hoped would be a more palatable topic. "They're trying to help me with the Hollow Creek problem ... which actually might have something to do with our other problem."

Mom took a moment to absorb the information and then nodded.

"Fine. We purposely don't have people in the rooms right now. Gunner and Scout are in on the big secret, so that will work out fine."

"*Ahem*." Minerva cleared her throat. "Nobody asked me if I thought it was wise to include other witches in the proceedings."

I disliked her greatly. I barely knew her, but her personality reminded me of sandpaper on glass. You would think that a midwife would at least make a pretense of pleasantness. Minerva proved that supposition wrong with every word she uttered.

"Why does it matter?" Mom challenged.

Minerva blinked. "What do you mean? I'm the one handling the birth."

"Technically, I think Clove is handling the birth," Gunner interjected, causing me to smile.

The stare Minerva leveled on him could've peeled paint. "Who are you again?"

"They're friends of the family," I replied. "They're working with me on a project."

"Aren't you the one getting married to the man with long hair?" Minerva was back to staring at me and I hated it.

"We call him Landon," I said.

"It seems to me you should be focused on your wedding."

"Right." I looked to Mom for help. Minerva was clearly throwing her weight around. Mom seemed to think we needed her — I wasn't so sure — but I had bigger worries than Clove's baby. "I need them."

Mom turned testy. "Bay, I won't refuse to let Gunner and Scout stay in the inn. Don't be ridiculous."

"They're roiling the energy," Minerva insisted.

"They're just standing here," Mom countered. "They haven't done anything but talk. They're hardly roiling up the energy in the house."

"Clove could go into labor any second."

"And when she does, I guarantee Scout and Gunner won't be part of it," Mom snapped. "They're here to help us with another situation. They have nothing to do with Clove. They'll be working with Bay. She doesn't even live under this roof."

"Yes, but ... ."

"No." Mom was having none of it. "The coven sent you here and we're grateful for your expertise. We haven't dealt with a doubly magic infant in ... well ... ever. That's what you're supposed to be focused on. That doesn't mean our lives cease to continue. We have other things going on.

"We have a wedding in a few days," she continued. "There's a magical explosion happening at Hollow Creek. The people in this town are at risk of some sort of contagion that's forcing them to kill others. It's time to get some perspective.

"Now, we want Clove to be as comfortable as possible for the birth. We're all looking forward to greeting the newest member of our family. But you are not in charge of this inn. We need room to live our lives."

Minerva, her eyes glittering slits of annoyance, worked her jaw. "I see."

"Focus on Clove," Mom ordered. "That's why we brought you in ... and for a hefty fee, I might add. You're being well paid for your services. You're not the center of our world."

"Ha!" Aunt Tillie jabbed a triumphant finger in Minerva's direction.

"As for you." I knew there would be fireworks when Mom swiveled to face Aunt Tillie. "Stop throwing magic around inside. Leave Minerva alone. You're baiting her. In fact, I think you need something to focus your considerable energy on."

"I'm not weeding the garden," Aunt Tillie barked. "I told you that an hour ago."

"Oh, you're going to weed that garden if I have to stand watch over you," Mom warned. "It can wait at this point. You need mental stimulation because you're feeling unloved. You will help Bay with her project."

I timidly raised my hand. "I have a problem with that," I said as Gunner hid a laugh.

"Suck it up." Mom's flashing eyes warned me that she wasn't going to put up with a single argument I had to offer. "Dinner won't be served for an hour. Find something to do until then."

"I'll check Scout and Gunner in." I was anxious to get away from my mother, so I moved toward the check-in counter."

Gunner whipped out his credit card. "Let's do that."

"Don't be morons." Mom shoved Gunner's hand away. "They're helping us. They're not paying for a room. Just program two keycards — give them room eight so they're nowhere near Clove's suite in case she does go into labor tonight — and be on your way."

"I ... well ... okay." I grabbed two keycards and glared at my mother's back. I wasn't used to her being this testy, especially with me.

"Once you've finished that, find something outside to do for an hour." Mom ordered. "I don't want Aunt Tillie doing ... well, anything she finds fun inside this inn for the next hour. I want her out of my hair."

"Hey!" Aunt Tillie had solid survival skills most days, but they weren't on display today. "I don't need a babysitter."

"Well, you've got three of them." Mom turned to the hallway. "I want one hour of quiet in this house. That means all of you — every single one of you — needs to shut up for the next sixty minutes." Her eyes lingered on Minerva before throwing daggers at Aunt Tillie. "That's all there is to it."

I pressed my lips together as I programmed the keycards and silently handed them to Gunner and Scout.

"So, are we all agreed?" Mom asked as she straightened.

"Totally." Gunner was the only one with the courage to answer. "I live to serve you."

Mom smiled. "I'm making fried chicken this evening. An old family recipe that's a lot of work, but everybody loves it. There will also be homemade potato salad, coleslaw and chocolate cake."

"I want you to be my mom," Gunner crooned.

"I can barely handle the children I have," Mom said. "I would trade all of them for you, though." She patted his cheek.

Now it was my turn to be offended. "You only have one child."

"And yet it feels like ten." She jabbed a finger at Aunt Tillie as she started down the hallway. "I wasn't joking, Bay. Aunt Tillie is your responsibility for the next hour. Keep her out of trouble."

Now she was just messing with me. Nobody could make Aunt Tillie do anything she didn't want to do.

. . .

"THIS PLACE IS COOL," SCOUT OFFERED TEN minutes later as I showed her around Aunt Tillie's greenhouse. For lack of anyplace better to hide — the library was far too close to the kitchen (and my mother's wrath) for my liking — we decided to retreat to Aunt Tillie's sacred space.

"We had it built last year," I explained as Aunt Tillie threw herself in an easy chair in the corner and pouted. "When did you get that?" I pointed to the chair.

"I ordered it a month ago. It arrived yesterday," Aunt Tillie replied. "I need a place to rest my tired bones."

"Because you're old?" Thistle asked as she breezed into the greenhouse. I'd texted to warn her about risking my mother's fury and so she'd headed straight out to join us when she arrived.

"Because I'm a warrior on the front lines of the fight between good and evil," Aunt Tillie replied. "I'm only middle-aged."

"Right." Thistle brandished a piece of paper. "Here's a list of the ingredients we need for the ritual."

I took the list and scanned it. "We need belladonna."

"I have some in the corner." Aunt Tillie pointed. "What's this ritual?"

"I have no idea," Thistle replied. "I found it in a book. The situation described — although not in enough detail if you ask me — suggested this ritual for breaking up a magical dam."

I pictured the scene at Hollow Creek and shrugged. "It can't hurt."

"That's my philosophy," she agreed as she headed to the corner Aunt Tillie had indicated. "What's going on inside? Why does Winnie want us out of the house?"

"You've met Aunt Tillie," I replied.

"Hey!" Aunt Tillie's eyes were full of fire when they landed on me. "I'll make it so your hair won't lay flat the day of your wedding if you're not careful."

As far as her threats went, it was tame. I also knew she wouldn't follow through. Despite all her talk, she had a good heart. She wanted Landon to be happy on his wedding day.

"Aunt Tillie and Minerva are fighting," I explained. "Minerva says

Aunt Tillie is roiling the birthing atmosphere, and Aunt Tillie just doesn't like her."

"She's evil," Aunt Tillie said. "You kill evil with fire. Maybe you should call Stormy to come for dinner."

"Yeah, I think I won't."

"What's the deal with Minerva?" Thistle asked as she walked to the potting benches and grabbed a knife to shred the belladonna.

"She's the devil," Aunt Tillie snapped. "I already told you."

"Yeah, but what's really the deal with her?" Thistle was precise as she made her cuts. "She's with the Bay City coven, right?"

I nodded. "That's what Mom said. She doesn't feel powerful. I've been around her three times now and she just seems mean. There's not much magic being thrown around when she's in the room ... except by Aunt Tillie."

"She's like those people in the Harry Potter books," Aunt Tillie offered.

"Muggles?"

"No. I know what a muggle is." Aunt Tillie rolled her eyes. "They're non-magical folk. She's like the ones who were born to magical families but have no power."

I knew what she was talking about. "That's weird. Why would the coven send a witch with no magic to help us?"

"Squibs," Gunner volunteered. He was in the corner studying a pot plant. Aunt Tillie grew them in the greenhouse over the winter so she would never run out. "That's what they're called in the books." He shifted his gaze to me. "Is this what I think it is?"

"I have glaucoma," Aunt Tillie answered before I could. "That's medicinal. Also, I'm allergic to oxygen and my eyes need protection. I used to wear sunglasses, but those plants serve the same purpose."

He barked out a laugh. "Sounds made up but knock yourself out."

"I still don't understand why the coven would send a non-magical midwife to help with the birth of Clove's baby," I argued. "I mean ... if they're worried this baby is going to be something special, don't we need a powerful midwife?"

"Maybe Minerva's magic only comes out when there's a birth,"

Thistle suggested. "Either way, I don't like her. I want her gone. Clove needs to squeeze out that kid so we can get rid of her."

"Well, I don't think we can force the situation," I said. "That baby is going to come when it feels like coming. It's like Aunt Tillie: stubborn and obnoxious."

"Oh, you're definitely on my list," Aunt Tillie warned. "I'm going to make your husband-to-be allergic to bacon if you're not careful."

That would be a fate worse than death for Landon. "Can you make it so he's only allergic after three slices? I want to force him to make better food decisions."

"No. That makes you happy."

"Well, I had to ask." I ambled over to Thistle. "Do you have everything you need?"

"Yup. After dinner we can head up to the bluff. It might work and it might not, but we have to try something."

I was right there with her.

CHAPTER Fourteen

"You can't conduct a ritual without me!"

Someone — and there would be hex to pay, let me tell you — had fixed Clove's phone so she could talk to all of us from upstairs without having to leave her bed. It was an app that we all had to sign up for. It required we all go into a room together and talk, and Clove had made herself the moderator so she could mute whomever she didn't want to hear from. Everybody was in the same room together, and the noise level was deafening.

"You can't be part of this," Mom argued as she sat in her spot at the table, rubbing her forehead and sipping from a glass of wine. She looked wrecked.

"You have to hit that little microphone icon to talk," Thistle offered helpfully. "She can't hear you."

"What?" Mom made a face. "Well, this is just stupid." She hit the microphone and repeated what she'd previously said.

"You can't cut me out of this," Clove insisted, fury evident in her voice. "I'm still a part of this family."

"Of course, you're a part of this family," Marnie soothed, opting to use Mom's phone instead of her own to speak. Clove had muted her five minutes earlier and refused to remove the speaking ban.

"How are you even talking?" Clove demanded. "I said I didn't want to hear from you again."

At the risk of incurring Clove's wrath, I inserted myself in the conversation. "We're all in the same room, Clove. It's easier if we use one phone instead of eight so we're not all talking over one another and straining to hear."

"It's not easier for me," she snapped. "I'm in charge, and I say you can't conduct a ritual without me."

I felt sorry for her. She'd been trapped in that bedroom for two days now. She could only get up to use the bathroom. We'd all stopped by for visits, but then we got to carry on with our normal — or paranormal — lives.

"Can't we do something?" I implored.

The question was directed at Mom, but Minerva answered. "Absolutely not!" The midwife vehemently shook her head. "She's on bed rest for a reason. She'll give birth any moment. What happens if she goes out there and her water breaks?"

"That might be a concern if we were in town," I shot back. "We're on the family property. If her water breaks, Sam and Landon can carry her back to the inn and we'll go from there."

"Oh, I don't want to carry her if something is already broken," Landon complained. "That sounds gross."

I pinned him with a dirty look. "You're an FBI agent. Weren't you trained for situations like this?"

He shook his head. "Are you honestly asking if I was trained to help monitor an expectant mother during a magical ritual when she's going to give birth to a magical baby that might be born in swaddling orbs?"

Sure, if he said it like that it sounded ridiculous. "I was talking about the water breaking thing."

"We were trained on dummies."

Thistle's hand shot in the hair.

"Don't even," Mom warned, jabbing a finger at her. "There's a reason you were muted first."

Thistle huffed but wisely kept her mouth shut.

"I'm not saying Clove should be involved in the ritual," I said.

"Frankly, we don't even know what we're going to be dealing with. She could go up there in a wheelchair or something. We don't have to cut her out of everything."

"And where do you suggest we get the wheelchair?" Mom challenged.

"Those chairs on the back patio have rollers," Clove said. "You can just roll me there."

Marcus, always practical, seemed to be considering the conundrum. "Those rollers are tiny, and the ground is uneven. It would take us hours."

"Not if Aunt Tillie uses magic," Landon said, shrinking when Mom hit him with her darkest glare. "I mean ... I probably shouldn't stick my nose into this."

"Then don't," Mom hissed.

Landon continued as if he hadn't heard her despite his obvious discomfort, proving he was either brave or stupid. "Bay, Thistle and Clove work well together. This is a ritual they've never done. Even if Clove isn't part of it, Bay will feel better if she's out there."

That was mostly true. "I don't think it's fair for her to suffer. Besides, a little action might help push her into labor. I can't be alone in hoping for that baby to freaking crawl out of there and greet the world."

"They don't crawl when they're newborns," Minerva said.

I stared at her. Was she serious? "I was being theatrical," I said.

"Of course, you were." Minerva shook her head. "This whole family is theatrical. That's what you do."

"Totally," I agreed. "We're theatrical just to irritate you."

"Bay, don't." Mom pinched the bridge of her nose. "It's best Clove stay upstairs. She's safer there."

"Yeah, but we all know we're going to perform the ritual and then hang out up there all night," Thistle argued. "Is it fair for us to party up there when she's miserable down here?" It was rare for Thistle to put somebody else's needs at the forefront of an argument. I couldn't help being impressed.

"It's not fair," Clove said mournfully. "I feel like a leper. Nobody loves me."

"I love you," Sam said from somewhere near Clove. "I'll stick close to you all night."

"You're the reason I'm in this position in the first place," Clove groused. "Aunt Tillie warned me that all men were dirty perverts, but I didn't believe her. Now look at my life. I'll be bedridden forever with another human being inside of me. I'll be stuck here until she's thirty at this rate."

"That sounds unlikely," Sam countered. "I think you're just feeling emotional."

"Do you want me to kill you?" Clove barked.

My eyes were imploring when they landed on Mom. "We have seven witches in this room. How can we not be able to figure out a way to get her to the bluff?"

Mom pursed her lips, making a face I hated from childhood. "Fine. But if she goes into labor, the men have to carry her down from the bluff … and be quick about it."

"I don't want to carry her if something breaks first," Landon warned.

I pinned him with a look that said, "Shut up or die."

"But I will gladly do it because there's nothing I want more than to keep this family happy," he said quickly.

"Let's do this." I pushed myself to a standing position. "If we're going to yuk it up on the bluff, we can't cut Clove out of it. She's part of this family and belongs with us."

ULTIMATELY, THE PLAN TO ROLL CLOVE TO the bluff didn't work. One look at Marcus told me he wanted to say "I told you so" and start drinking. Instead, he, Landon and Sam managed to get their arms around Clove and carry her the rest of the way. Then they settled her on a blanket, far from the action just to be safe, and retrieved beers from the cooler Aunt Tillie had floated up from the inn.

"She's like five feet tall," Landon hissed in my ear when he appeared at my side. He was breathless and sweaty. "How can she weigh that much when she's only five feet tall?"

"I heard that!" Clove's voice was accusatory when it came from my phone.

"What the ...?" There was betrayal on Landon's face when I lifted the phone so he could see that the app Clove had made us install was still operational.

"She doesn't think she'll be able to hear what we're doing from so far away," I explained. "I promised to keep it going."

"Oh, well, great." Landon pressed the cold beer to his forehead. "I'll make you pay for this later."

"See," Clove said, her voice clear despite how far into the hills we were. "Men are dirty perverts, each and every one of you."

"Yes, Clove," Sam said in his most amiable tone. "I got you iced tea."

"I want wine."

"You can't have wine until after you give birth." Sam pleaded.

"What if it kicks me into labor?" Clove's voice was a conspiratorial whisper. "They don't have to know. Just go over there and steal that bottle from Aunt Tillie's hand."

"I heard that," Aunt Tillie snapped.

Clove didn't appear bothered. "She's old, Sam. You can take her."

"No wine," Mom barked. "Clove, we've already gone out of our way to get you up here. It's time for you to be quiet ... and grateful."

"Oh, right," Clove groused. "Like that's the way the Winchesters do things."

Mom pressed the tip of her tongue to her lip and took a moment, as if calming herself, before smiling at me. "Do your ritual. We need to get this over with."

"I'm on it." I moved with Thistle and Scout to the center of the circle. Thistle had copied the instructions from the book and had a huge bag of ingredients in her hand. "What do we do?"

"What we always do," Thistle replied. "We drop the ingredients on the ground and chant."

I glared at her. "But ... should we do it here? Are you certain this shouldn't be done at Hollow Creek?"

"We're not taking Clove to Hollow Creek," Mom warned.

"Definitely not," Landon agreed. "I'll throw out my back, and that won't make for a happy honeymoon."

"Pervert," Clove muttered through the phone.

I smiled because I couldn't help myself. "Well, I guess we can do the ritual here. If it doesn't work, we can try it again at Hollow Creek tomorrow."

"It didn't say it had to be in a specific spot," Thistle argued, although one look at her face told me she no longer believed the ritual would work now that the obvious had been pointed out.

I hesitated, briefly wondering if we should even waste our time. Then I simply held out my hands. "Let's try it. We'll consider it a dry run. It's not like we're going to run out of herbs."

"Where did we land on that pot in the greenhouse?" Gunner asked. "If we're going to be playing herb games, maybe we should have some fun."

Landon and Chief Terry shot twin looks of disgust in his direction, something that wasn't lost on Scout.

"You probably shouldn't talk about pot in front of law enforcement," she said in a low voice.

"Why? It's legal in Michigan now."

"I don't even know what he's talking about," Aunt Tillie said. "What's this pot he's referring to?"

"Oh, that was weak," Gunner chided. "I expected more from you."

"Then stop talking about my private business," she growled. "Are you new? Come on!" She flicked his shoulder and shook her head. "I thought you were better than this."

"Let's just get this over with," Mom ordered. "If it won't work — and now everybody thinks it won't — then let's stop pretending we're going to do something serious and start drinking. It's been a long day."

Was I the only one who thought drinking when Clove could go into labor at any moment was a bad idea? A quick glance at my female relatives told me that, yes, I was the only one who cared.

As if reading my mind, Landon leaned in. "I'm not helping them carry Clove back to the inn. She's heavy and I'm afraid something will break all over me."

I pinned him with an exasperated look. "Seriously? What happens when I'm pregnant?"

"What do you mean?"

"If I want to be carried when I'm pregnant, are you going to make a big deal out of it like you are now?"

"No. If something of yours breaks all over me, I'll thank my lucky stars that you loved me enough to carry my offspring in the first place and do whatever you want. Clove doesn't love me. This is Sam's responsibility."

My phone crackled, reminding me the app was still open.

"You're helping or I'll be the one killing you, Landon," Sam threatened.

"And I am not that heavy," Clove sniffed. "All the weight I've gained is for the baby."

"Oh, right," Thistle complained from the spot on my right. "Like you're going to have a seventy-pound baby."

"Thirty pounds!" Clove was so shrill her voice carried across the bluff. We no longer needed the app. "I've only gained thirty pounds."

Thistle planted her hands on her hips and glared through the darkness. "Dude, I've spent more time with you than anyone since you got knocked up."

"I beg to differ," Sam interjected.

Thistle pretended he hadn't spoken. "You gained thirty pounds before you even told anyone you were pregnant."

"That's true," Marnie said. "I thought you were stress eating because Sam was cheating on you or something."

"Hey!" Sam was affronted, and rightly so. "I would never cheat on her."

"They did lie about Clove being pregnant," Thistle said. "And not little lies. Big, fat lies ... kind of like Clove's butt."

"That did it!" Clove slapped her hand against the ground. "I'll make you eat dirt."

"Come over here and say that," Thistle taunted.

"Aunt Winnie." Clove used her most wheedling tone. "Make Thistle come over here so I can shove dirt in her mouth."

Mom's sigh was so drawn out she sounded like a tire slowly deflating. She started nodding, taking me by surprise. "Thistle, go over there and let Clove shove dirt in your mouth."

Thistle snorted. "That's not going to happen."

"Do it or I'll send Landon over there to arrest you," Mom threatened.

"Yeah, that's not going to happen either." Landon had completely lost interest in the ritual. He'd also already drained one beer. He placed the empty bottle in the cooler and grabbed another, offering me his most charming smile as he cracked it open and began to drink.

Mom glared at Landon for so long I thought her eyes might pop out of her head. He refused to look at her, however, and the one-sided stare-off was starting to seem funny because it was going on so long. Finally, she turned her attention to Chief Terry. "It's on you," she said.

"I believe I've been rendered temporarily deaf," he said as he moved to the cooler.

"You heard me just now," Mom pointed out.

"Fine, I simply don't want to do it."

To my right, Scout and Gunner had their heads bent together. Gunner was laughing so hard his shoulders shook.

"I freaking love this family," he said as he moved to stand with the other men. "Do you guys do this often?"

"In the summer, once a week," Landon replied. "Usually, we go through about a vat of wine, enough so that I don't care when the clothes come off."

Gunner froze with a beer halfway to his mouth. "What?" he said, his voice a soft squeak.

"Oh, yeah, the wine is evil." Landon took another pull on his beer. "Once the women drink enough, they get naked and dance."

"I am not doing that," Scout announced. She glanced around. "Why don't the men get naked? I might play if the men got naked too."

"I'm not getting naked," Marcus said. "I draw the line at naked dancing."

"He won't even get naked in the shower," Thistle offered. She had also lost interest in the ritual. In fact, she'd dropped the baggie on the ground and was now studying the box of wine bottles that Aunt Tillie had conjured to the top of the bluff. "He doesn't believe showering is a tandem sport."

It was dark, the only lights coming from the bonfire and the twinkle net Aunt Tillie had thrown out before our arrival. The ambiance was moody and warm. Despite that, the flush creeping up Marcus's cheeks was obvious. "Thank you for sharing our private business, Thistle."

For her part, Thistle was blasé. "You're welcome."

"I was being sarcastic."

"You're bad at it."

"I'm confused," Twila interjected. She already had a bottle of wine in her hand and looked unsteady on her feet. Of course, Twila was one of those people who floated through life. I often wondered why she didn't fall down more often because she was so lost. "Why wouldn't you shower with Thistle, Marcus? I'm not saying it's necessary for every shower, but she's a cute girl. Are you frigid?"

"I can't believe we're having this conversation," Marcus complained, looking to Landon for help. "Do you want to chime in here?"

Landon shrugged. "I love showering with Bay."

"Oh, nobody needs to hear that," Chief Terry complained. "This conversation is inappropriate."

"She has this shower gel. It smells like coconut in the summer and pumpkin in the fall. Oh, and she has candy cane shower gel around Christmas." He beamed at me. "I'm going to find bacon shower gel for her and turn it into a party."

"I don't believe this," Chief Terry snapped.

Everybody ignored him.

"You're in big trouble, Thistle," Marcus growled. "How would you like it if I told everyone that you prefer I paint your toenails because it turns you on?"

My mouth dropped open. "Oh, that's weird and kinky."

"It's not," Thistle shot back. "It's normal."

Landon slipped his arm around my waist and nudged me toward one of the empty blankets outside the fire circle. "Do you want to get drunk with your future husband and make out?"

I hesitated. "We really should try the ritual."

"It won't work here, Bay. Even I know that."

"Yeah, but ... ." I blew out a sigh, resigned. "Maybe a night off will do us some good. We can't get falling down drunk, though."

"Absolutely not. We'll get responsible drunk." He led me to the blanket. "Besides, I'm more interested in the making out. This is probably the last time we'll be able to do it up here before we're married. The next time I get to third base on the bluff, you'll be my wife."

I laughed so hard I snorted. "I see you've thought this through."

"I just want you tonight." He was earnest. "If these other people are hanging out too, I'll muddle through. But you're the main course."

I nodded and leaned into him. "I think we have the components for a perfect evening."

"You read my mind."

CHAPTER Fifteen

"Oh, geez."

Landon's voice sounded ragged when consciousness reclaimed me the next morning. It was only after thinking about it a good thirty seconds that I realized he wasn't in bed. Slowly, I dragged myself to a sitting position, cringing when I saw my hair in the full-length mirror on the wall. I looked as if I'd been in trapped in a wind tunnel all night.

"Ugh."

Landon appeared in the bedroom doorway, shirtless and with his customary morning stubble. Normally that was a turn-on for me, but he looked so pale this morning. "Are you okay?" He crawled onto the bed face first and pulled the pillow over his eyes.

"I don't know." I held up my arms to test them, groaning when a random pain in my side made itself known. "Did you tackle me into bed last night?"

"I believe I did." He peeked out from under the pillow. "I was going to wow you with my romantic prowess, if memory serves."

I glanced down at my sleep outfit. I was still in everything but my pants from the night before. "I don't think that happened."

He chuckled. "No, we decided to say schmaltzy things to one another — that was my idea — and passed out after five minutes."

"I don't know whether I should be sad or grateful that it didn't happen. I wouldn't remember it."

"I'm right there with you." He rubbed my arm and shot me a rueful smile. "You know I love you?"

The change in topic threw me. "That's the rumor on the street."

"I need you to know that you're my angel. I look at you and see beauty ... grace ... and the strongest person I've ever known. Nothing could ever change the way I feel about you."

He sounded as though he was about to drop a bomb on me, and when I glanced at my reflection again, I had to wonder about the statement. "I look like I've been hit by a train."

He chuckled. "I like when you look a little wrecked in the morning. It reminds me that you're human underneath all that magic and delightful snark."

"Landon, I'm getting worried." I decided to put it out there. "You're saying wonderful things, but I can't help feeling you're about to add something terrible."

"Oh, no." He grimaced as he shook his head. "I meant everything I said. It's just ... I have this fear."

I focused my full attention on him even though my head was throbbing. "What are you afraid of? You're not going to call off the wedding?"

He pinned me with a dark look. "Don't even joke about that."

"Okay, what aren't you saying?"

"You're my angel," he repeated, "but your family consists of devils. That's the only thing that can explain that wine. I know it's going to knock me on my ass and yet I still drink it. In the moment, I don't care what it'll do to me, or that I'll regret drinking it twelve hours later. I'm afraid that the devil gene will somehow take hold later in life and steal my angel."

I laughed so hard tears came to my eyes. "And here I thought you were about to say something serious that might derail our lives." I swiped at the tears. "I guess I should know better than that by now."

"You really should." He grunted as he sat up, leaning in to rub his nose against my cheek. "I will never want to derail our lives, Bay. I love this life. I love you. Even though they're devils, I love your family."

"I love you too, but I maintain the wine hangover is your fault. I tried to convince you to go back after two glasses."

"I don't remember you putting much effort into that."

"Well, then you're remembering incorrectly, because I begged."

"Oh, please." He rolled his eyes ... and then looked as if he regretted it. "Ow." He rubbed his forehead. "You were having as much fun as me. Even though the ritual never happened, I think the family needed the time together as much as anything else."

"Everyone is tense," I agreed. "It's like ... life is closing in on us. I want to focus on the wedding, but it's impossible knowing there's a horrible magical entity out there being used to kill people. It feels like some sort of macabre game."

"We have zero leads. All we know is that it started at the high school."

An image of Amelia popped into my head. "Speaking of that ... I ran into an old friend when I was at the school with Scout yesterday." I told him about my conversation with Amelia.

"You mentioned that yesterday," he noted, his hand on my back. "You said you didn't want to focus on her."

"What if that's a mistake? What if she's doing this?"

"What if she isn't?"

"You said it yourself. We have nothing else to go on. We should at least test the waters with her."

He pursed his lips and then nodded. "Okay. We need breakfast and coffee first. Then we can head over to her house. It can't hurt to talk to her. If she's involved, she might let something slip. She hates us enough to want to boast."

"Pretty much," I agreed, blowing out a sigh before angling my head. "Do you want to give romance a try before breakfast? It might cure the hangovers."

"Normally I would be all over that offer, but I can't romance you without kissing you."

"So?"

"So, I just threw up." His expression was hangdog. "That's what I was doing in the bathroom."

"I'm sorry. Do you want to sleep a bit longer?"

"No, I want breakfast. I think that's the only thing that's going to make me feel better."

"It sounds like there's an insult buried in there," I teased. "Usually, I'm the only thing that can make you feel better."

His eyes sparked with mirth. "You make me feel like a king every day we're together, but a hangover is a specific pain. I need food ... liquids ... and aspirin, not necessarily in that order."

"Then we should get on that."

"Yeah." He didn't move to get out of the bed. "Just one thing, Bay."

I waited, knowing in my heart he was about to embrace the schmaltz once again. The run-up to the wedding had turned him into a romantic fool. I wasn't complaining. I liked him when he was feeling soft and cuddly.

"One day we're going to have a house on the lake. We'll have kids — I figure at least one, maybe two at the most — and they'll have left to start their own adventures. Even then, when we're old and gray — although I'm still hot and virile — I'll love you with every breath I take. Nothing, and I mean nothing, will ever tear us apart."

A lump formed in my throat. "I feel the same way about you. I'm going to be hot and virile when I'm eighty, so we'll be a good fit."

He grinned. "It's you and me forever, right?"

"Right."

"Good." He leaned in and rested his forehead against mine.

It was a nice moment, even though we couldn't kiss. Then I got a whiff of his breath. "You really need to brush your teeth if you want to be this close to me." I pulled my head back and found him glaring.

"Where did the love go?"

"I think you left it in the toilet bowl this morning."

IT TOOK US LONGER THAN NORMAL TO get ready for the day. The walk to the inn was meandering. We held hands, smiled at one another as the birds chirped, and groaned continuously as we walked the five-minute path.

"I feel old, Bay," he said as he held open the door to the family living quarters. "Like ... really, really old."

"You can't be old. You just said you're virile."

"Oh, I'm virile." He gave me a pat on the rear end and then pulled up short when he caught sight of Aunt Tillie. Today, she'd decided to forego camouflage altogether. She was dressed in what looked to be an antique military outfit ... complete with bayonet. "Going after the Redcoats?" he asked.

Aunt Tillie brightened. "How did you know?"

"Just a guess."

I cocked my head as I regarded her. "Has Mom seen that outfit?"

"I don't answer to your mother," Aunt Tillie snapped. "How many times do I have to tell you that?"

"Until I believe it."

"Well, believe it." She squared her shoulders. "If I did care about your mother's opinion, I might be trying to get under her skin because she warned me that I couldn't wear anything in my closet to your wedding."

Ah, now we were getting somewhere. "Are you wearing that?" I wasn't opposed to it. The photos would look weird, but I figured they would be odd anyway given the circumstances ... and Clove's impressive girth.

"I'm considering it." Aunt Tillie's smile told me she was fully prepared to drive my mother over the cliffs of insanity this morning.

"I thought you wanted to be the flower witch," Landon countered. "Isn't that what you were babbling on and on about two weeks ago? Bay got you a dress so you'll fit in with the wedding party. Now that Clove likely won't be able to stand up for Bay, I figured you could serve as another bridesmaid."

I hadn't even considered that. "Oh ... I don't have enough attendants." I shot him a worried look. "You have two brothers and Marcus. I have Thistle ... and Thistle."

Landon was calm. "Clove will probably be there. She just might not be able to stand up."

"I still don't have enough attendants." Now I was frustrated. "Why don't I have more friends?"

He chuckled. "You have friends."

"Obviously not."

"Ask Scout or Stormy."

"I can't do that." I was exasperated. "It's the last second. They can't get dresses. On top of that, they'll know I asked them because I was desperate this close to the ceremony."

"I don't see the problem." Landon clearly wasn't in the mood to play out some huge drama this morning, especially when it involved dresses. "Why does it matter if we have an even number of attendants."

"Because I don't want you to win."

"Oh, well ... ." He exhaled heavily. "The attendants thing will work itself out. We'll force Aunt Tillie into a dress if it comes to that."

"I'm wearing what I want to wear," Aunt Tillie shot back. "I'm also bringing props."

Landon eyed the bayonet and then muttered something under his breath. His full attention was for me. "We have enough to worry about. You can't melt down about this. I won't allow it. Besides, you have a bigger issue to deal with."

"And what's that?" I was honestly confused.

"Who is walking you down the aisle to give you away?"

I froze. I'd expected him to bring up this subject months ago. Instead, he'd left me to dwell on it until I'd turned myself into a basket case. "What do you mean?" I asked evasively.

"Oh, don't do that." He wagged a finger. "Normally the father gives away the daughter. You, however, have two fathers. One of those fathers has attitude with the other. The other father won't say anything because he doesn't want to put pressure on you. He would never admit to being hurt if you don't choose him, but he's the one you want to walk you down the aisle."

It didn't take an expert to figure out what he was saying. I loved my father despite the fact that he'd spent years away from me after divorcing my mother. We'd made inroads in the last year and were in a good place. That didn't change the fact that Chief Terry helped raise me and was one of my favorite people in the world.

"I'm not going to have anyone walk me down the aisle," I said. It was the only acceptable conclusion I'd been able to come to. I couldn't hurt either of them. "It's an antiquated custom."

Landon folded his arms across his chest and fixed me with a dark look. "That's not what you want."

"I ... think it's for the best."

"It's not what you want, though. I want you to have what you want."

"Maybe they could take turns," Aunt Tillie suggested as she practiced with her bayonet, swiping it in a wide arc and narrowly missing Mom's favorite porcelain table lamp. "Jack can start and then hand you off to Terry."

I'd considered that, but it felt as if I was taking something away from my father. "I ... can't."

Landon's expression fell. It was as if he could read the torture occurring in my soul. "Bay, do you want me to talk to your father?"

That was the last thing I wanted. They'd only recently managed to get on good terms, thanks to a great deal of effort on both their parts. They'd done it for me because it was what I needed. I couldn't risk that relationship or ask Landon to do something I wasn't comfortable with.

"No. I don't need anyone to walk me down the aisle." It was the only solution I could fathom. "Just ... let it go." I started toward the kitchen, but he gripped my hand tightly.

"It's okay," he reassured me. "The wedding day will be perfect."

"Totally," Aunt Tillie agreed as she swung the bayonet around again. This time she clipped the lamp, but Landon caught it before it hit the floor. "Don't mention that to Winnie," she ordered as she marched to the kitchen.

Landon shook his head as he returned the lamp to its perch. "Should I be worried that she wants to be armed for the wedding?"

"She doesn't want to be armed for the wedding," I countered. "She wants to annoy my mother this morning. They're at war, but neither will admit it because it will look like a sign of weakness if they own up to the fact that the other can irritate them."

"See ... devils." He tapped my chin and leaned in for a kiss. I thought he was going to suggest stealing a plate of bacon and returning to the guesthouse for the romance he'd promised — and then failed to deliver — the previous night. Instead, he was sober when he pulled back. "I'm okay talking to your father."

Exasperated, I pulled away. "Well, I'm not okay with it." I didn't mean to be irritable, but I couldn't help myself. "Just let me make my own decisions on this, okay?"

He searched my face, perhaps thinking that I was going to send him a message of some sort, and then nodded. "Okay. It's up to you."

"It is."

"I just want you to be happy." He stroked his hand over my hair. "We're only doing this once, Bay. I want to get it right. You already had the best proposal any woman ever received from a man. I want the wedding to match."

I choked on a laugh. His proposal was definitely one for the books. "I'll take it under consideration." It was the best I could do. "Now, let's get breakfast. If we're going to face off with potentially murderous teenagers this morning, we need fuel."

"Good idea." He squeezed my hand as we walked into the kitchen, skirting around the island and not batting an eye even though Mom and Aunt Tillie were in the middle of a screaming match.

"You're not wearing that outfit!" Mom raged. "What did we talk about?"

"You said no leggings at the wedding," Aunt Tillie fired back. "As you can clearly see, these are not leggings. So, under your aforementioned declaration, I am breaking no rules."

"Do you want me to make a new rule?" Mom was beside herself. "I'll do it."

"Then I'll just find something else to wear. You can't control me."

Landon's smile was easy as he pushed open the swinging door that led to the dining room. "So ... my family is arriving today. I know we have a lot going on, but we really do need to make time to see them. My mother will melt down otherwise."

His mother's meltdowns were nothing compared to the shenanigans my family offered. "Let's talk with Amelia and then plan the rest of the day. I think she's going to give us an idea of what we're dealing with right away. She's not very subtle when she's up to something."

CHAPTER
Sixteen

"Terry said we can interview Amelia on our own," Landon said as he met me in Clove's room. He grinned when he saw my cousin in the bed. Her stomach was so big at this point she could barely see over it. "Do you think it's possible you're going to give birth to the world's biggest baby?"

Clove murdered him with a glare. "As soon as this kid is out, I'm going to murder each and every member of this family. You've been warned."

"Aw." He shot her a charming wink. "Does that mean you think of me as family? That's really sweet."

Clove's eyes were so squinted I was surprised she could see. "Yup. I'm definitely going to kill you first."

Landon leaned over and pressed a friendly kiss to her forehead before studying her stomach again. "Can I ...?" He held out his hand to ask if he could touch the huge bump.

She nodded. "You're the only person who bothers asking now. Last week, complete strangers in town touched me without asking. I don't want strange people touching me."

"Oh, so you're the exact opposite as you were in high school," I teased. "Back then all she could talk about was strange men touching her," I explained for Landon's benefit.

Sam, who was in bed with Clove, lifted an eyebrow. "I'm not sure I want to know."

"Definitely not," Clove agreed. "Besides, Bay is making that up. I didn't want strangers to touch me. I knew all the boys I wanted to touch me."

Sam made a face. "I'm not sure that makes it any better."

"Whatever." Clove shifted, a quick bolt of angst coming into her face.

"Are you okay?" I asked, instantly alert. "Are you in labor?"

She shook her head. "My back hurts. I'm in bed constantly. It's no longer comfortable." Her gaze was imploring when it locked with mine. "I need this baby to come, Bay. I just .... can't do this much longer." Her eyes filled with tears.

Clove was always dramatic. She could muster tears faster than anybody I'd ever met when she wanted to garner sympathy or get us out of trouble. But these tears were real, and they clawed at my heart.

"I'm sorry." I reached over and snagged her hand as Landon touched her stomach. He seemed amazed as he stared at the huge beach ball that used to be her flat midriff. "Just keep reminding yourself that you'll have a baby when this is over."

"And then what?"

The question caught me off guard. "You'll have a baby, who will grow up to be a toddler, who will grow up to be a little girl. That's what you've always wanted."

"What if I was crazy to want that? Have you ever considered that I was nuts this entire time?"

"Only a few hundred times." I beamed at her. "I'm not sure what you're worked up about. I can't fix the problem if I don't know what it is."

"It's never going to be the same." Clove was earnest. "When I first got pregnant and started getting cut out of things, I told myself that it was only for a while ... until I gave birth. But that's not true. Once the baby comes, I'll be cut out of the dangerous things because I'll have a baby I have to stay home with."

I flicked a glance at Sam and saw the concern in his eyes. This obviously wasn't the first time she'd voiced this particular concern.

"Clove ... ." I searched for the right words. Then I opted for the truth. "You know what? You probably are going to be cut out of a few things. You don't like the dangerous stuff anyway."

"I like it better than having to hear about the adventures you and Thistle are having without me."

"You're still going to have adventures with us." I believed that with my whole heart. "I guarantee that Sam will be a great babysitter."

"I've been informed that it's not babysitting when the child is mine," Sam said, grinning. "I'll be happy to have the baby with me. I'm going to be finishing up the tanker in the months after she's born. She can come to work with me, and you can run around with your cousins, Clove. You don't have to be with her twenty-four-seven."

"Shouldn't I be?" Clove looked legitimately torn. "Isn't it my job to take care of my baby?"

"When you think about our childhood, what do you remember?" I asked.

She shrugged. "Mostly I remember you and Thistle making fun of me."

"Yeah, I'm pretty sure you and Thistle made fun of me," I countered.

"And I'm pretty sure Thistle remembers it as the two of you making fun of her," Landon replied, withdrawing his hand from Clove's stomach. He had a look of wonder on his face. "I could feel the little foot. That is ... miraculous."

"We're not having a baby for at least two years," I warned him.

"I know. We'll just spoil Clove's baby and then go home to get a full night's sleep."

Clove glared at him before turning back to me. "Why did you ask what I remember?"

"Because the memories I have mostly involve Aunt Tillie," I replied. "She was our primary babysitter, and we went on adventures with her every day. Your daughter will go on adventures with us.

"The first year will probably be a little difficult," I continued. "She'll be more vulnerable at the start. That doesn't mean we're going to cut you out of adventures. I won't stand for that."

Clove's lips pursed into a pout. "I want to go on an adventure now."

I laughed as I stood. "You're on the biggest adventure of your life now. Just because the adventures won't be the same for a few months doesn't mean they won't be great. Have a little faith."

Clove couldn't be placated. "I wish she would get here. I don't want her coming at your wedding. That wouldn't be fair."

I couldn't disagree with her, but she had no control over that, and guilting her to force her into labor before the baby was ready to come would help nobody. "If she comes at the wedding, I bet it will be a story we remember forever."

"But if she doesn't come today, it would be great if you could keep her in there until after the wedding," Landon added. "You know ... just to be fair. I want Bay to have her day."

Clove sniffled. "I want Bay to have her day too. I don't know what to do." She grabbed her stomach and gave it a hearty squeeze. "Get out here right now! I mean it! I'm in charge."

I laughed so hard tears sprang to my eyes. "It will happen soon, Clove. Then we'll both be embarking on a whole new adventure."

"And only Thistle will be left behind," Clove mused. "That sounds fun."

Despite Clove's misery, the real her was intact. "It's coming, Clove. Get ready. Your whole life is about to change. We'll still torture Aunt Tillie and Thistle. I promise."

She brightened considerably. "That's something to look forward to."

LANDON WAS GRIM AS HE PULLED INTO the Hart driveway, his eyes automatically scanning the front of the quiet house.

"How many times have we been here the last few months?" he asked as he pocketed his keys and exited the Explorer.

I shrugged as I joined him in front of the vehicle. "She's trouble."

"She is," Landon agreed. "Can I ask you something?"

I knew what he was going to ask and saw no reason to torture him by forcing him to say the words. "I'm not sorry we didn't kill them that night at Hollow Creek. The other girls seem to be drifting away from the darkness. Only Amelia remains a problem."

"Have you considered that you might still have to kill her?"

I swallowed hard. It wasn't something I wanted to think about. "I ... don't know."

He nodded as he moved his hand to my back "I never thought I would be considering ending the life of a teenager, but she could turn dangerous again, Bay. We have to be prepared."

"I know. Let's just feel her out now. If she's dangerous, we should know relatively quickly."

He gave my hand a squeeze before knocking briskly. Tina Hart seemed surprised to see us.

"Oh, I ... um ... ." There were bags under her eyes, as if she hadn't been sleeping, but there was resignation there, too. "What did Amelia do now?"

Landon was prepared. "Nothing that we know of. We're here to discuss a few things with her regarding Paisley Gilmore's death." It wasn't a lie — well, not completely — but it still made me squirm. Tina had no idea what her daughter had been dabbling in – and she showed no interest in learning.

Relief flooded Tina's features. "Of course. I should've realized you weren't done with Amelia. She's been so sad since Paisley died. She's even stopped talking to Emma and Sophia."

Landon feigned polite interest and I could practically hear the gears in his mind working. "She hasn't been hanging with Emma and Sophia?"

Tina was grave as she shook her head. "It's as if they've completely ended their friendship. I feel bad for her — to go through losing her two other friends in the wake of the tragedy she's already dealing with. But she doesn't want to talk about it."

Something occurred to me, and I spoke before thinking better of it. "Have you considered getting her professional help?"

Tina's forehead wrinkled. "I didn't know there was professional help for making friends."

I tugged on my limited patience and kept my face placid. "I mean for her emotional problems. It might help for her to talk to a professional about what she's feeling regarding Paisley's death."

Tina balked. "A shrink?"

"Or a psychologist."

"Well, she's not crazy." Tina was firm on that as she gestured to the living room. "She's in there. I'll be in the kitchen if you need anything." And just like that she disappeared, leaving an FBI agent and a local reporter to talk to her troubled teenager alone.

"She is a terrible mother," I muttered.

"She is," Landon agreed. "I have to wonder when she gave up. Was she always a terrible mother? Is that why Amelia ended up the way she did? Did she become a terrible mother because Amelia is a rotten kid?"

"That whole nature-versus-nurture thing throws me," I said. "Do you think I would be a different person if I'd grown up in another family? I mean ... what would I be like if Mrs. Little had raised me?"

Landon made a horrified face. "Oh, now I'm going to have nightmares." He pinned me with a serious look. "As for the rest ... you always would've turned into my Bay. I have no doubt of that."

I smiled, as I'm sure he'd intended. "I'm glad. You seem to like your Bay."

"I love her more than anything," he readily agreed. "Now, come on. Let's get this over with."

Amelia sat on the couch. She had the remote control in her hand and appeared bored by whatever she was watching on the television. When she saw us, her expression turned to annoyance. "What do you two want?"

"Most girls your age would be terrified by a visit from an FBI agent," Landon noted as he settled in one of the armchairs across from the couch. I followed suit, sticking close to him, and positioning myself in a spot where I could watch Amelia's reaction.

"I'm not afraid of you," Amelia snapped, haughty. "I have enough information to ruin the both of you."

"Is that so?" Landon's expression didn't change. "How do you figure?"

"I know what you are." Amelia's eyes were almost black when they landed on me. "I know your girlfriend is a witch and that you cover for her. That's enough to end both of you."

Landon wasn't bothered by the threat. "How do you think that's going to go? Are you going to call the head of the FBI, tell him that an agent in Hemlock Cove is covering for a witch with magical powers?"

Amelia hesitated and then shook her head. "He'll believe me because it's true."

"Are you going to tell him that you went to Hollow Creek, stole magic, faked your own kidnapping, and enticed an adult to help you run away from home while you're at it?" I asked.

Amelia's jaw swung back and forth until she held up her hands. "What do you want from me?"

"We want to know what you've been up to the last few weeks," Landon replied. "Your mother said you haven't been hanging out with Emma and Sophia."

"My mother is an idiot."

"Your mother looks as if she's not sleeping," I said. "Could she be worried about something?"

"What? Are you talking about me?" The laugh Amelia let loose was cold. "My mother has no idea what happened. She believed the stories we made up. She doesn't know about the magic."

"Are you still trying to enhance yourself with magic?" Landon asked.

Amelia pinned him with a glare that should've been out of her reach at her age. "What do you think?"

"I think you want power," Landon replied. "I think you got a taste of it when you stole that magic from Hollow Creek. I think you want more."

"Well ... then I guess that's your answer." Amelia held out her hands. "You're not here about Hollow Creek. You're here about Mr. Compton. He killed himself — and that was after Granger Montgomery brought the gun into the school — and you think it's somehow tied to magic. Don't bother denying it. I'm not an idiot."

"All signs point to the contrary, but we're here to listen to you," Landon prodded. "Tell us what you know."

For the first time since we'd entered the room, Amelia's expression changed. She seemed confused despite her veneer of bravado. "I ... don't know what you want." She licked her lips as she glanced between us. "Are you saying what happened at the school was magical?"

She didn't know. We were providing her with information. She might very well have been on the hunt for magic, but she wasn't involved in what happened with the contagion. She didn't even realize it was happening.

"We're saying what happened at the school was a tragedy," Landon clarified. "It's very sad."

"I've been crying myself to sleep over it every night," Amelia drawled. "I can't tell you how horrible it is to think about."

"You're a narcissist," Landon said. "It's possible you're also a sociopath. Either way, you're a horrible person. Not everybody is like you, Amelia. We want to know what people are saying about the incident at the school."

"The normal stuff," Amelia replied. "They say Granger melted down and Mr. Compton tried to stop him and somehow got shot. Granger is to blame for this."

"Will Compton took his own life," I interjected. "That's been covered in all the news broadcasts."

"Yeah, but reporters lie." Amelia was back to blasé. "They're just spreading that story because they don't want to ruin Granger's life. Everybody knows he's a murderer and that you guys are covering."

"Is that really what they're saying?" Landon asked.

She bobbed her head. "It's the truth. Everybody knows it."

He turned to me, a million emotions fighting for control. Finally, he forced a tight smile and stood. "Thank you for your time, Amelia."

"Is that it?" She was surprised. "You don't want to ask me any more questions?"

"Would it help?" I asked. I'd yet to stand. "Just out of curiosity, how hard have you been chasing magic? I know you haven't given up on the idea of being a witch. Where are you conducting your research?"

Amelia snorted. "Wouldn't you like to know."

"That's why I asked."

"I'm not telling you." Amelia's eyes flashed hot. "I'm in control of my own destiny. I'm going to do what I want to do and there's nothing you can do or say about it."

"Fair enough." I finally stood. "Just remember, Amelia, that you weren't born into this world. I was. No matter what you think you can do, I'll always be stronger. You'll never be able to outrun the leash I put on you."

"Or maybe you just want me to think that."

"You keep telling yourself that."

LANDON WAITED UNTIL WE WERE SAFELY IN his Explorer and out of earshot to speak again.

"What do you think?"

"She wants to be more dangerous than she is right now," I replied. "She has no idea what's going on at the school."

"I came to the same conclusion."

"We should talk with Sophia and Emma just to be on the safe side. I want to hear what they have to say about this rift. Otherwise, I think we're looking in the wrong place."

"I'll call Terry and have him meet us there," Landon said as he fired the Explorer's engine to life. "The other parents are more involved, and we might need his presence to soothe them."

"Amelia is an angry girl," I noted. "She's not smart enough to pull this off."

"No, but somebody is. We have to find out who."

"I don't even know where to start looking."

"Neither do I … and we're running out of time."

We could both hear it, the ticking of a clock as we tried to put the pieces together. We had a powerful enemy, and we were behind. We had to catch up.

CHAPTER
Seventeen

We went to Emma's house next, which turned out to be a good choice because she was in the yard with Sophia when we pulled up. We were barely out of Landon's Explorer when Chief Terry's vehicle pulled in behind us. I was surprised to see him despite Landon believing we needed him to placate Emma's parents. He looked tired.

"You should take the day off." I rubbed his arm when he drew close.

His lips curved as he regarded me. "Are you tending me?"

I shrugged. "You look tired."

"Don't worry. I'll have plenty of energy for your wedding. It's a big day for my little sweetheart." He winked and a jolt of guilt rolled through me. I wanted him to walk me down the aisle. Landon was right about that. Balancing what I wanted with what was best for my father was delicate business.

I flicked a quick glance toward Landon and found him watching me with unreadable eyes. He knew. He always knew everything. It was impossible to keep secrets from him. I didn't want to talk about it, though, so I forced a smile.

"I don't think they're involved," I said. "Amelia has attitude enough for ten people, but she's looking for magic to steal. I don't think she's found it."

"We don't know that she hasn't been back to Hollow Creek," Landon pointed out. "That's where she got juiced the first time. Seems to me that she would keep going back to recreate what happened."

"Yeah." I blew out a sigh. "Let's see what these two have to say and then do some brainstorming." I glanced back at Chief Terry. "Or you could go home and take a nap."

He leveled a glare on me. "I don't need to be mothered. I get enough of that from your mother."

I jolted at the pointed words. "Is something wrong? Is she being mean to you? I can talk to her if you want." I liked having him around for meals. He'd always been part of the family, but this was different. There was no wall of separation between him and us now.

"Bay, I don't think he's suggesting that he's going to break up with your mother," Landon said gently.

Chief Terry jolted. "Of course, I'm not going to break up with her. I didn't wait so long to find the perfect time to get together with her just to break it off. She's just ... she's very intense."

"She'll be better when the wedding is over ... and the baby is born ... and Aunt Tillie calms down."

Landon and Chief Terry snorted in unison.

"I've known Tillie longer than you have," Chief Terry pointed out. "She's never going to calm down. Even when she dies, she's going to come back and haunt us all. Don't kid yourself."

He wasn't wrong. "I just don't want you suffering."

He chuckled. "I was just thinking the same thing about you. I see the weight of the world dragging you down when you should be gearing up for your wedding."

"I'm not suffering," I reassured him. "Well, I had a hangover this morning and that felt especially painful, but don't worry about me."

He pressed a fatherly kiss to my forehead. "I can't help it. I want you to have your day." He turned gruff in an instant, jerking a thumb at Landon. "And this one is desperate to make sure Clove doesn't steal your attention by giving birth. It's becoming a bit ridiculous."

"If Clove goes into labor at the wedding, it will be fine." I'd thought about it a long time. I wanted my day, but that wasn't the most important thing. "The wedding will be great regardless. I'm more excited for the marriage than the wedding."

Landon slung his arm around my shoulders. "That's because you're marrying the best man in the world and you know he's going to be an absolute dream."

I laughed so loud I sounded like a donkey. "Oh, right," I said once I'd recovered. "That's exactly what I was thinking."

"Yeah, yeah, yeah." He returned to looking at Sophia and Emma, who hadn't moved since we'd pulled into the driveway. "Let's do this."

He took the lead and headed toward the girls, Chief Terry falling in directly behind him. That left me to bring up the rear, and I was more interested in watching the girls study us than throwing out questions.

"Hello, girls," Landon offered by way of greeting. "How are you doing today?"

I searched their faces for a reaction. As far as I could tell, the memory spell I'd performed on them had stuck. They showed no signs of lapsing into bad habits.

"We're fine," Emma replied, her body language stiff as she glanced between us. "Is this about Paisley?"

"We've closed the Paisley case," Landon replied. "We know who killed her."

"Brian Kelly." Sophia's gaze was dark. "I don't even get that. How did they know one another?"

Landon hesitated. Technically it wasn't Brian who killed Paisley. An entity had taken him over. But Brian was no longer a concern and the entity had been trapped in a garden gnome on the newspaper property. As far as the girls were concerned, Brian was a killer. That's all they needed to know.

"We're actually here about Amelia," Chief Terry interjected calmly. "We're wondering if you can enlighten us on her mood of late."

"We're not friends with her any longer," Sophia replied.

"She doesn't want to be friends with us," Emma added. "She says we're weak and didn't fight hard enough to remember. We can't figure out what she's talking about."

"Did she say what she wanted you to remember?" I asked.

Sophia's gaze was sharp when it landed on me. "No. She won't say. She just keeps repeating that we're idiots and she can't believe she was ever friends with us."

"She really hates you, too," Emma said, looking at me. "She has nothing nice to say about you."

"Does she want to hurt Bay?" Landon queried.

Emma looked confused by the question. "Like ... kill her? I think you're reading Amelia wrong. She talks about people, but she wouldn't kill anyone."

"Are you here because Amelia threatened Ms. Winchester?" Sophia's eyes were wide with wonder. She was clearly feeding on the gossip. "Are you going to throw her in jail?"

"That's not why we're here." Landon kept his demeanor flat. "We're here because Amelia has been hanging around the high school since the incident the other day." His response was smooth. Even though it wasn't an overt lie, it was stretching the bonds of credibility.

"Oh." Emma's forehead creased, as if she was thinking hard. "That's weird."

"Was she involved with Granger Montgomery?" Chief Terry prodded. "Did they interact at all?"

"We haven't been paying much attention to her because she's so mean to us, but I don't think she was friendly with Granger," Sophia replied. "I mean ... she once said he was cute, but she didn't think she could date him because he wasn't hot."

"You just know Granger is going to end up hot," Emma offered. "Like him." She pointed at Landon. She looked Landon up and down. "Were you always hot, or did you turn hot when you grew up?"

"I was always hot," Landon replied. "Even in elementary school, the girls were all over me."

"I can see that." Emma was blasé. "I can also see you being a geek. I mean ... you are marrying one of the Winchesters. Is that still happening?"

Landon smirked. "A couple of days. I can't wait."

"Bummer," Emma muttered. "You're the only hot guy in town

these days. Well, you and Marcus from the petting zoo. But he's with a Winchester too."

She talked about me as if I wasn't there and I didn't like it.

"Well, I'm happy with my Winchester," Landon said. "We need more info on Amelia. Are you certain she had no ties to Granger?"

"Pretty sure," Emma confirmed.

"What about Will Compton?"

"Mr. Compton?" Sophia's expression was hard to read. "He was the hottest teacher in school."

That was interesting. The girls were at an age when everything revolved around the way people looked. I had hope they would get over that, but there was a definite ripple between them at mention of the teacher who had taken his own life.

"Was he?" Landon kept his grimace in check. "Did Amelia agree with you about that?"

"Everybody agreed," Emma replied. "Like ... everybody. He was young and had great hair."

"He was single," Sophia supplied. "All the other teachers are married."

"Well, that's a bonus." Landon feigned brightness. "Did Amelia have a crush on him like you guys do?"

The look Emma shot Landon was withering. "We don't have crushes. We're adults. Adults don't have crushes."

"I had a crush on Bay the moment I saw her."

"Yeah, but you guys dated."

"Not right away. I crushed on her from afar for weeks before she agreed to date me." He shot me a wink. "Isn't that right?"

"I didn't know you had a crush on me," I said. "I thought you were just being your usual charming self."

"Well, now you know. I had a complete and total crush on you." Landon turned back to the girls. "Crushes are normal. If Amelia had a crush on Will Compton, we need to know about it."

Emma's forehead creased in confusion. "You think Amelia had something to do with Mr. Compton killing himself?"

"We're trying to sort through all the information," Landon replied. "If Amelia had a crush on her teacher, we need to know."

"Well, I don't know what to tell you." Emma held out her hands. "She talked about how cute he was, but every girl in school talked about that. We have Mr. Landry to look at most of the time, so Mr. Compton was great when he came in."

Landon slid his eyes to me. "Mr. Landry?"

"He's been around since long before I was in school," I explained. "He's ancient."

"Ah." Landon nodded. "Okay, well ... what is everybody saying about what happened at school?"

"Nobody knows anything," Sophia said. "All we know is that Granger went into the school with a gun and is now in the hospital. People are saying he's crazy. Mr. Compton is dead. Some people say he shot himself and other people say Granger did it and you're covering up for it because you don't want it to make national news."

Landon's lips curved down. "Are people really saying that?"

"Of course. Why would Mr. Compton take the gun from Granger and kill himself? It makes no sense."

Landon's gaze was heavy when it locked with mine, propelling me to open my mouth. He gave me an almost imperceptible shake of the head to silence me. He didn't want me correcting the assumption.

"Is anyone saying anything else?" Chief Terry asked. "We're especially interested in Amelia."

"Amelia has completely shut us out," Emma replied. "She wants nothing to do with us."

"We don't want anything to do with her either," Sophia added. "She's too intense. She's no fun now. Ever since the stuff with Paisley, she's been intolerable."

"Good riddance," Emma said. "We don't need her."

And that was that. Emma and Sophia were far removed from whatever Amelia had planned. They weren't good enough actresses to bamboozle us.

"Thank you." Landon unleashed a devastating smile on the girls, making them blush. "That's all we needed to know."

. . .

EMMA AND SOPHIA ESCAPED INTO THE HOUSE once we finished with them. The three of us stood in the driveway talking.

"They don't have anything to do with this," Chief Terry said as he dragged a hand through his hair, the bags under his eyes reminding me again that he was exhausted.

"I don't think Amelia has anything to do with it either," I said. "That's not to say she wouldn't involve herself in something like this, but she doesn't have any magic at her disposal right now."

"And we want to keep it that way," Landon said. "This whole thing is a mess. We have no idea who we're even supposed to be looking at."

"It's frustrating," Chief Terry agreed. "What do you guys say to heading to town for an early lunch? We can brainstorm over patty melts at the diner."

"I'm not eating a patty melt but I'm up for lunch." Landon flicked his eyes to me. "You okay with that?"

I nodded. "I could eat."

"Good." Chief Terry started for his truck. "We'll meet up at the diner." He was almost to the door of his service vehicle when I noticed something odd. The tires appeared to be rolling, not fast, but definitely rolling, and the truck was heading straight toward him. At first, I thought it was an optical illusion, but then I heard the telltale crunch of gravel.

"Chief Terry!"

He looked at me, the tone of my voice alerting him that something horrible was about to happen.

I reacted on instinct, stepping forward and unleashing a tsunami of magic. There was a terrific crunch as the magic hit the front of his truck, stopping it only two feet from him.

Chief Terry's eyes went wide. "What the ...?"

I couldn't release the magic. Something was propelling the truck forward. If I stopped, the truck would hit him. "Move," I gritted out.

Landon jabbed a finger at Chief Terry. "Get out of there right now!"

Chief Terry didn't have to be told twice. He raced from between the two vehicles, not stopping until he was safe on the lawn. "What is happening?"

Landon shook his head as he watched me. "Bay?"

"Someone is here," I growled, striding forward with a purpose.

When Landon realized I was positioning myself between Chief Terry's truck and his Explorer, he was livid. "Get out of there right now." He moved to intercept me, but I shook my head. "Your life is not worth risking for either of those vehicles," he snarled. "Move."

I wasn't worried about the vehicles. "I need to see." I placed my hands on the front of Chief Terry's grill and closed my eyes, magic briefly washing over me. Most of the magic was mine, but a dark edge rolled beneath my white magic, and it was powerful. "Someone is watching us."

Landon turned his eyes to the trees surrounding the house. "Do you want me to go over there and search?"

"No."

"I can."

"We both can," Chief Terry offered. "Also, I agree with Landon. Move away from those vehicles. I don't want you putting yourself at risk."

I readjusted my magic, the shift in my output momentarily overwhelming whoever was playing with us. "I've got this." It was with a great deal of force that I shoved at the truck. I shouldn't have been able to move it — physically, I wasn't an imposing specimen — but I easily pushed it back five feet.

"What is happening?" Landon was breathless. "Are you doing that?"

I nodded.

"How?" he demanded.

"I need to break the spell." I needed to prove to myself as much as to them that I could do it. "I ... here it comes." I groaned as I funneled everything I had into fighting the dark wave that was so desperately trying to push the police vehicle into me.

Now the two streams of magic collided, a terrific bolt of lightning hit the trees to the east. It was followed almost immediately by a rumble of thunder. The downpour that followed was intense.

"Well, this is just great," Chief Terry complained as his truck rolled to a standstill fifteen feet from where it had started. "I can't believe you just went all Hulk on my truck, Bay."

I lowered my hands. Instinctively, I knew the magical assault was over. I ignored the rain as I peered into the trees. The presence I felt was dark, evil to the core, and it lingered for several moments. Then, just as quickly, it was gone.

"What do we do?" Landon demanded.

I pushed my damp hair out of my eyes. "She's gone," I said. "It's okay."

"She?" Landon cocked an eyebrow. "The *she* from the school?"

"That would be my guess."

"Who is she?" Chief Terry asked. "Did you just beat her?"

"She's still out there. She's powerful, but she's not as powerful as I am."

"That's good?"

I shrugged. "It's something to think about. She's going to keep coming."

"Then we have to stop her."

"If you have an idea on that front, I'm all ears."

Chief Terry licked his lips as he turned his attention to Landon. "I don't like this."

Landon was grim. "Join the club. There's an evil ... something ... trying to kill my fiancée days before our wedding. There's nothing to like about this situation. Nothing at all."

CHAPTER
Eighteen

Scout and Gunner were outside the diner when we parked. We followed close behind Chief Terry during the drive in case he was attacked again. Once we were safely on the sidewalk, I moved back to his truck and magically scanned it. I couldn't detect anything.

"What's going on?" Scout asked. She was good at reading body language, and it was apparent that she recognized something had gone down during our morning interviews.

"Nothing good," Landon replied, rage simmering beneath his calm facade. "Everything sucks."

Sympathetic, I rubbed his shoulder. There was little I could do to correct his evaluation of the day. "You guys missed breakfast this morning."

"Yes, well, Tillie's wine is clearly the devil's brew," Gunner offered. "We slept in ... and I can't remember the last time wine knocked me out that hard."

I chuckled. "You're just not used to it. If you hang around with us more often, you'll build up a tolerance."

"Right," Landon said dryly. "That's why we woke up with hangovers."

"Fair point." I ran my hand over the grill once more. "Someone tried to take Chief Terry out." I launched into the tale, catching them up, and when I finished, I realized the anger I'd been trying to hold at bay was about to come out. "Whoever it was wanted to hurt him because they knew he was important to me."

Chief Terry grunted. "Don't blame yourself for this, Bay," he said. "We don't know this is happening because of you."

"Who else?"

Chief Terry looked to Landon for help. "Do something to make her feel better."

"I'm upset too," Landon replied. "Like ... really, really upset. Not only could you have been hurt, she could've been as well."

"Don't worry," I said. "We'll get you a bacon grilled cheese for lunch."

He didn't immediately respond, and when I risked a glance at him, I found him glaring.

"What?" I was immediately on alert. "Are you mad at me for some reason?"

"I'm mad you said that," he replied. "Bacon doesn't make up for the fact that you could've been hurt."

"Oh, geez." I pinched the bridge of my nose to ward off the incoming headache. It was going to be a big one if I didn't get this situation under control. "I only moved in front of the truck because I knew I could counter the magic."

"And what if there's more than one person behind this?" Landon challenged. "What if other magic was added to the mix and you couldn't fight it off? Maybe that was the plan from the start."

"That didn't happen."

Landon kicked a stone back into the gravel parking lot and turned his back to me. It wasn't a dismissal. He was trying to get his emotions under control.

"It's an interesting way to go at you," Scout mused as she stepped up to touch the truck. "I have to believe somebody either followed you or went looking. What were you doing right before it happened?"

"Talking to those girls I told you about, the ones whose memories I modified."

"Hmm." She leaned forward and rested her ear on the hood of the truck. "There's no magic here now."

"Did the truck tell you that?" Landon asked. He seemed confused by Scout's actions. "Is it talking to you?"

"Yes, and it's a salty beast." Scout grinned at him when she straightened. "Trucks don't talk. No matter what Stephen King tells us, vehicles don't have feelings."

"Awesome." Landon's tone was dark. "What are you doing?"

"Trying to get a feel for the magical remnants. Not much here."

"I'm afraid," I admitted out of the blue. "I was already afraid because everybody here has a gun and could be forced to use it against someone they love. Now we have to be afraid of our cars too? This is just ... not good."

"Oh, it's going to be okay." Annoyance forgotten, Landon pulled me in for a hug. "Just don't stand between two vehicles when one of them is magically possessed. You shortened my life by ten years."

I patted his back, thankful for the hug. "I don't know what to do."

"I do." Scout was a doer. She didn't ask for permission. She simply did what she thought was right. I admired that about her, even as she placed her hands on Chief Terry's vehicle and infused it with magic. "Anybody have any lipstick?" The question was clearly for me. I nodded.

"Sure." I rummaged in my purse and came up with a tube.

"This isn't your wedding lipstick or anything, is it?"

"No. Why?"

"Because I'm going to use it all." Scout drew a symbol I didn't recognize on the hood of the truck and then added a burst of her magic to the mix. The symbol flared and then disappeared.

"What was that?" Landon asked, his arm around my waist.

"It's a protection rune," Gunner replied. "We have them on all of our motorcycles. It solves certain ... problems."

"Like I won't get into an accident now?" Chief Terry looked happy at the prospect.

"Meaning that nobody else can curse your truck," Scout countered. "You can still get into an accident if you're an idiot driver."

Scout moved to Landon's Explorer and repeated the ritual. "We need to hit every vehicle you guys have to be on the safe side."

I nodded and gestured to the parking spots across the street. "That's Thistle's car." I pointed toward the stable. "And Marcus's truck."

"Bay's car is in front of the newspaper office," Landon added.

Thistle's car and Marcus's truck were protected in a few minutes. When we got to my car, however, Scout lingered. "This thing is already cursed."

Landon threw up his hands. "Of course, it is. Let's just junk it and buy a new one after the honeymoon."

Mirth flooded Scout's features as she put her hand on the hood. "Or we could just kill the previous curse and then protect it."

Landon refused to match her smile. "I can't let Bay drive that car knowing there was a curse on it. I'll go insane."

"Buddy, you're halfway there." Gunner grinned as he moved behind Scout. "Do you know what sort of curse we're dealing with?"

"No." She was pensive. "It's weird. I ... have never seen anything like it, and I've seen a lot of curses." She pursed her lips. "You know what? We'll leave this for now. You can't drive it." Her gaze was serious when it locked with mine.

"I don't want to die, so no problem," I reassured her. "I can ride with Landon. His vehicle is safe."

"And we'll hit all the other vehicles at the inn after lunch," Landon added. "I want everybody safe."

"We should probably head out to the Dragonfly, too," I added. "Your parents are arriving today and we can multi-task with the visit. We'll keep your parents and brothers busy while Scout protects all the vehicles."

"I would feel better knowing everybody is protected," Landon said. "I don't want you in that car until this is completely over with. Promise me."

"I promise. I don't want to die before I get to marry you."

"I don't want you to die period." Landon was serious. "Just ... no, no, no."

I leaned into him and grinned, a hint of movement catching my attention. When I turned, I found Mrs. Little heading up the walkway, Kristen at her side.

"This won't be good," Landon muttered.

"Ugh." Chief Terry made a disgusted sound deep in his throat. "Let me." He stepped in front of the women and unleashed a tight smile. "Do you need something?"

Mrs. Little pulled up short. "Does it matter?"

"Bay is having car trouble," he replied. "We might have to tear the car apart to get it running."

It seemed like an odd thing to say, but I kept my expression placid as I nodded. "Yes, it's acting up."

Mrs. Little's face was blank. "What do I care about Bay's car?"

Kristen had the grace to at least feign concern. "I'm sorry about your car. If this is a bad time, we can come back."

"For what?" Landon asked.

"I was hoping to place an ad." Kristen appeared so uncomfortable I felt sorry for her. She wasn't to blame for any of this. Mrs. Little was using her as a weapon against my family and she didn't even know it. "Bay said I didn't need one, but Mrs. Little says it's good to design one right away."

"We can put an ad together," I offered as I stepped onto the sidewalk, sending Landon a silent cease-and-desist order. "What did you have in mind?"

"Something basic." Kristen clasped her hands together in front of her. "But I feel that we're interrupting something important."

"Oh, don't worry about that," Mrs. Little admonished. "These reprobates are always up to something. If you wait for them to act normal, you'll never get anywhere."

Landon's response was to blow a raspberry in her direction. It took everything I had to contain my laughter.

"I recognize you." Mrs. Little turned her attention to Scout and Gunner. "You were in town a few weeks ago. People say you were hanging out by the cove doing something illegal."

Scout's smile was enigmatic. "Well, if people said it, I guess it must be true."

"They weren't doing anything illegal," I argued. "They were just ... hanging around with us."

"I stand by my statement." Mrs. Little folded her arms across her chest, impatience radiating off her. "Do you want to show us inside, Bay? Kristen wants the ad in next week's edition."

I wanted to tell Mrs. Little to shove it.

"Do you have any sales you want to run?" I asked Kristen, forcing myself to be professional even though I wanted to pop Mrs. Little in the face. "I can mock something up and email you suggestions. Then you can pick the one you like."

Kristen looked relieved. "That sounds great." She pulled a business card from her purse. "My email address is on here."

"Awesome." I shoved the card into my back pocket. "I'll do the mockups this afternoon. Then you pick the one you like and tell me the size. I'll include the pricing information when I send it."

"I would think that you'd offer Kristen a discount since she's a first-time customer," Mrs. Little interjected.

"Do you give people a break on the first unicorn they buy at your store?" Scout asked. "I mean ... you seem to think Bay should do it, so I assume it's a tried-and-true business practice for you."

Whatever Mrs. Little was expecting, it wasn't that. Her eyes momentarily flashed dark, and she moved her jaw. She didn't like Scout's cheekiness, and she didn't want to be painted as a hypocrite in front of Kristen. She needed as many allies as she could get. "Of course, I offer a deal — twenty-five percent off your first purchase."

"Awesome." Scout started toward the Unicorn Emporium without further prodding. "I can't wait to buy something for my cabin."

"Make sure it's pink and gaudy," Gunner called to her back. "If it won't make my father itchy then it's not the right purchase for us."

"I'm on it." Scout flashed a thumbs-up and continued walking.

Mrs. Little's eyes were wild as she glanced between Scout's back and me. It was obvious she blamed me, but there was nothing she could do to change how things had played out. She wouldn't risk Scout causing a scene ... and there was little Scout loved more than causing a scene.

"I'll be right back." She darted after Scout, calling out to her as they crossed the street.

I fixed a kind smile on Kristen to distract her. "I'll have those ad mockups to you as soon as I can."

"Thanks for that." Kristen let loose a small wave. "I hope your car is okay."

"I'm sure it will be fine." I waited until she was gone to speak again. "So ... lunch and then car protection detail?"

Landon nodded. "Is it wrong that I can't wait to see which unicorn Scout buys?"

I was kind of looking forward to that too. Scout never half-assed anything. Whatever she had planned for Mrs. Little, it was going to be big.

"THIS IS SPARKLES," SHE ANNOUNCED when she withdrew the unicorn from the fancy canvas bag she'd received from the Unicorn Emporium. The item she held up was about twelve inches tall and featured an explosion of pastel colors that would've made the Easter bunny retch.

"He's awesome," Gunner said as he rested against a tree in front of the Dragonfly. Once lunch was finished, we decided a trip to the Dragonfly was warranted. Nobody was leaving The Overlook, so the vehicles there could wait until we wound our way around again this afternoon. Just in case, we'd sent Chief Terry to make sure they didn't leave ... and to take a nap. I was still worried that he looked so tired. "I can't wait to introduce him to my dad."

"I think your father will love him." Scout grinned at the unicorn. "He was her central display in the store. I took him even though she really didn't want to sell him, and then made her give me twenty-five percent off. She was so mad."

"I think you still overpaid," Landon said as she shoved the unicorn into Gunner's hand. "He's ugly."

"Sparkles is a she," Scout replied as she fished in her pocket for the lipstick. "She'll make a great cursed object for my collection."

"You have a collection of cursed objects?" I was intrigued. "May I ask why?"

Scout shrugged. "I just like them." She inclined her head toward the inn. "Incoming."

When I turned to look, I found my father traipsing across the lawn. He didn't look happy.

"I've got this," Landon said as he moved to intercept him. "Hey, Jack." He held out his hand for a proper greeting. "My parents here yet?"

"They're due any minute," Dad replied. He shook Landon's hand, although it was clear he was confused by our presence. "Why are you hanging around Warren's SUV?"

I could've lied. Sometimes I thought my father might prefer it. The magic was beyond him, and he didn't pretend otherwise. But we'd forged a new start, and I refused to go that route. "We have a situation."

"Of course, you do." He exhaled heavily, as if settling himself. "Why did I think that you two would make it to your wedding without another situation arising? Clearly I'm an idiot."

"We were hopeful ourselves," I said. "In a nutshell, we're making sure nobody can curse your vehicles. There was an incident a few hours ago with Chief Terry's truck. Luckily nobody was hurt, but now we want to make sure everyone stays safe."

"I see." Dad's eyes fell on Scout. "You're new."

"Oh, I'm sorry." I made quick introductions. "Scout and Gunner are helping us with our little problem."

"That makes me nervous." Dad planted his hands on his hips. "You've got me convinced that you can do anything without help. If you need help ... ." He trailed off.

"It's okay," I reassured him. "We're going to figure it out. Nothing will derail this wedding."

"Nothing," Landon agreed. "I don't care if I have to get out and push something. It's happening, and we're going on our honeymoon with nothing hanging over our heads. I'll make sure of that."

"Good." Dad patted Landon on the shoulder and then turned to the driveway as a vehicle pulled in. "Are these your parents?"

Landon swiveled quickly, a smile overtaking his features. He hadn't seen his parents in months. They'd visited us about eighteen months ago and we'd been down for several day trips since. This would be their first significant visit since the poltergeist affair.

Landon started toward them, practically glowing with happiness.

"You need to do their car too," I said to Scout in a low voice before crossing with him.

"I've got it," she promised. "Just get them inside. I'll handle the rest."

"We can have tea and scones," Dad offered. "Please join us," he said to Gunner and Scout. "I'd like to get to know you."

"Absolutely," Scout promised. "Just let me finish this."

I left them to their task and hurried to catch up. Connie and Earl Michaels were all smiles when they saw me.

"There she is." Earl drew me into a bear hug before I could utter a greeting. "I can't believe you're almost my daughter." He gave me a loud kiss that made me burst out laughing.

"We're so glad this day has finally come." Connie gripped her son's arm so tightly I was certain she was leaving marks. Her eyes were glassy when they locked with mine. "This wedding is going to be beautiful."

"It is," I agreed, even though I couldn't help picturing a magical assault that triggered Clove's labor in the middle of the ceremony. "It's going to be a beautiful day."

"It is," Landon confirmed.

"And then, after that, grandchildren." Connie clapped her hands and bounced up and down.

"I think we're going to enjoy each other for a bit first," Landon hedged.

"I want grandchildren." Connie linked her arm through his and tugged him toward the inn. "And magical grandchildren to boot? That's going to be the best thing ever."

I smiled as she dragged Landon inside, opting to remain behind and help Earl with the luggage.

"Is something wrong?" Earl asked as he handed me a suitcase. He looked concerned.

"Everything is fine," I promised. "We're almost there. The wedding is going to be great."

Now I just had to follow through. We were nowhere near solving this one, and the wedding was barreling down. I needed a break.

CHAPTER
Nineteen

Landon needed time with his parents. If we were normal people, he would be able to take time off work and hang out with them to his heart's content.

We were pretty far from normal people.

That didn't stop me from suggesting he visit with them a few hours. Just him.

"I don't know." He looked pained. "Where are you going?"

"I want to talk to Granger's parents," I replied. "I understand they're camped out at the hospital."

"How are you going to get there? You can't walk to a different town, and I need my vehicle in case a call comes in."

I pointed to Scout and Gunner, who were loitering at the front door of the lobby. "I figured I would go with them."

Landon chewed his bottom lip, debating.

"I'll be safe with them," I promised. "Their bikes are already warded."

He sighed and pulled me in for a hug. That was the moment I knew he really needed time with his parents. He was willing to separate even though a threat stalked Hemlock Cove. "Text me if you get anywhere."

I nodded. "We'll figure this out." I sounded like a skipping record.

When I wasn't saying those exact words to him, he was saying them to me. We were both desperate to come through for one another, but we had nothing to go on.

"We will." He gave me a soft kiss. "I love you, Bay."

"I love you too." I gave his butt a playful squeeze. "I promise I will be perfectly safe."

"Just make sure you ride with Scout," he said in a voice that was loud enough to carry. "I don't want Gunner to get ideas."

"Oh, will you let that go?" Gunner made a face. "I have my own woman."

"Yes, and I so love being referred to as if I'm a possession," Scout sneered. "Ready?" she asked me.

"Yeah. We need answers. I don't know if we'll get them with the Montgomerys, but it can't hurt to try."

CALEB AND ANDREA MONTGOMERY WERE IN THE FIFTH FLOOR waiting room of the hospital when we arrived in Traverse City. Hemlock Cove and the surrounding towns were too small to have their own hospital — some towns didn't even have urgent care facilities — so we were accustomed to driving a distance when it came to tapping hospital resources.

I hesitated in the open archway, briefly debating if I was making a mistake. They had a lot to deal with. Would I be adding to their grief and worry? I had no choice. I needed to know if they could help me.

"Excuse me." I kept my voice low as I approached them.

Andrea lifted her eyes to me first, confusion etching across her face. Then, after a beat, her gaze cleared. "I know you're only doing your job, Bay, but we don't have a statement for you."

I didn't know her well. I knew her husband even less. I was determined to get through this, so I plastered a wan smile on my face. "That's not why I'm here."

Gunner and Scout hung back, sitting on a nearby couch. They weren't part of the interview, but they were close enough to hear what was being said.

"I don't know if anybody told you, but I was in the room with

Granger when it happened," I explained. "I just ... wanted to see how he's doing."

Realization dawned on Andrea's face as she flicked a look toward her husband, who didn't even acknowledge my presence. He looked beaten down. Perhaps Granger's turn had hurt him in ways from which he could never recover. I truly hoped that wasn't the case.

"I knew that," Andrea said, managing a brief smile. "I meant to thank you for whatever you did to stop Granger from ... well, whatever he was going to do. I just haven't had a moment to think."

"It's okay." I ran my hands over the fabric of the cheap waiting room chair. It was an itchy blend and it only served to make things more uncomfortable. "I don't know how much you've heard, but ... Granger seemed confused when I talked to him."

Caleb stirred. "They said he acted like he was on drugs. Granger doesn't take drugs."

"I don't think it was drugs," I hedged. The truth might be worse, I reminded myself. It was better to acknowledge that I didn't know anything about Granger's state of mind that day rather than say the wrong thing. "He seemed ... muddled. It was as if he didn't know where he was. He kept saying that 'she' wanted him to do it, and then he complained that she wasn't there to help him. Do you know who he was referring to?"

Andrea shook her head. "He didn't have a girlfriend. Or doesn't I should say. I don't know why I keep referring to him in the past tense."

I knew why. The child they raised was essentially dead, no matter how things turned out. His life would never be the same.

"You're the reason we still have him." Andrea's smile was watery. "I don't know what you did to talk him down but ... I'm so grateful."

"I did what was necessary."

"No." She dabbed at her eye with a crinkled tissue. "You did way more than that. You ... saved him. Nobody else would've gone in that school knowing there was a teenager with a gun on the loose. You made sure he didn't shoot someone.

"It's going to be hard enough for him to come back from this," she continued, her voice cracking. "He's no longer my little boy. But he can be helped, and we have you to thank for that."

I didn't want to be thanked. "I ... just did what I felt was necessary." I barreled forward. "Just out of curiosity, can you tell me if Granger had some sort of personal relationship with Will Compton?"

"The teacher who died?" Andrea's forehead creased. "I don't even think Granger had a class with him this year. I would have to check to be certain, but he never mentioned Mr. Compton."

That wasn't what I wanted to hear. "What about Granger himself? How was he acting in the days before what happened?"

"He was ... sullen." Andrea dabbed again. "I didn't like his attitude. He's a teenager, so he always has attitude, but this was different. He was withdrawn, spending all his time in his room. He wouldn't interact with us at all."

"It's drugs," Caleb interjected, shifting on his chair as he reversed his earlier course. The first thing he'd said to me was that drugs weren't possible. Now he was saying otherwise. His voice was gravelly. "I told you that he was on drugs days ago, but you didn't want to hear it. There's no other explanation. His personality was so different."

I pressed my lips together, debating. "Drugs can definitely change someone's personality. Did they run a drug panel on him?"

Andrea bobbed her head. "The first panel came back negative. The doctor said they have to send a more extensive panel to a different lab. Sometimes kids take drugs that don't turn up on a normal panel. It's not as if Hemlock Cove is a hotbed of drug activity. The doctor believes that whatever Granger took is probably something available locally."

In a weird sort of way, it made sense. Unfortunately, I knew it wasn't drugs. Granger Montgomery had certainly been influenced by something. I couldn't tell his parents that it was magic unless I wanted to end up strapped down in the bed next to Granger.

"Has Granger spoken to you at all?" I asked.

Andrea's lower lip trembled. "No, and it's breaking my heart. What was the last thing he said to you?"

"He was just angry that 'she' wasn't there. He wanted her to be there and she wasn't. He fought me when I knocked the gun away." That was part of the story Landon and I agreed upon. I had to be the one who knocked the gun out of Granger's hand when people asked.

Explaining that a ghost had done it for me wouldn't go over well. "Then I started wrestling with him. I yelled at Will to unload the gun."

I swallowed hard. I was days removed from the incident and yet it felt like only minutes when I allowed myself to give in and feel. "Mr. Compton picked up the gun, stared at it a moment, and then put it to his own head before pulling the trigger."

"Did he say anything?" Caleb asked, his eyes bloodshot and brimming with tears. "Did he say why?"

I shook my head. "No. He just said he was doing it for 'her' and then he was gone. Right up until that moment I thought he was fine. I was wrong."

"You're a hero, Bay." Andrea gripped my hand. "You did what nobody else was willing to do. You saved our son. It's not your fault you didn't realize what was happening. It's not as if you're some all-powerful being."

No, but sometimes my magic made me feel as if I should do more than I could. "I hope Granger gets the help here he needs," I said.

"The doctor says it's going to take time," Andrea said. "We have that time, thanks to you."

"I'll keep in touch," I promised as I stood. "Granger will need your strength. If it becomes too much, take a break. You're right about this fight taking a long time. There's no easy fix."

"Our lives will never be the same."

Sadly, I knew she was right.

I DIDN'T KNOW WHAT I WAS FEELING when we emerged from the hospital. I meandered to a spot in the shade under a willow tree — a memorial bench placed there — and sank down.

"You can't take on their pain, Bay," Scout said as she moved in front of me. "They're filled with horror ... and fear ... and doubt. That can't be your horror, fear and doubt."

"No? I keep wondering what would've happened if I hadn't gone into that school."

"I'll tell you what would've happened. That kid would've killed someone. His programming wouldn't have allowed for anything else. He might've killed multiple people."

"Scout's right," Gunner stressed. "You did the right thing. You got those other kids out."

"What if Will Compton intervened because I went in the school when I shouldn't have?" I challenged.

"What if Will Compton was supposed to die at Granger Montgomery's hand and there was no way you could stop him without more information?" Scout challenged. "Stop kicking yourself for something you couldn't possibly know."

I laughed. "You sound like Landon."

"Well, don't tell him because it will only go to his head, but he's smart when he wants to be." Scout let loose a small smile and shifted in such a way that her shadow stretched long on the ground. "He's got a big head and an even bigger ego, but that doesn't mean he's wrong."

When she shifted again, the shadow didn't move with her.

I frowned.

"Now, those parents are sad," she continued, swinging her hips. The shadow remained immobile. "I feel horrible for them. They're looking at things the right way. They still have their son. It's going to take a lot of work to get him back, but he's alive. That's better than the alternative."

She flapped her arms when she realized I wasn't looking at her, instead remaining transfixed by her shadow. "Earth to Bay."

The shadow didn't move again.

"Hold up," Gunner leaned closer to the shadow. "Is that ... Bay's shadow?" Even as he asked the question it was obvious he recognized how stupid it was. "Scout." He moved quickly, grabbing her around the waist and tackling her to the ground at the moment the shadow's hand raised up to grab her by the throat.

The shadow missed, and when it shifted, red eyes flared to life. For a moment, all I could think about was Peter Pan's shadow, and how it would act if it was evil rather than mischievous ... and then it was on me.

The shadow hissed as it tackled me with enough force that I fell backward off the bench. I hit the ground hard enough that the oxygen was knocked out of my lungs. I was stunned and yet I fought back. It was a short grappling session, because Scout appeared behind the shadow and grabbed it by the throat.

"I. Don't. Think. So." Her voice was gritty, as if being raked over sand, and her fury was evident as she began pouring magic into the thing that had knocked me from the bench.

I recovered quickly, realizing what she was going to do, but it was already too late to stop her. "Scout, no!"

The shadow began disintegrating. Piece by piece, it flaked away. I would say that the pieces blew away in the wind, but there were no pieces. The shadow simply was no more once Scout overpowered it.

"Well, that was new," Gunner said once he'd recovered. "I'm not sure what just happened."

He wasn't the only one.

"WHY DID YOU CALL ME INSTEAD OF Landon?" Chief Terry asked when he arrived. It felt as if I should report what happened to someone, but there was nothing Chief Terry could do.

"He's with his parents," I replied, lowering my eyes. "I didn't want to drag him away. I should've thought about it. You were taking a nap, weren't you?" If I felt guilty before, it was doubling up on me now. "I'm so sorry. You need your rest."

"Knock that off." He jabbed a finger in my direction to let me know he meant business and then studied the ground by the bench. "I'm not elderly, Bay. I still have a few good years in me left."

I was contrite. "I just ... want you to be able to dance with me at the wedding."

He stilled. "Let's not get worked up over little things," he suggested. "Don't tie yourself up in knots over dances ... and walks down the aisle. Worry about the big things."

"That's what I've been telling her." Scout was blasé. "By the way, whatever that shadow was, it wasn't meant to sustain for more than a brief burst of time. It was like a magical assassin somebody unleashed. There wasn't enough power in that thing to sustain itself for more than another hour or so."

"Then why was it here?" I asked. "Why attack now?"

"Maybe because you haven't gotten in your car," Gunner suggested. "Maybe because you saved Chief Terry earlier. I'm not sure anybody can answer that until we know what's fueling this mess."

I dragged a hand through my hair. "My stomach is constantly upset today ... and not just because of the hangover. The wedding is almost here, and if things don't go perfectly Landon will melt down. Clove's vulnerable because she can't get out of her bed. How am I supposed to solve this?"

Rather than shower me with sympathy, Scout made a face. "We're going to kick this thing's ass and party it up at the wedding. Don't be an idiot."

"We don't know what we're fighting."

"We'll figure it out."

"How?"

"I just know we will." She slung an arm around my shoulders and tugged me tight against her side. "Did I mention I'm part pixie?"

I nodded as I swiped at the tears cascading down my cheeks.

"That means I can do magical things ... and with pixie dust, no less."

"I thought you didn't have any pixie dust handy. That's what you told me when we were looking for Evan that day."

"That doesn't change the fact that I'm an amazing witch. There's no way I'm going to let your day be ruined."

I laughed through the tears. "Now you sound like Landon again."

"Like I said, he's smarter than he looks." She gave me another hug before releasing me. "I have an idea. I'm going to bring a few more people in for research. We don't know everything yet, but we know more. I work with some of the smartest people in the world. We're going to figure this out."

I hoped beyond hope she was right. I was starting to despair, and that wasn't like me. I wanted my wedding and the happiness that was supposed to come after. I refused to settle for anything less.

CHAPTER Twenty

At The Overlook, Scout and Gunner started doling out protection spells on every vehicle in the lot. My attention, however, was drawn to Landon as he stood next to the front door, arms crossed. He watched us work but stayed put.

"He looks like he's steaming mad but in a cold way," Gunner noted as he watched Scout work. "Do you think he knows?"

I had no doubt he knew. "Chief Terry told him."

Gunner checked over our shoulder a second time. "How can you be sure?"

"I grew up with Chief Terry." I flicked another look back at Landon and found him focused on me, his expression unreadable. "He's a law-and-order guy."

"You weren't breaking the law," Scout argued as she studied the tube of lipstick. She'd made it through the last vehicle. "The good news is that you won't have to worry about the vehicles going all *Christine* on you. The bad news is that your lipstick is no more."

I smiled as I accepted the empty tube. "It's fine. I rarely wear lipstick anyway."

Scout moved to stand on my right, her gaze following mine to Landon. "Do you want me to beat him up for you?"

I laughed. "No, I just ... don't want to fight."

"He won't fight," Gunner said.

"What makes you say that?" I was honestly curious.

"Because he loves you more than anything."

"That's usually why he picks a fight."

"Yeah, well, he's not doing it today." Gunner moved his hand to Scout's waist and slipped his finger through her belt loop. They were in sync with one another, and it always made me smile when they interacted. They were both alphas, yet they worked well together, picking and choosing their battles. I liked to think that Landon and I were the same way ... at least most of the time.

"Why won't he do it today?" I was wasting time because I didn't want to walk up the sidewalk to the inn.

"Do you really not know?" Gunner sent me a sidelong look. "When he looks at you, do you know what he thinks?"

"Probably that he wishes he had a way to make me smell like bacon forever."

Gunner laughed. "You guys play some kinky games with bacon. It's fine. Scout and I play those games with this gas station chicken in Hawthorne Hollow. It's divine."

"It's surprisingly good," Scout agreed. "We eat it in bed and then wipe our greasy fingers all over one another, which totally excites the cat."

"I'm not sure what that has to do with Landon being angry."

"It has nothing to do with Landon," Gunner replied. "I just like thinking about Scout and chicken. Anyway, when he looks at you, he convinces himself that no man has ever loved a woman as much as he loves you."

"You're saying that's not possible," I said. "You think he convinces himself of that, so it makes him worry more."

"I'm saying he loves you more than any man has ever loved his partner. Ever." Gunner's grin widened. "He loves you with everything he has, Bay. I know you called Terry because you didn't want to worry Landon, but that feels like a slap to him."

I blew out a sigh. "I just want him to have his day."

Gunner laughed. "That's what he wants for you. You're the love of his life."

"So ... what do you suggest I do?"

"Tell him the truth," Scout suggested. "You want him to be happy as much as he wants you to be happy. He has to understand that."

I hung my head and scuffed my shoes against the pavement as I walked to him. Scout and Gunner cut around the side of the building so they could enter the inn through the back door. I didn't blame them. I wouldn't want a ringside seat either. "Hey." I made an attempt at a smile as I called out to him.

"Hey." He leaned in to kiss me. "All the vehicles warded?"

I eyed him with bubbling suspicion. "All the vehicles but mine at the newspaper office. Scout is still debating if we can use the curse that's on the car against the person coming after us."

"As long as you don't drive it." He ran his hands up and down my arms and then pressed his forehead to mine. "How was the rest of your day?"

This was a trap. He expected me to lie to him. There was no way I was falling for that. "Um ... interesting. We were attacked by a shadow, but you already know that because Chief Terry tattled on me."

His expression was unreadable when he pulled back. "Are you only telling me about it because you know Terry told me?"

"I had every intention of telling you regardless. I just didn't want to interrupt your afternoon with your parents."

"Ah." His smile was wide and yet there was an emotion in his eyes I didn't recognize. "Well, since I know you're curious, my afternoon with my parents went well. My brothers are here. Everybody is inside getting reacquainted with your family."

"Group dinner," I said, rubbing my forehead. "I guess I should've seen that coming."

"Is there something you want to say to me before we go inside?"

I hated being put on the spot. "I love you." It was the easiest thing to say. It was also true.

"I love you too."

"I'm not sorry for calling Chief Terry instead of you," I added.

He arched one eyebrow. "Why is that?"

"Because you needed time with your family. You're wound really tight these days. I thought it was best you hang out with them."

"I see."

"Oh, don't say it like that." I lost my fight against the frustration and threw up my hands. "I hate when you get passive aggressive. I just ... didn't want you to worry. Between that and your parents being here, I was desperate to give you a few hours to decompress."

He slid his arm around my shoulders and tugged me to his side. "Here's the thing, though ... ." He broke off and licked his lips before continuing. "You're the most important thing to me. As much as I want to spend time with my parents and relax before the wedding, you're more important."

"I know but ... ."

"Shh." He pressed his finger to my lips and gave me a warning look. "You and I go above and beyond when it's time to protect one another. Sometimes that causes miscommunication. I don't want that happening today."

"What do you want?"

"For you to know that I appreciated being able to spend time with my parents. I also love you so much it hurts. Don't make yourself small because you think you're giving me what I need. I want you to be big."

My forehead creased. "Um ... ."

"Yes, that came out weirder than I thought it would," he acknowledged. "We're just going to let it go."

I laughed as he pulled me tightly against him. "I don't know what to do," I whispered. "We're running out of time."

"We'll figure it out."

"What if we don't?"

"We will."

"How can you be sure?"

"Because you're getting your dream wedding if I have to handle every little detail myself. You've earned this."

"I've earned you?"

"Of course. You've also earned this." He pulled back and pressed his hand to the spot above my heart. "I want you to always be happy. This wedding is important to both of us. Yes, the marriage is more important, but I want you to have your day. I know you think it's funny, and you're worried about how intense I am, but I need you to be able to get everything you want for at least one day of your life."

It was a sweet sentiment. "Have you considered that I already have everything I want? Between you ... and the newspaper ... and my family ... and my friends, what else could I want?"

"Wedding cake and scallops wrapped in bacon," he replied.

I laughed so hard I was surprised I didn't spit on his face. "Oh, I love you." I threw my arms around his neck and held tight. "I was always going to tell you about the shadow," I said. "I was just buying time."

"I know. Don't buy time again until we've put this behind us, okay? It feels too big."

"Deal."

THE DINING ROOM OVERFLOWED with people. Connie was on her feet and across the room in a shot to hug me.

"I hear you fought a monster today. Are you all right?" She petted me as if I was a small dog.

I glared at Landon, who suddenly found something interesting on the wall to stare at.

"Heard about that, did you?" I fought to remain calm. Landon's family knew about my witchy origins. They seemed fine with it ... at least so far. "May I ask how?"

"Oh, Landon told us." She waved off the response as if it was nothing. "He was upset when he heard — I'm sure you understand — and might've let his opinion on the incident be known."

I slid my eyes to Landon. "I can imagine exactly how he let his opinion be known."

"Don't give me grief," Landon warned, his expression practically daring me to pick a fight. "I got myself under control and we made nice in the parking lot. You can't pick a fight after the fact."

"I didn't realize that was one of the rules."

"Bay ... ." He pressed his lips together. "Talk to my mother," he instructed. "She's been gushing about how excited she is to have you for a daughter-in-law. She was just saying at lunch that Daryl and Denny will never marry partners she likes more than you."

"I did say that," Connie confirmed.

"She did," Daryl agreed, his eyes filled with mirth. "I can't wait to fall in love with a woman and tell her that she never has a chance against you. It should go over well."

They were a lovable lot, their jokes staider than the ones I had to put up with in my family. Even though I was annoyed with Landon for opening his big, fat mouth, I found myself smiling. "It's nice to be loved."

"We love you too," Mom said as she carried a huge platter of food into the room. "We just don't love you as much as they love you. There might be a lesson in there."

I grinned. "What sort of lesson?"

"Much like your Aunt Tillie, you're better in small doses." She pressed a kiss to my cheek and then beamed. "I hear you beat up a shadow monster today and then tried to hide it by filtering the information through Terry. Do you really think that's smart so close to your wedding?"

Annoyance bubbled up. "Speaking of Chief Terry, where is he?"

"Taking a nap," Mom replied. "I texted to wake him. He should be down in a second." Her attention landed on Scout and Gunner, who looked torn about joining us. "Why are you acting weird? Sit down."

Scout balked. "This seems like a family thing."

"What did I just say?" Mom's annoyance was obvious. "Sit down. It's Mexican night."

"I do love Mexican food," Gunner noted. "Is that homemade guacamole?" He looked like he might start dancing when he saw the platter Twila carried from the kitchen.

"And homemade salsa," Twila confirmed with a wide grin.

"We make our own tortillas, too," Marnie added as she exited the kitchen with three huge baskets of warm tortillas.

"We're staying," Gunner announced as he plopped down in a chair next to Denny, a minister. It was an interesting pairing.

Scout shot me a rueful smile. "I'm sorry he's such a glutton."

"Well, since mine is a glutton too, I'll forgive you." I slid into my normal chair and glanced to the right as Chief Terry settled next me. "Hello, tattletale."

"Be as angry as you want," he replied. "Landon needed to know."

"I was going to tell him," I insisted. "I was going to get him full of tacos and tequila first."

Landon made a face. "No tequila. I'm off drinking until the wedding."

"Will marrying me drive you to drink?"

I expected him to say no. Instead, he bobbed his head. "Most definitely." He grabbed some tortillas, taking the time to deposit extra on Aunt Tillie's empty plate. "Speaking of driving me to drink, where is Aunt Tillie?"

"Upstairs," Mom replied, her gaze momentarily going dark. "She's decided that Minerva shouldn't be trusted. She's taken to spying on her ... and by spying, I mean she's hiding in the closets and jumping out when Minerva passes to scare the demon out of her."

I could only feel it was better Aunt Tillie focus on Minerva than me. "That's ... terrible."

"Don't even." Mom looked as if she wanted to be cross but couldn't manage it. Instead, she smiled. "It is kind of funny."

"Poor Clove." Connie clucked her tongue. "I can't imagine how uncomfortable she is."

"You don't have to imagine," Landon replied. "You can go upstairs and she'll tell you exactly how unhappy with life she is right now. She's not shy about it."

"She's just ... having a rough time," I corrected. I might've been annoyed with Clove and her attitude — and it was fine for me to voice that annoyance — but it wasn't okay for other people to say anything. "I don't blame her. If I was as big as her and still had a drug-free birth to look forward to I'd be in a foul mood too."

"Drug-free?" Connie looked appalled. "Are you kidding me?"

"Nope."

"But ... why?" Connie looked to Mom. "That's torture ... especially for an overdue baby."

Mom's glare was pronounced when it landed on me. "Thanks for making me out to be the bad guy."

"I didn't say you were the bad guy," I protested. "I was standing up for Clove."

"Why is anybody standing up for Clove?" Aunt Tillie asked as she breezed into the room. She was still in her war uniform, but thankfully weaponless.

"What happened to your bayonet?" Landon asked.

If his family thought that was a weird question to ask, they didn't show it.

"I have no idea what you're talking about," Aunt Tillie sniffed, though I didn't miss the glare she shot Mom. "A bayonet would be a ridiculous weapon to carry around in this day and age."

"Yes," Mom agreed darkly. "It would."

"You have a bayonet?" It took a lot to rattle Chief Terry where this family was concerned, but he went pale. "You can't take that downtown. I'll have to arrest you."

"What did I just say?" Aunt Tillie barked. "It's not a practical weapon. I have a shotgun. I'm sticking with that."

"You'd better not." Mom's eyes flashed. "You'll be in big trouble if you have another shotgun."

"I didn't say I had *another* shotgun," Aunt Tillie clarified. "I said I had a shotgun."

"I took that shotgun and put it away. The same with that bayonet."

The only thing up for debate was where Mom was hiding the things she confiscated from Aunt Tillie. I knew my great-aunt was on the hunt for them, so wherever Mom had stashed it had to be good.

"Are bayonets even legal?" Daryl asked. He'd filled his plate with three huge tacos and seemed eager to dig into them.

"No," Landon, Chief Terry and Gunner replied in unison.

Daryl flicked his eyes to the tall shifter sitting at the other end of the table. "I'm sorry. I'm still unclear who you are."

"They're friends of mine," I replied hurriedly. "They're ... um ... helping me with something."

"Something witchy?" Connie asked, her eyes sparkling.

"Well ... ." This conversation was making me itchy.

"I thought you said that things were going relatively well."

Connie's tone was accusatory as she focused on her son. "Isn't that what he said, Earl?"

"Things *are* going well," Landon reassured her. He looked tired. "Bay and I are in love and we have everything under control."

Connie didn't look convinced. "We should talk over cocktails after dinner."

"Sounds like a great idea," Aunt Tillie agreed.

"Nobody asked you," Landon shot back.

"Landon," Connie scolded. "Be respectful of your elders."

Landon's eyes were accusatory when they locked with mine. "I can't help blaming you for this."

"What did I do?" I demanded, reaching for the pico de gallo. "I've been sitting here minding my own business."

"She's your great-aunt," Landon argued. "She just has to get everybody worked up."

"That's kind of true," Gunner agreed, "but that's what I like about her."

"Can't you be good for one meal?" I implored Aunt Tillie.

"Nope." She shook her head, as if it wasn't even a consideration. "By the way, while Landon is getting his butt chewed by his mother, I have a mission for you."

"No." I vehemently shook my head.

"What did I just say?" Aunt Tillie was in no mood for an argument. She expected to be kowtowed to and that's all there was to it. "I'm the matriarch of this family. What I say goes."

I had no idea what she was planning but I knew it wouldn't end well.

"I totally love this family," Gunner enthused, his mouth full of taco. "We definitely need to visit more often."

Scout looked torn on the issue. She wisely kept her mouth shut.

CHAPTER Twenty-One

"What are we doing?"

True to her word, Aunt Tillie insisted I stick close to her after dinner. Landon reluctantly retreated to the library with his family — something that looked like it caused him actual pain — and I was left to deal with Aunt Tillie.

"What did I say?" Aunt Tillie demanded as we approached the back stairs. There was no warmth in her eyes as she regarded me.

"You're being a real pain," I muttered.

"It's fun," Gunner countered from behind me. After loading up on tacos and cake he demanded to be included in the adventure. Scout opted to visit Evan — just to be on the safe side — leaving me to entertain her boyfriend.

"Is that why you stayed here instead of going with Scout?" I asked.

He shrugged, his smile faltering. "They need time alone."

I patted his arm. "You're worried."

"I'm ... concerned," he admitted. "She won't recover if she can't somehow pull Evan back into this world. She makes herself sick over him."

"And you make yourself sick over her," I mused. "Love is all kinds of wacky."

He laughed. "Evan won't hurt her. At least ... I don't think he will.

Whenever I see him, he's lost. I think he might hurt himself, but there are times I see him looking at her and know that he would cut off his own hand before purposely hurting her."

"How do you feel about that?"

Gunner snorted. "Are you my shrink now?"

"She's just a busybody," Aunt Tillie replied, glaring at each one of us in turn. "This is a stealth mission. As you might recall, that means no talking when we go upstairs."

I didn't bother to hide my eye roll. "What are we going to do upstairs?"

"Crawl into the belly of the beast."

"Is that a metaphor for something?" Gunner asked. "You guys don't really keep a beast upstairs, do you?"

"What do you think?" I asked.

He shrugged. "Nothing you guys do surprises me. You have a pig you dress in tutus. Your great-aunt has a bayonet. I totally want to play with that by the way."

Aunt Tillie bobbed her head to acknowledge the request.

"You don't do anything normal," he continued. "I like that about you. I always thought that it was abnormal to grow up in such a weird world, but you make me look like the poster child for sanity."

I was fairly certain there was an insult buried in there. It was also a compliment in a weird way. "You really do fit in with this family," I said. "You could be a male cousin."

Gunner beamed. "I'm guessing you don't have male cousins."

"Nope. All females. The genetics in this family are strong."

"It's still neat. I'm sure Landon won't mind having only girls to parent."

"Would you mind?" I was honestly curious.

"Not at all."

"Some men might."

"Only jerks." Gunner's grin was as charming as ever. "Here's the thing." He leaned close. "Weak men put value on the sex of a child. Strong men find value in loving whatever child they have. You have a strong man."

It was a profound statement for a guy with salsa on his cheek.

"That's a really nice way of putting it," I said when I'd run it through my head three times. "Scout is lucky to have you."

"That's what I tell her every morning."

"You're really lucky to have her."

"That's what I tell her every night when we go to sleep."

I wanted to hug him. Before I could, Aunt Tillie pushed between us.

"What did I say?" she demanded. "We have to be quiet to fool the beast."

"Oh, geez." I dragged my hand through my hair and glared at her. "This had better be good."

The trip up the stairs was done on light feet. Despite his size, Gunner was surprisingly graceful. Once we got to the second floor, Aunt Tillie dimmed the sconces on the wall with her magic and motioned for us to follow. I didn't have to ask where. The second she turned the corner that led to Clove's room the answer was clear.

"No." I snagged her by the back of her shirt and held steady as she struggled against my grasp.

"Let me go," she demanded, her eyes blazing. "It's time to slay the beast."

"Isn't that Clove's room?" Gunner asked. "Wait ... she's not the beast, is she?"

I shook my head. "No. It's Minerva."

Gunner shuddered. "She is one creepy lady. She has eyes like a bug, one of those killer bugs that take over the New York subway system in that movie twenty years ago."

Aunt Tillie wordlessly held out her fist to bump against his. Gunner obliged.

"She's not a bug," I argued. "She's not a beast either. She's just a woman who finds little joy in life." I rethought the statement almost immediately. "Or little joy in us, which I can see. We're an acquired taste."

"We're total jerks when we want to be," Aunt Tillie agreed. "I'm serious. That woman cannot be trusted with the next generation of Winchesters."

"Why?"

Aunt Tillie straightened. "What do you mean why? She's evil."

"She's the beast," Gunner clarified. "Just out of curiosity, is she an ancient beast or a new one? That will influence how we deal with her."

I smacked him lightly on the side of the head. "Don't encourage her."

"I can't help it. I love her." He was so earnest it took everything I had not to laugh.

"Minerva has a job to do," I reminded Aunt Tillie. "She's here to make sure Clove's baby is born safely into this world. She doesn't have to be a laugh a minute to do that."

"She's evil," Aunt Tillie insisted. "She's going to kill us all in our sleep."

"Like the bugs in that movie," Gunner agreed solemnly. "I wish I could remember the name of it."

"*Mimic*," I replied, my temper flashing. "It was called *Mimic* and it was not very good."

"It traumatized me when I was a kid." Gunner was solemn. "True horror doesn't haven't to be good."

"Oh, I can't even." I gave him a shove back toward the stairs. "Don't get Aunt Tillie wound up. She makes things up in her head. There's nothing wrong with Minerva that a good cocktail wouldn't solve. If you want to fix things with her, Aunt Tillie, then let her drink some of your wine."

"You don't get evil liquored up," Aunt Tillie argued. "You kill it with fire."

"That's true," Gunner agreed.

I put everything I had into the shoves I gave them. "Enough is enough. Leave Minerva alone. We have other things to worry about."

I was almost to the stairs when I heard a telltale click and jerked my eyes to the hallway. The only people staying in this part of the inn were Clove, Sam, and Minerva. Otherwise, it was emptied out because of the impending birth. The noise I heard was obviously from a door closing, but which one? Was it Clove's room? Did Sam hear us and retreat when he realized Aunt Tillie was on the prowl? Was Minerva sending a message that she knew we thought she was weird?

My heart gave a little twist at the thought she might've heard us.

She'd done nothing to earn our ire ... other than be a little bland. If we'd hurt her feelings, I would feel bad.

"Are you coming?" Gunner demanded from the stairwell when he realized I'd stopped. "There's cake on the main floor."

"You've already eaten cake," I reminded him, abandoning my worries about Minerva. She was a grown woman who assisted witches in labor. She'd obviously been insulted a time or two. "I don't think Scout would be happy with you having seconds."

"Then we won't tell her."

"Yeah, Bay," Aunt Tillie muttered. "Stop being a kvetch. It's embarrassing."

MY DREAMS WERE DARK. I FOUND myself in a hedge maze and no matter which direction I turned I couldn't find my way out. To make matters worse, a baby was crying in the distance. I could hear it ... and something inside of me was desperate to find it. No matter how hard I ran, I couldn't manage it. No matter how hard I looked, there was nothing to find.

Frustration finally grabbed me by the throat and when I woke in my own bed I was sweating and fighting tears.

"What is it?" For once, Landon didn't cling to sleep. Instead, his senses told him I needed him, and he was wide awake when I started rubbing my face. "A nightmare?"

I nodded, swiping the back of my hand over my forehead. "I'm sorry for waking you."

"Yes, it's quite the hardship," he drawled. "There's nothing worse than waking up with the woman I love." He rubbed my back. "I'll have to divorce you over this."

His words made me feel like a bit of an idiot. "We're not even married," I reminded him. "You can't divorce someone if you're not married."

"Yes, well, I'll have to marry you and then divorce you." He leaned close, his grin devastating. "Because there's nothing in this world that will ever stop me from marrying you."

"But divorce is allowed?" I teased. "These are some interesting rules we live by."

"Oh, divorce isn't allowed either. I was just making an empty threat." His fingers were gentle when they brushed my face. "Tell me what's torturing you." He was far too observant sometimes. Was it the FBI agent who could so easily see beneath my bravado or was it the man who loved with his whole heart?

"It was a dream." I leaned into him so he could have easier access to rub my back. I wasn't above milking my nightmare for a massage. "I ... was in a maze — a hedge maze."

"Like in *The Shining*?"

"How did you know?"

"Aunt Tillie had it on the other day. You mentioned you always thought the maze was cool and thought your mom and aunts should plant one for the guests on the grounds."

"Was I drunk when I suggested that?"

"Yes."

"Well, that explains that." I offered a rueful smile. It didn't last. "A baby was crying. I couldn't get to it. I could hear it calling to me, but I couldn't find it."

"Clove's baby?"

"I ... don't have any proof of that."

"But you feel it." He stopped rubbing and slipped his arm around my waist. "Have you considered this wasn't one of your witchy dreams and was instead an anxiety dream?"

"Go back to massaging me," I ordered.

He chuckled but did as I instructed. "The wedding is almost here. My family is in town and they're sticking their nose into the magic stuff. Clove might explode soon if that baby doesn't willingly make an appearance. Mrs. Little is purposely positioning a store to interfere with Hypnotic's business. There's a weird vampire hybrid living here now. You're tearing yourself up over Chief Terry not being able to walk you down the aisle."

I jerked up my head. "Why do you keep coming back to that?"

"Because it's what you want."

"It's something I can't have." I was firm. "If I ask Chief Terry, I will break my father's heart."

"That's his fault. He shouldn't have left you as a kid."

"Well, I can't change that, but I can't hurt him. I won't be able to take it."

Landon studied me for a long moment. "I don't want to force you to do something you don't want to do."

"Good."

"I want this day to be everything you've ever dreamed of, Bay. There are no do-overs when you marry me. This is it. We're doing it once. Period."

"I only want to do it once," I promised. "As for the other thing ... I can't." It made me sick when I thought about it. "Please don't push me."

He growled and then nodded. "This is your decision. I won't get in the way."

"Thank you."

"Just one more thing." He held up a finger as he regarded me. "What if they both walk you down the aisle?"

"And then punch each other out at the end of the walk? Yeah, I don't want to deal with that either."

"Fine." He kissed me. "I want what you want. If you want Terry to walk you down the aisle, tell me now and I'll make it happen."

"I don't want to hurt anybody."

"Except yourself," he muttered. "Do what you want. I won't push you."

I forced myself to be bright and cheery. "That will be a nice change of pace."

"Yeah, yeah, yeah."

I HEADED STRAIGHT UPSTAIRS TO CHECK on Clove when we got to the inn the next morning. Landon explained he didn't want to be near Clove in case she really did explode and shower him with goo, which meant he would have to be trained when it was my turn to go through the baby rigamarole. I let him off the hook. He was dealing with his own stress.

Clove was alone in the bedroom when I let myself in after a soft knock.

"Hey." I smiled, but she looked miserable, so I stowed it quickly. "I'm so sorry this is happening. How can you not be in labor yet?"

"I think the baby hates me," Clove replied. "I think she ... just really, really hates me."

"Don't be ridiculous." I shook my head. "That baby loves you. I'm positive of that. Why else would she want to stick so close to you?"

"Because she wants to punish me, Bay. There's no other explanation." Tears flooded Clove's eyes and she grabbed one of the extra pillows to hide her face. "This is supposed to be a beautiful thing. That's what everybody keeps telling me. Do I look beautiful?"

"I can't see you through the pillow."

She didn't remove it from her face.

"Clove, you're always beautiful," I reassured her, resting my hands on her stomach. I wanted to comfort her. The baby shifted, something igniting inside her, and magic flowed through her into me.

I jerked back my hands as a series of images flooded my mind.

"What was that?" Clove demanded, whipping the pillow from her face. "What did you do?"

I hesitated and then shook my head. "I didn't do anything."

"I saw ... something," Clove insisted, all trace of tears gone from her face. "You showed the baby something."

"No, I didn't." My heart refused to return to its normal rhythm, and I tentatively reached out to touch her stomach a second time.

"Don't," Clove demanded. "It's freaking me out."

"It's not me," I insisted. As frightened as I was by what I'd seen, I couldn't stop myself from looking again. "It's the baby, Clove. She's trying to show me something."

"What is she trying to show you?" Clove's lower lip trembled.

"Do not do that," I snapped. "I can't take you crying on top of everything else."

"Oh, well, as long as you're happy, that's all that matters. That's what everybody keeps saying. They say I have to have the baby now so I don't steal your day. Do you know how hard I'm trying not to steal your day?"

"Maybe that's why the baby hasn't come yet." Carefully, I rested my hands on her stomach and concentrated. "You're too worried about me to focus on anything else. Forget me. If you have the baby in the middle of the ceremony, we'll be fine. We'll still get our happily ever after."

"But I'll have been the horrible person who turned your wedding into my memory."

"I'll survive." I muttered to entice the baby to show me the images again. "Just try, little one."

And she did.

I saw Sam and Clove laughing on the couch at the Dandridge. They looked happy, carefree, and even though it was clear Clove was pregnant she hadn't yet fallen into despair.

I saw Aunt Tillie and Landon arguing as Clove watched them at breakfast.

I saw Thistle and I needling one another over Clove's choice of baby names.

And then I saw what I was searching for. I looked long and hard, devouring what the baby had to show me. When I pulled back my hands, I was flummoxed ... and yet I knew what I had to do.

"I know I said I was on your side about having the baby in a hospital, but that's one powerful little girl," I said as Clove watched my face for signs I was going to melt down. "She knows that Hollow Creek is a problem. She somehow knows that it's more of a problem than we've realized until now."

"I saw that too," Clove supplied. "What are you going to do?"

"We have to end the threat at Hollow Creek. We can't do anything else until we do that."

"Do you think that's why I'm not in labor yet? Is the baby afraid something is going happen to her because of what's going on at Hollow Creek?"

"I don't know, but I'm going to find out." I hugged Clove. Hard. "Just hold on. If we can solve the Hollow Creek problem, you're going to get your baby."

She nodded, blinking back tears. "Then what are you waiting for?"

"Landon needs his bacon before we can go out there."

"You tell Landon to suck it up. I want my baby ... and you need your day."

I grinned. "We can share the day, Clove. Don't worry about that, not even a little."

CHAPTER
Twenty-Two

"They're on their way," Scout announced when she popped into the dining room for breakfast. I'd stopped by her room to talk to her after Clove's baby showed me what needed to be done at Hollow Creek.

"How long?" I asked, checking the clock on the wall.

"Within the hour," Scout replied. She'd called her entire Spells Angels group to join with us because we needed firepower. They had a lot at their disposal. "What about your friend?"

"Stormy?" I smiled. "I texted her. She's on the way."

"What's the plan?" Mom asked as she sat in her chair. I didn't miss the fact that she had her phone next to her ... and it was open to the app Clove made us download.

"What's that?" I pointed, annoyance bubbling up.

"That would be your cousin Clove." Mom's tone told me that arguing about including her in the conversation wouldn't go well. "She wants to hear what we're doing, and because her baby provided this epiphany that we're operating under, it's only fair to make sure she knows what's about to happen."

It was a practical response and yet it irked me. "She doesn't need to get worked up."

"I'm not worked up," Clove barked through the app. "I'm eating my breakfast like a good girl. Then I will go to the bathroom like a good girl. And then I will crawl back into bed even though I hate this room with a fiery passion ... like a good girl."

"Just let her do it," Thistle muttered, shaking her head. "If you're right and the reason Clove hasn't gone into labor yet is the threat at Hollow Creek, then she needs to be involved."

I leveled a steely-eyed glare on her. "I can't believe you just turned on me. I thought for sure you'd take my side."

She shrugged. "I get why you would think that, but we're on the clock. It's easier not to argue."

"Fine. We need to cast a net. If the circus folks were here, they'd know how to do it. The baby ... *showed me* ... what to do, if that makes sense."

"It doesn't make sense," Minerva sniffed. I hadn't realized she was sitting at the table. "That baby doesn't even know she has a nose yet. How can she show you how to take down this magical threat you keep yammering about?"

I really disliked her, so it was hard to keep my temper in check. "Clove's baby has demonstrated multiple abilities the last few months. I have no reason to believe she doesn't know what she's talking about — er, showing me — in this instance."

"And what does it matter?" Thistle challenged. Her hatred for Minerva was off the charts. She would argue with the woman just to argue at this point. "There's no harm in trying, is there?"

"Of course not," Mom replied. "We have to try. If we ever want the Clove we all love and adore back, we need to end the threat at Hollow Creek. Like Bay, I have to think the baby needs us to do something for her if we ever want to meet her ... and this is what she needs."

"Clove really is intolerable," Marnie said. "We need to do this."

"I heard that!" Clove's voice was shrill when it filtered into the room. "I'll have you know that I'm creating human life out of nothing at all, and I'm doing it completely on my own."

Sam cleared his throat from somewhere next to Clove, causing me to smile.

"Oh, you barely contributed," Clove hissed. "We all know I'm doing the heavy lifting."

"I have a plan," I insisted loudly, hoping to drown out a potential fight. "We have an army coming to help. It's going to work."

"What do you need from us?" Mom asked.

She wasn't going to like my answer. "I need you guys to stay here," I replied, cringing when her eyes narrowed. "I'll be taking Thistle and Aunt Tillie, but we need protection here for Clove ... just in case."

"Okay, but ... I'm not comfortable with that. If something happens to you down at Hollow Creek, we won't be there to help."

"It will be fine," I reassured her. "I'll have an army with me. You don't have to worry."

"Oh, right." Mom's eye roll was pronounced. "You do realize I've been in this family longer than you. I know darned well that this is going to be more difficult than you're letting on."

She wasn't wrong, but we had no choice. "We can't leave Clove unprotected."

"You'd better take me along," Clove barked. "I mean it. I want to know exactly what's happening, and in real time."

I looked to Thistle, hoping she would argue against it. Instead, she sighed and nodded. "I'll have my phone. This will work out."

"Great." Clove sounded happy. "If you guys hold up your end of the bargain, I might have a baby by the end of the day."

"And then Bay might be able to be the star at her own wedding," Landon muttered.

"It's all going to happen just as we want," I insisted. "Trust me."

SCOUT'S CONTINGENT OF MAGIC-WIELDERS were already parked at Hollow Creek when we arrived. One look at Rooster Tremaine's face — he was the leader of her group — told me things were bad.

"What's wrong?" I strode directly to him and planted my hands on my hips.

"When was the last time you were here?" he asked, not bothering with niceties.

"Yesterday. Why?"

"This place is unbelievable."

I moved past him, getting my first clear view of the creek, and my mouth dropped open. "Holy ...!"

He nodded. "That is a big ball of magic."

It did indeed look like a big ball of magic. The shards were no longer separate and floating. They'd coalesced to create ... well, it was difficult to fathom what they'd created. The ball of magic had to be twenty feet across and the way it shimmered under the sunlight told me that the magic was building into something ultra-powerful.

"This is off the charts." Craig "Doc" Davidson, the Spells Angels recruit Scout referred to as the computer geek, flushed with excitement. "It's pulsating beneath the surface."

"We have to take it down today," I announced.

"Definitely," Rooster agreed. "If this thing blows ... who knows what could happen."

"Who is talking, please?" Clove's prim voice came out of Thistle's phone.

"What is that?" Rooster made a face when Thistle held up her phone.

"That would be my very pregnant cousin," I replied. I was beyond frustrated. "She's on bed rest and her baby is the one who showed me what to do."

"Wait, we're following the plan of a baby?" Marissa Martin, my least favorite member of Scout's team, straightened. "Who else thinks this is a bad idea?" She raised her hand.

"Who said that?" Clove demanded, fury dripping from Thistle's phone.

"Why is your cousin listening in on the phone?" Rooster asked.

"I can't keep up with who is talking," Clove snapped. "I need everyone to introduce themselves before they speak and then indicate that they're done speaking when they're finished so I don't accidentally interrupt someone. I don't want to be rude."

"Yes, that would be the true tragedy of the day," Thistle drawled.

I glared at her and then sent a pleading look to Rooster.

"Oh, well, this is the stupidest thing ever," Rooster muttered. "Um ... this is Rooster. I would like to know why we're following the orders of an infant who hasn't been born yet."

Clove waited a beat to respond. "I need you to sign out so I know not to talk over you."

"Right." Rooster shook his head. "This is Rooster, I'm done speaking."

I pressed my lips together to keep from laughing.

"Bay says the baby showed her things," Landon interjected. "I have to think the baby knows what she's talking about. Why else would she get involved?"

"This is Marissa, and I think this is stupid." The witch in question had a pinched face that made me think of eating lemons. She was following the rules, though, so I refrained from shoving her face into the dirt until she stopped talking. She was related to Mrs. Little, which only made me hate her more. "Also, I'm done talking."

"Well, we think you're stupid, so that works out great," Scout drawled. "This is Scout, by the way, and I think this entire setup is delightful."

I glanced over my shoulder at the sound of a vehicle, smiling when I saw Stormy Morgan and her boyfriend Hunter Ryan exiting his truck. They looked excited ... and maybe a little worried. "Here's the rest of our team."

"Bay, you need to introduce yourself," Clove scolded.

"Don't you recognize my voice?"

"That doesn't matter. Rules are rules."

"Oh, whatever." I turned to greet the newcomers. Stormy was a new witch, but her fire magic was strong and we would need it for what I had planned. "Thanks for coming guys."

"No problem." Stormy gave me a friendly hug. "Lots of people I don't recognize." She seemed nervous, and I couldn't blame her.

"I'll handle introductions," Rooster offered. He ran through his people quickly and then waited for Stormy to introduce herself. Then he turned back to me. "What do you want us to do?"

"I need a magical net," I explained, narrowing my eyes when I realized Mama Moon, the former leader of Spells Angels, was at the water's edge with Aunt Tillie. They knew one another from a long time ago but their interactions weren't always friendly. "What are they doing?"

"Bay!" Clove's voice was so shrill I had no doubt she would crawl through the phone and strangle me if she could.

"Fine." My annoyance couldn't be contained. "This is Bay. I want to know what Aunt Tillie and Mama Moon are doing at the water's edge. I'm out."

"Nothing good," Thistle mused.

"If Bay has to follow the rules, so do you, Thistle," Clove called out.

"The second that kid is out of you I'm dragging you outside by your hair and making you eat a dirt sandwich," Thistle threatened.

"That's the meanest thing you've ever said to me," Clove sniffed. "The baby doesn't like when you're mean to me."

Thistle threw her hands in the air. "Here we go."

In an attempt to take control of the situation, Landon cleared his throat, attracting multiple sets of eyes. "This is Landon. We need the plan explained so we can stop doing ... *this*." He gestured to the phone. "I've seen some wacky things since I fell in love with you, Bay, but this takes the cake. I mean ... there's a big ball of magic in the creek. Oh, and I'm out."

My eyes went wide as I focused on him. "You can see it?"

"It's hard to miss."

"But ... if you can see it, that means anybody can see it."

Realization dawned on his face. "You're right. We're in big trouble here." He pulled his phone from his pocket. "I'll call Terry and have him shut down the road."

"If someone really wants to get out here, I don't think anything will stop them. Oh, this is Rooster, and ... I'm done speaking."

Clove's insistence on people introducing themselves was ridiculous.

"We need to do this now," I insisted.

"Bay!"

"Clove, I will kill you," I snapped back. "Just ... stop. We need to get this done. I don't think you understand what we're dealing with." *And hopefully you will never have to see it, because it would give you nightmares*, I silently added.

"I'm Doc and I'm taking photos," the enthusiastic assistant offered. "This is a magical marvel that should be studied."

"It can't be studied." I was firm on that. "We need it down ... now."

"This is Rooster, and Bay is right." The Spells Angels leader was grave. "What do you want us to do?"

"We need to build a net." Describing what was needed wouldn't be easy. "Scout, Mama Moon, Aunt Tillie, Thistle and I will create the net. We need to completely cover that ... thing. Once we have, Stormy will add her magic to the mix and burn it."

Stormy whipped up her head. "Um ... you want me to burn that thing?" She looked terrified at the prospect.

"Yes. Can you do it?"

She swallowed hard, risked a glance at Hunter, and then nodded. "I guess I can."

"That's Stormy?" Clove asked. "Nobody is following the rules."

"That's Stormy," I gritted out, my glare for Thistle. "This is really your fault."

"She just wants to be included," Thistle whined.

"Since when do you care about that?"

"Since ... I don't know. She's sad and I don't like when she's sad."

"I think Thistle just admitted she's a big old softie," Gunner interjected. "I didn't see that coming. Oh, this is Gunner, and ten-four."

He was having way too much fun with this. "We need to feel it out as we go. It's going to be trial and error. The rest of you need to serve as backup in case the magic shatters again and tries to escape."

"And then what?" Rooster asked. "What happens if the magic does escape?"

I didn't want to think about that. "Let's just make sure that doesn't happen."

Everyone got into position. Thistle handed her phone off to Landon because she was going to need both hands and then positioned herself between Aunt Tillie and me. Mama Moon moved to Aunt Tillie's other side and Stormy stood between Scout and me.

"Here we go." I nodded to Aunt Tillie.

Her response was to wrinkle her nose. "Why are you looking at me?"

"She wants you to start," Thistle snapped. "You're always claiming you're the most powerful witch in the Midwest, so prove it. Throw out your net."

"Oh, I'll make you pay later, Mouth," Aunt Tillie grumbled as she focused on the sphere. "Scout and I have been talking. She has a karma spell she's willing to show me. You're going to be crying when I'm done with you."

I slid my eyes to Scout. "You're teaching her spells?"

Scout shrugged. "She asked."

"From now on, when she asks for spell help, the answer is always 'no,'" Thistle barked. "Giving her access to new ideas is terrifying. You have no idea what she could do with that little tidbit."

"Oh, I have ideas." Aunt Tillie grinned as she held up her hands. "*Expando.*"

The first wave of magic bounced off the sphere, causing Aunt Tillie to frown. "We can't penetrate that ball," she muttered.

"Then build the net just outside of it," I ordered. "Stormy's magic will do the rest."

Aunt Tillie planted her feet again. This time when she unleashed her magic it took up position just outside the sphere. Mama Moon joined her, and then Thistle threw her contribution into the mix.

"Look." Scout pointed to the east side of the sphere. "The magic is fraying. I'm next. I need to stabilize it."

I watched with wide-eyed wonder as Scout let loose a wave of pink magic. It was like radioactive goo that slowly inched over the glittering net that had already been set. I held my breath as the magic solidified into a hard wall. There was no glow to it. In fact, it looked like the world's biggest wad of chewing gum.

"Well, that's Hubba Bubba fantastic," Landon muttered from behind me.

"I'm next," I said. The magic I threw into the mix involved a protection spell. I wasn't trying to protect the sphere, I was making sure it couldn't escape. I cocked my head as I tested various sections of the net. It was working, but the sphere hadn't yet reacted to what we were doing.

"It's up to you." I turned my eyes to Stormy and found fear there. Determination was obvious, too. "Just ... get inside the shell. When you can get between the net we've built and the sphere, set everything in there on fire."

Stormy nodded, clutching her hands at her sides. Behind her, Hunter watched. He was obviously keen to stand as her protector. He also knew he had nothing to offer but love for Stormy.

"Here we go." Stormy let loose a breath and unfurled her magic. It was slow going at first — she was still a novice, after all — but once she figured out how to get between the net and sphere, she was ready. "How much magic should I use?"

"As much as it takes."

"Go in hot," Aunt Tillie ordered. "You're a hellcat, for crying out loud, do what you were born to do."

Stormy drew her eyebrows together in a show of concentration. She hadn't yet learned about control. Instead of testing the sphere, she unleashed a torrent of magic so hot the air felt as if it was catching fire as it began to blow our hair.

"Holy ...!" Landon was breathless behind me. "The mercury just shot up twenty degrees."

"What do you feel, Stormy?" I asked. "Are you winning?"

She didn't respond, instead narrowing her eyes and feeding more fire into the trap. The bubblegum outside began to sweat ... and melt in some places. The net held, and when the hard coating we'd built began to fall away, I could see inside.

The sphere was retracting, shrinking into itself. The smaller it became, the more it started to pulse.

"It's going to make one attempt to escape," Rooster called from somewhere on my left. If I had to guess, he was flanking Mama Moon. "Lock that net down," he roared.

Everyone doubled their magical output at the same time the sphere exploded outward. This time the fragments that tried to escape had nowhere to go. Stormy increased her magic, to the point I felt I might faint from the heat, but the fire burned so quick and bright that the fragments had nowhere to go. It was like a nuclear wall of energy consuming everything in its path.

Screams erupted as the fragments were eaten by the fire ... and they had our voices.

"What is that?" Clove screamed from the phone. "Was that Bay?"

I'd forgotten Landon still had the app open.

"They're gone," Rooster announced when the screaming stopped. "She burned them all."

"That's great," Aunt Tillie said dryly. "Now what? Stormy is still funneling magic into the sphere."

Stormy was indeed funneling magic into the sphere. Now that she'd started, apparently she couldn't stop. We couldn't drop the net for fear Stormy would set the world on fire.

"Hunter," I kept my voice even, "you need to get her to stop. We're good now."

Hunter's face went ashen. "How am I supposed to do that?"

"Just ... talk her down. You're the only one who can."

He took a timid step toward his girlfriend, as if fearing what was to come, and then caught himself. The next step he took was more forceful. "Stormy, you're done. You can stop now." He wrapped his arm around her waist and pressed himself to her back. "Come back to me please."

It was as if a switch had been flipped. Stormy stopped funneling magic into the net and sagged back into Hunter. She was exhausted but her eyes were full of exhilaration.

"Point it up," Aunt Tillie ordered. "Let the fire burn out in the sky without touching anything."

I nodded in agreement, my stomach clenching as we angled high. We all dropped our magic at the same time, watching as the huge ball of fire hurtled into the sky. It looked like a second small sun.

Then it was gone, the only sound left was that of our ragged breathing.

"What happened?" Clove demanded.

I glared at the phone. "This is Bay. I declare this creek magic free. Oh, and over and out."

CHAPTER
Twenty-Three

"Come here." Landon slipped his arms around my waist and tugged me to the ground, pulling me on his lap to bury his face in my hair. "That was ... intense."

I smiled and shut my eyes, sucking in a cleansing breath. The air still reeked of smoke. "We did it."

"*You* did it."

"Oh, no." I shook my head, forcing my eyes open to check on Stormy. She was unbelievably pale as Hunter sat with her on the ground, his hands roaming her back as she rested her cheek on his shoulder. "I didn't do anything."

"Don't." Landon's tone was firm as he stroked my hair. "It was your idea. You might've needed help, but that's what makes you you. Ego isn't a thing with you. Results are."

"Yeah, well ... I'm just glad it's done." I closed my eyes again and snuggled close. "Is it wrong that I kind of want to thump my chest and do a little dance?"

"King Kong style?"

I shrugged. "Maybe."

"You can be the king of the bedroom jungle tonight." His lips brushed my cheek, and then he frowned when a muffled sound came from under his knee. "Oh, crap." He rummaged until he came up with

Thistle's phone. The app was still active, and Clove was apoplectic on the other end of the call.

"What is happening?" she shrieked.

I took the phone and glared at the little icon she'd put up as her avatar. It looked like stick figures. I tapped it. The image enlarged and showed me three little girls — witches — standing in front of a storage shed. I recognized the shed and the witches. It was us, when we were younger, in front of the shed we'd appropriated as our fort.

I thought I might cry.

As if reading my mind, Landon took the phone from me and tapped the microphone. "Everybody is okay, Clove," he reassured her. "The magical fragments are gone. Nobody was hurt."

"This is Rooster," the Spells Angels chief said, inching closer to us. "Did you go into labor?"

"No," Clove sniffed. "I'm still big as a house. I was kind of hoping that the baby would just magically appear when you guys won."

That was so Clove, a dreamer of the highest order. "I think you're still going to have to do the whole sweating-and-pushing thing," I said.

"And pooping," Thistle added as she came over to retrieve her phone. "Don't forget the pooping."

Landon's expression reflected horror. "Stop saying that. I'll never want a baby if you guys don't stop freaking me out."

"Why?" Thistle's expression was blank. "You're not the one who's going to poop in front of people. That will be Bay."

A shudder ran through me. "Can we not talk about this?"

"Definitely," Rooster agreed. He pointed to the creek. "We're done here? We finally solved your problem?"

I hesitated, unsure. "Well ... the magical fragments are gone," I hedged. "We don't know if that thing I saw in the dream is still out there. We don't know if more shadow assailants will show up. We also don't know who was controlling the 'she' that caused Granger Montgomery to lose his mind."

"So ... how do we figure out the rest of it?"

That was a good question. I didn't have an answer.

. . .

"HOW ABOUT A NAP?" Landon asked after getting me settled in my office an hour later. The Spells Angels team remained at the creek to run some tests. Scout and Gunner were in charge, ordering Doc around as he collected samples and tested the atmosphere. They hadn't suggested that they were leaving town yet, and I was thankful for that ... at least for now.

Thistle left to open Hypnotic, all the while arguing with Clove regarding the day-to-day operations of the store once the baby decided to make an appearance. Hunter took Stormy home, saying something about a day in bed being warranted for both of them. As for Aunt Tillie and Mama Moon, they were hardly sly when they announced they were going for a nature walk. It was obvious they had other plans, but nobody questioned them. If they wanted to wreak havoc on the world, they'd earned it.

That left me and my future husband, a man who seemingly couldn't stop hovering now that we were away from the others

"I don't need a nap," I reassured him, patting his arm. "I'm fine."

"What if I need a nap?" His eyes danced with mirth. "I love a good nap. What's more, I love a good nap with my favorite girl."

"Don't you have things to do?" I didn't want to send him away, but I didn't need a babysitter. "I mean, you're still investigating a suicide at the high school. I think that takes precedence over a nap with me."

"Just for the record, nothing takes precedence over a nap with you," he argued, brushing my hair from my face with soft hands. "That's going to be my favorite thing to do for the rest of my life."

"And here I thought yelling at the Lions on Sundays was your favorite thing to do," I teased.

"That's just habit. I only like doing that because you curl up with a book on the couch next to me and it allows us to spend time together while doing different things."

That's why I liked fall Sundays as well. His interest in sticking close to me now was a problem, however. "I'm okay." I wrapped my hands around his wrists and stared directly into his eyes. "Don't worry about me. The big problem is handled."

He shook his head. "You said it yourself. Somebody harnessed the magic out there."

"But the magic is gone."

"Does that mean the person who stole that magic is no longer magical?"

I hesitated, unsure. "Probably not," I conceded, "but that magic can no longer be used against us. Whoever is out there could take off now that he or she knows there's no more magic at the creek to tap into."

"Or maybe he or she doesn't care and will push harder to finish whatever agenda is fueling this assault on our family."

Since I largely agreed with him, I couldn't continue to argue. "What about your parents? They haven't even been in town a day. You should spend time with them."

"I plan to. I want to spend time with you first."

I cocked an eyebrow. "We're talking a real nap? You're not going to turn this into one of your handsy naps?"

He shook his head. "No. I just want to hold you ... and rest my eyes for an hour. You're tired. I can see it. So am I. We'll regroup in an hour. We'll figure out the best way to find whoever stole the magic from the creek."

He made it sound so easy. "How are we going to figure it out when we have nothing to go on?"

"You have me believing you can do anything. It'll work out. You've already done the hard part."

He believed it, which had him relaxing, so I wanted to believe it too. I just couldn't be certain. What if the person who had tapped into the magic at Hollow Creek was more powerful than we imagined?

"Fine." I gave in. He knew I would. "We'll take a nap. But no funny business."

"I'll save my stand-up routine for after dinner," he promised, setting the security alarm and pulling me toward my office. "You need to close your eyes and let what happened at the creek go."

I balked. "I'm fine. We fixed the problem at the creek. That's something to celebrate."

"We're not done yet. We don't have a clear path to the wedding. It's going to happen, though. I have faith."

"You're full of faith," I said, cupping his cheek as he pulled me onto the couch, situating us so my head was on his shoulder, his arms were around me. "You have more faith that anybody I've ever known," I said as my eyes drifted shut. Now that I was horizontal, the sleep I didn't think I needed stalked me.

His voice was soft. "Before you, I had faith in the system. I believed in law and order and that's about it. Now that I have you, I believe in so much more."

"Like what?" I murmured.

"I believe in you. Nobody, ever, has shown me the things you've shown me. You make me want to be a better man."

He'd said it before, but it never failed to make me go warm all over. "You're already the best man."

"Of course, I am. How else would I deserve you? And make no mistake, Bay, I deserve you. It's you and me forever."

"Shh." I pressed my finger to his lips. "You can deserve me again in an hour."

I SLEPT HARD, and when I woke, Landon was snoring lightly in my ear. He had one arm thrown over the top of his head and the other wrapped lightly around my waist.

I carefully extricated myself from his embrace and padded into the lobby. The lights were turned low to dissuade visitors, and the doors were locked. The building was quiet, just as I liked it.

Then I heard the low murmur that signified the television in the lunchroom was on. I headed in that direction, grinning when I realized Viola was watching her afternoon soaps.

"Isn't it early for *General Hospital*?" I asked, glancing at the clock on the wall, confused.

"There is no set time for television shows any longer," Viola replied. She appeared to be kicked back in a chair but because she was ethereal, she floated above the chair. "The episodes are available by streaming. That's how I watch it now."

"Good to know." I moved to the Keurig on the counter and hit the button so it could warm up. I needed caffeine. "I didn't realize you were here."

"I haven't been here that long." Her gaze was speculative as she looked me up and down. "I saw you and Landon in your office. It's kind of cute how you guys snore in tandem."

I was appalled. "I don't snore."

"Keep telling yourself that."

"I don't." I was almost positive that was true. "I'm ... just a heavy breather."

"Uh-huh."

"Landon snores."

"I really don't care which one of you snores." Viola glanced at me again. "Something has changed out there."

The way she said it caught me off guard. She'd been goofy in life and her ghost often went off on tangents. She was rarely serious.

"What do you mean?"

"It's as if someone turned off the power," Viola explained. "Before — a year ago or so — there were pockets of power. You could follow them. The biggest was The Overlook."

I lowered myself into the chair across from her. "You can register the power in this town?" It was a new development, something she'd never mentioned.

"I don't know if I would use the word register," she said. "It's more like ... I can feel things. I can't always explain what I feel but feeling the things humming around me is easy."

"What do you feel today?"

"As if the power has been shut off."

"Okay, well ... ." I thought about the scene at Hollow Creek. "Maybe we did shut off the power," I mused after a beat. "We let what was happening at the creek grow out of control so long that it was starting to feed other individuals."

"I don't know what you did. I just know that things are back to the way they were. I can still feel your power, but I can't benefit from it."

"Were you benefitting from what was happening at Hollow Creek?"

"I don't know if I would say I was benefitting," she said. "Sometimes I could feel a pulsing, like a lightbulb flashing thanks to a poor electrical connection." She waved her finger around the side of her head. "I could feel it here." She moved her finger down to her heart. "And here. It's gone now."

"Is that good or bad?" I was honestly curious.

She shrugged. "I ... don't know how to make you understand. Things have been powered down a bit, but there's still something out there. I can feel it, like a magical shadow crawling inside my brain looking for answers."

I narrowed my eyes. "A shadow?" I thought back to the previous day, to what had happened outside the hospital. "Can you tell me where the shadow originated?"

"No." She shook her head. "There's no pinpointing it. Sometimes it's nowhere. Sometimes it's everywhere. It's very weird."

"It sounds weird." I got up again to make a cup of tea. "What about everybody else in town? Do you know who is magical and who isn't? Can you tell when you're around them?"

"Sometimes." She bobbed her head. "It's easy with your family ... and some of those people you've brought in. There's a new man in town who feels like he should be magical, but he's shadowed too. When I get too close to him, all I see is blood."

Evan. She had to be talking about Evan. "You don't have to worry about him." Even as I said it, I wondered if it was true. I didn't know the day-walking vampire who had been partially healed. I only knew that Scout wouldn't have left him here if she believed he was a danger. I believed in Scout, so I had to believe in Evan. "He might've been dangerous at one time, but not any longer."

"What about the other shadows?"

"I don't know, but we'll figure it out."

I took my tea when I left. I intended to wake Landon — he would be angry at himself if he slept the whole day away — but my attention was drawn to the red flashing light on the security panel when I entered the lobby. No alarm was sounding, yet something had tripped the alarm. When I looked at the panel display, I realized that it was alerting me somebody had tried to get in through the front door.

"Probably a client," I murmured to myself as I switched off the security system and unlocked the door. Most of my regulars dropped their ad changes off in envelopes and left them in a bin outside. I planned to grab what had been dropped off and then retrieve Landon. When I pulled on the door handle, however, it wouldn't budge.

"Weird." I fiddled with the lock and tried again. This time I felt a small surge of magic transfer from the door to me, forcing me to jerk back my hand. I waved it around, frowning at the numbness, and then tried again.

This time the response was almost instantaneous. I was thrown back with enough force that I hit the desk with a resounding thud, my tea mug shattering on the floor.

"What was that?" Viola asked, popping into existence at my right.

"I ... don't ... know. Can you leave?"

"Leave the building?" Viola looked as if she was having trouble understanding the concept. "I'm in the middle of my show."

"Just see if you can get in and out," I instructed.

"Fine." She let loose a sigh. "But you owe me."

I watched as she tried to disappear. She faded to almost nothing and then her image solidified. Alarm raced over her features. "I can't leave."

I nodded, grim. "I figured that was the case. I can't leave either."

"What does it mean?"

"We're trapped."

"But ... ."

"I don't know what it means other than that," I said, rolling my neck. "I just know that we're trapped."

CHAPTER
Twenty-Four

"Landon!"

I didn't think he could help but I didn't want him separated from me if we were under some sort of magical attack. I yelled his name three more times as I studied the door. Finally, he wandered out in bare feet, a surly expression on his face.

"Yes, my love," he drawled. His hair was messy from his nap, but he managed a smile. "Do you want to get romantic with me now? For the record, you don't have to yell. Next time just wake me with kisses."

I glared at him. "We're trapped."

His smile slipped a little. "Is this some sort of new game we're playing? If so, I need to know the rules."

"Is he slow?" Viola asked.

"He's not slow," I snapped.

Landon's eyes narrowed. "Are you talking to a ghost?"

"Viola," I replied. I had to catch him up ... and fast. "She can't get out. I can't get out. The door won't open. It's magically sealed."

He walked forward and grabbed the handle, grimacing when he couldn't get it to turn. "We are trapped."

I wanted to shake him. "Did you think I was making it up?"

"No, I just ... ." He took a breath and held up his hands. "Let's not freak out."

"I'm not freaking out." I wasn't. Mostly. "I want you with me in case ... ." I didn't finish the statement. There was no reason to. He knew why I wanted him with me.

His FBI face snapped into place. "Tell me what we're dealing with." He moved to the front window and peered out. "I don't see anybody."

"That doesn't change the fact that we're trapped." Something occurred to me, and I felt in my pocket for my phone. It wasn't there.

"On the floor by the couch," Landon said, reading my mind. "I put them on silent so we could sleep."

I hurried to my office, grabbing my phone and checking for bars. There were none. Landon trailed into the room after me. He was grim when he checked. "No service."

He pressed his lips together and then looked at my desk. "What about your computer?"

I sat in my desk chair and booted it, letting loose a relieved sigh when I realized it was getting internet service. "So ... why are our phones not getting service but the computer is?"

"Maybe someone cast a spell and didn't think about it." He moved behind me. "Send a mass email."

I clicked several of my contacts and started typing.

"Tell them to be careful if they approach because they could be attacked," he instructed. "Tell them to get Scout. She's strong enough to fight off whatever this is."

"We hope," I muttered.

"Add Clove," he ordered.

I shook my head. "She can't do anything to help us."

"No, but how many members of your family check their email regularly? Clove is bored and constantly on her phone."

That was a good point. "Anybody else?"

"Terry."

I balked. "He doesn't have magic. He could be ambushed if he comes here and has no way to protect himself."

"Bay, he's a professional." Landon's tone was soft but no-nonsense. "He won't come without backup. If you feel you need to include that, do it. We need someone to recognize we're in trouble."

My heart gave a little heave. "Okay. Anybody else?"

"Contact your father — they're on the computer for reservations quite often — but then my parents would get involved and that's an added level of nonsense we don't need." He moved his hands to my neck and started massaging. "Sent?"

I nodded and leaned back. "Are we just supposed to wait?"

"I don't know. What does Viola say?"

I glanced around, frowning. We'd lost the ghost in the mad dash to my office. "She's not here." I got to my feet and slid my phone in my pocket. Until whatever spell we were dealing with had been knocked out, it was useless. I still felt better having it with me. "Let's check the other doors."

"Now we're thinking." He linked his fingers with mine as we moved to the east-side door. The magic sizzled when I tried the handle and I yelped as I pulled back my hand.

"What's wrong?" He looked at my fingers, frowning at the red patches popping up. "What is that?"

"Magic. I felt a tingle when I first tried, a little jolt. This is worse." I licked my fingers to ease the pain. "Whatever spell we're up against is getting stronger."

"Well, you're a superhero. I have no doubt we'll figure it out."

He had more faith in my abilities than I did right now, but I nodded all the same. "Okay. Let's do this."

"Next door. I'll touch it."

When we reached the west side of the building Landon slid in front of me to make sure I didn't injure myself again. He frowned when the knob refused to budge. "Do you think we can break through the door?"

"Are you going to do one of those macho things and kick it?"

"It's worth a shot." He braced his hands on either side of the door frame and lifted his leg. He delivered a blow next to the handle, but nothing happened. He tried again, exhaling heavily as he lowered his leg. "I don't think that's going to work."

"We could start a fire," I suggested. "I mean ... it's wood. It has to burn."

"It's fiberglass," he corrected. "Do you really want to risk a fire when we're trapped inside? That seems a bit reckless, especially since we've emailed for help. Even if it takes an hour or two for somebody to read our messages, we'll be okay."

He was missing the obvious point. "Do you really think somebody cast a spell on the building to simply lock us inside?"

"I ... don't know." He straightened and glanced over his shoulder. "Is somebody in here with us?"

I pictured the shadow from the hospital. "It's likely not a person."

His jaw shifted back and forth as he regarded me and then nodded in understanding. "Okay, ... you said that the shadow thing attached itself to Scout's shadow. We need to find a place in the building where there are no shadows."

I doubted that would work but doing something was preferable to doing nothing. "The lunchroom."

He put his hand on the small of my back and trailed me, making sure not to leave too much room between us in case we were attacked. When we got to the lunchroom, we found Viola sitting in her chair watching *General Hospital*.

"Are you kidding?" I snapped, dumbfounded. "I thought you were trying to find a way out of the building."

Viola shrugged. "There is no way out. I checked all the doors. I figured if we weren't doing anything else I might as well see what Anna and Robert are up to. This show is so much better now that they've incorporated some of the oldies. But the mob is still disgusting. Have I mentioned I hate the mob?"

"The mob is stupid," I agreed as I turned off the television. "We can't focus on that right now. We need to focus on our problem.

"Aw." Viola let loose her patented hangdog expression. "It was just getting good."

"Yes, well, we have other things to deal with. I need you to search the building. If you see a shadow that doesn't belong, come back and tell me."

"I don't want to search the building."

"Go!"

Viola regarded me with unreadable eyes. "Is that an order?" she asked.

I hated being backed into a corner. Using my magic to strip free will from the ghosts I could command wasn't my favorite activity. I only did it as a measure of last resort now.

"It's a favor," I said. I would force her if I had to, but I wasn't keen on the prospect. "There's something in this building, Viola. It will kill us if it can. If it does, the only person in town you'll have to talk to will be Aunt Tillie. Is that what you want?"

Viola made a face. "Definitely not." It was with a great deal of resignation that she finally got up. "Why can't you guys ever have a normal day? Has it occurred to you that danger follows you everywhere?"

"It has occurred to me. It's part of being a witch. Just ... please find it."

"And it will look like a shadow?"

"Probably. It's a shadow that can move independently of a host to catch the light."

"Got it." She was gone in an instant.

Landon was quiet, but I could feel his heavy gaze on me. "You know you could force her to do what you want without begging."

"I don't feel right about it. I already forced her to protect me once this week when I went into the school."

"Your heart is way too soft." He kissed my temple. "I guess that's why I love you more than anything."

"I also have a mother who cooks like an angel and fills you full of pot roast."

"Ah, pot roast. Do you think we can talk her into cooking it for the wedding?" He looked hopeful.

"Believe it or not, she's figured out a way to make pot roast bites. She's putting a bit of breading around them and baking the pot roast inside."

"I think I just orgasmed."

That earned a grin. "You're so easy to please."

"Honestly, I'm not. I just needed a moment of levity. Why do you think I talk about bacon so often?"

"You love it."

"I do but there are times when I feel overwhelmed regarding the things you face on a daily basis. I can't let the fear rule me. I need to talk about something mundane instead of freaking out. The bacon is an ongoing joke."

"I get it." I patted his arm and then looked up when Viola reappeared. "Anything?"

"I can't see a shadow," she replied, "but there are people outside."

My heart skipped. "Do you recognize them?"

"I recognize Tillie and Thistle. They have a blond woman and a tall man with long hair with them. They seem to be arguing."

"Oh, good." I hurried to the front door, peering through the side window. Sure enough, I heard voices in front of the door ... and they didn't sound happy.

"I'm telling you the best way to handle this is to blow the door off the hinges," Aunt Tillie said. "I've got this."

"Hold on." I could just make out Scout's voice. She sounded agitated. "Let's not go the nuclear route unless we absolutely have to, okay?"

"Let's definitely not do that," Landon yelled through the door, flashing me a quick smile. It was obvious he was relieved. I was still unsure. The cavalry had arrived, but things still felt off.

"Are you guys okay?" Thistle scrambled closer to the window and pressed the side of her head to the glass. "You're lucky I was responding to some online orders when your email came through. Otherwise, I might not have checked for hours."

"Email is a stupid way to tell us you're about to die," Aunt Tillie chastised.

"We're not about to die," Landon argued. "In fact, we were taking a nap when it happened. It feels like a fluke that we even know we're in trouble."

Even as he said it, the hair on the back of my neck stood on end. I felt another presence, and it was close.

I took one step back and scanned the lobby. The lights were low because that's how I kept them most days. I didn't encourage walk-ins.

The lobby seemed normal. I looked it over again and again. Nothing was out of place ... and yet I couldn't shake the feeling that we were being watched. "Viola," I called out, doing my best to keep my voice even. "Can you come up here please?"

Landon remained focused on the activity outside, barking orders at Aunt Tillie. It was better he focus on that than what I feared was about to happen.

Viola floated into the lobby. "What? I just want to watch my show. I ... ." She trailed off and cocked her head, her eyes focusing on the potted plant in the corner. "Where is the light for that shadow coming from?"

I moved to my left, angling my head to study the shadow. She was right.

"Son of a hex," I muttered, my breath clogging in my throat as the shadow detached and pulled up to its full height.

"We'll figure it out, Bay," Landon said absently, turning. His eyes went wide when he realized what I was looking at, his hand automatically going to the spot on his waist where he kept his service weapon. He'd removed it when we settled down for our nap. It was still on the floor of the office, but it wouldn't help anyway. "Bay ... ." He sounded as if he was at a loss.

I couldn't focus on him or his fear. I had to deal with this. "*Congelo.*" The curse came out as a hiss as I raised my hands.

The shadow, which had started advancing, froze in place. The eyes, red orbs of hate, fired hotter.

"We're not alone in here," Landon snapped to our rescue team. "Get this door open right now."

Ever calm in the face of a fight, Scout refused to panic. "Is it another shadow?"

"Yes."

"Tell Bay to rip it apart from the inside."

"Like I just know how to do that," I grumbled. I took another step toward the shadow, carefully watching the creature's arms for signs of movement.

"Bay, don't get too close," Landon ordered. "We don't know what that thing is capable of."

We didn't, but I knew what I was capable of. "*Gutta,*" I whispered, watching as the creature's eyes went wider. There was only one thing I knew to do. I strode up to it, waited to see if it would attack, and then placed my hands on either side of the shadow's head. "*Gutta.*"

The shadow rippled, almost as if phasing in and out of existence.

"Bay." Landon sounded desperate. "Be careful." He didn't order — or beg — me not to continue. He stood at my back, ready to fight an enemy he couldn't beat. He would die for me. I would for him.

"*Gutta.*" I unleashed more magic into the shadow, as it flickered again. Then I tried something new. "*Incaendo.*"

The shadow threw back its head, a thin wail escaping, and then burst into flames. I instinctively covered my face as the flames flashed hot for a brief moment and then were gone.

There was one breathless moment of silence to follow ... and then the front door flew open thanks to Gunner throwing his huge body at it. He looked momentarily triumphant and then frowned when he lifted his nose. "What's that smell? Are you guys barbecuing in here?"

My shoulders sagged as I slid my gaze to Landon. He was unbelievably pale but managed a smile as he pulled me in for a hug.

"You are absolutely terrifying," he muttered into my ear as he rocked back and forth. "You're a total badass and I love you."

"I love you too." I closed my eyes and then flashed a smile in his direction. "That was fun, huh?"

"That is not the word I would use."

"Yeah, me neither." I turned my attention to Aunt Tillie and Thistle as they piled through the door. "Hey, guys, glad you could make it."

Thistle scowled. "I take it the spell at Hollow Creek didn't fix our problem."

"I think we fixed one problem," I replied. "I want to check the creek to be sure. We still have another problem, though. Somebody is conjuring shadow assassins."

"Ooh." Aunt Tillie sagely bobbed her head. "I've always thought I would make an amazing assassin."

"You could do it professionally," Landon added as he dragged a hand through his hair. "We need to figure this out. We're not in the clear yet."

"Definitely not," I agreed, snagging gazes with Scout. She seemed more intrigued than frightened. "Any ideas?"

She shook her head. "No, but there has to be a way to figure out what we're up against. Maybe we need someone who thought like a diabolical killer for a time."

I knew who she meant. "Evan?"

She nodded. "I'll see if I can get him to come to town."

I balked. "We can go to him."

"He needs to rejoin the human race. Hiding does him no good. He can come to us."

CHAPTER
Twenty-Five

Landon and Gunner remained behind to fix the front door of the newspaper office. Even though Gunner was puffed up about opening the door, Landon had the unenviable task of explaining his success was due to my destroying the shadow the same moment he threw himself against the door. From what I could tell, it had turned to a testosterone conversation by the time we left, making them promise to text every twenty minutes or we would come looking for them.

"We don't need no stinking females to save us," Gunner called out as Scout and I headed toward Hypnotic, adopting an annoying braggadocios voice. "We're manly men. We've got it covered. You females should go do some shopping ... or talk about periods."

I cast him a dubious look over my shoulder, but Scout was laughing so hard I knew he was joking.

"He likes to defuse the tension with inappropriate jokes," she explained as we walked. "He learned it from his father."

"Does he like his father?" From the things Gunner had said, I had to believe there was some tension.

"Graham raised him alone for a long time, and I think that they were kind of ... I don't know ... angry at one another." Scout turned serious. "When you break it down, they weren't really angry with each other, if you know what I mean."

"I'm not sure I do."

"They were angry at the situation. Gunner's mother tried to hurt him when he was a child — she was mentally ill. After she was locked away, they were grieving. Their way of dealing with the grief was to take it out on one another."

Sadly, I understood. "How is that working out for them now?"

"They love each other but snipe a lot. Graham and I get along for the most part, and he always swoops in to help whenever there's trouble. There are a lot of different types of love."

I flicked my eyes to the opposite side of the road, where Aunt Tillie was watching Mrs. Little's store. She was alone now, no sign of Mama Moon, but I sensed trouble. "Kind of like how we feel about Aunt Tillie."

She laughed. "You guys are well aware that you love her. Your way of communicating is through snark. It's harder for Gunner and Graham, but they seem to be making inroads."

"Do you think your relationship with Gunner has helped?"

"Love is hard to pin down." She shot me a rueful smile. "I mean ... there are a lot of different ways to love someone. I love Gunner more than I ever thought possible. I love Evan, too, just in a different way. That doesn't mean the love I feel for Evan is any less significant. It's just ... different."

She was struggling. She didn't talk about it much, but I could see it. "You don't have to push things with Evan," I said. "Maybe the smart thing to do is take a step back and let him come to you."

"I'm afraid if I do that, he'll fall off the map."

"Well, then keep doing what you're doing. You might get lucky and have some sort of breakthrough with him."

"That's what I keep hoping for."

THISTLE WAS BUSY BEHIND THE COUNTER. She'd left it unwatched when racing to help us.

Scout had called Evan before we left The Whistler, and although he'd initially put up token resistance about coming to town, he eventually relented. We'd barely had a chance to get comfortable on the couch before he entered, his hair disheveled and his eyes wild.

"Do you know that old witch you hang out with has cast a spell on the unicorn store and is making the door open every sixty seconds?"

As far as greetings went, it was a winner. "Please refer to Aunt Tillie as 'that old witch we hang out with' to her face before leaving," I pleaded. "She'll love it."

He didn't look bothered by the suggestion. "That unicorn lady keeps running to the door to close it and screaming that she knows Tillie is doing it. She sounds like she's losing her mind."

I couldn't get worked up over that. As far as spells went, this was a mild effort on Aunt Tillie's part. Perhaps she was slipping ... or just bored. "Aunt Tillie will lose interest after a few minutes," I said, waving my hand. "She likes messing with Mrs. Little at least once a week. If she doesn't, she gets grumpy. It's like a mood booster or something."

"Sounds weird."

"It's definitely weird," I agreed, inclining my head toward one of the empty chairs in the center of the store. "Why don't you sit down?"

Evan scanned the store. He seemed interested in some of the items on the shelves but remained where he was. He picked the chair closest to Scout — he would never admit it, but she was a security blanket of sorts — and then gripped the arm rests as he regarded me.

"I don't socialize much," he said.

Was that an apology or a caveat? It seemed unnecessary however you looked at it. "That's okay." I flashed a grin in his direction. "I'm related to people who socialize every day of their lives and they're still bad at it."

"That would be the old witch you were referring to earlier," Thistle offered helpfully.

"And you," I added, snickering when Thistle threw a stuffed bat at me. I caught it in mid-air and studied it. "Since when do you guys carry toys like this?"

Thistle shrugged, noncommittal. "I got it for Clove's baby. I haven't wrapped it yet."

"You got her a stuffed bat?"

"Well, our mothers told us when we were little that bats delivered babies." A small smile played at the corners of her mouth. "I thought it would be a fun joke ... but only after she's sweated and screamed for eighteen hours to push out that kid."

"I don't think it will take that long," I argued. "I mean ... that kid is so big at this point that she might be able to crawl out."

"That's what I said." Thistle laughed to herself. "Don't mention that in front of Clove. She has zero sense of humor."

Evan shifted on his chair, uncomfortable with the small talk. "I don't want to be rude, but I didn't come here to listen to you go on about some witch baby. Scout said you needed something."

"But he doesn't want to be rude," Scout said dryly, sending her former partner a scathing look. "I know socializing is difficult for you, but it's normal to enjoy some niceties before getting to the nitty-gritty."

"Thanks so much for the explanation," Evan drawled. "Tell me what you want. I'm uncomfortable down here."

I studied him and then looked to Scout. I figured she should be the one to lead the conversation. She knew him best, after all.

"We have some issues," Scout began. She proceeded to lay everything out for him. When she finished, she kept her eyes on his face to gauge his reaction.

"That's a lot to take in," he said, shaking his head. "Are you certain you took down the magical fragments at Hollow Creek?"

"As certain as we can be," I replied. "There was nothing there when we left, not even a whiff of magic. We'll check on our way home, but I'm fairly confident that problem is handled."

"That's good. It sounds like that was the big problem."

My eyebrows drew together. "Did you miss the part where I was locked in my newspaper building and a shadow attacked?"

"Yes, but you handled that without breaking a sweat." Evan didn't sound bothered by the talk of shadows. "You don't look battered and bruised, which means it was just a normal day for you."

"Not exactly," I muttered.

"It wasn't all that difficult," he insisted. "I'm guessing you've faced worse."

"She's getting married in a few days," Scout argued. "She wants this done."

"So ask yourself the obvious question." Evan sounded like a pragmatic therapist as he leaned back in the chair and steepled his fingers on his stomach. "Who would want to hurt you the most in the run-up to your wedding?"

"We don't really have any outstanding enemies right now," I hedged.

"Obviously you do. Someone has either pegged you as a threat or someone needs to be taken down a notch. These shadows — and I'm willing to bet they're different entities rather than the same resurrected one — have gone after you twice now. Yes, Scout was involved in the first attack, but the shadow was going for you."

I opened my mouth to respond and then snapped it shut. He was right.

"You're a necromancer," he continued, not taking a breath. "You can control the dead. Is it possible you tapped the wrong ghost and upset a family member?"

"I guess anything is possible," I replied. "I think I would know if that were the case, though. Nobody in this town can keep a secret."

"Then what else could it be?" Evan crossed his legs, offering a smile that looked more like a grimace when Thistle delivered him a cup of tea. "Thank you."

"Can you drink that?" Thistle looked nervous as she hovered at his elbow. "I mean ... you don't need me to track down a chicken and drain it to feed you, do you? I want to be a good hostess and all — my mother would melt down if she thought I didn't offer you anything — but I draw the line at killing a chicken."

Evan was silent several seconds and then he did the one thing I didn't expect. He burst out laughing. The sound was so raucous it echoed, and when I darted a look to Scout, I found her beaming. She covered it quickly, but her delight was obvious.

"I can drink the tea," Evan said. "I wasn't sure, but ... I can. I've been testing things."

Scout perked up. "You have?"

"Yes. I can eat, but I don't know if it helps or hurts. It doesn't really taste like anything so there doesn't seem to be a point, but I can eat."

"Maybe the point is to ease you back into human life," Scout suggested.

"I'm not human."

Her smile slipped. "Well, it's good to know you're testing things." She tapped the arm of the couch. "Let's get back to this. Do you think a normal human could tap into the magic at Hollow Creek to create shadow assassins?"

"Shadow assassins?" Evan shook his head. "Only you would think that's a real thing."

"Not only me," she countered. "Tillie thinks it's a thing too."

"Oh, well, Aunt Tillie," I muttered, my eyes moving to door of the shop when the wind chimes sounded. I sucked in a breath and steeled myself for mayhem when Mrs. Little stormed through the door. "Here comes trouble," I groused.

"Definitely," Thistle agreed, glaring at the older woman as she stomped directly in front of me and planted her hands on her hips. "Nobody is in the mood for whatever you're selling right now, Mrs. Little," she warned. "If you're here to be an asshat, just turn yourself around and ... go elsewhere."

Mrs. Little didn't bother acknowledging Thistle. She'd made it clear — on more than one occasion — that she believed Thistle was a mini Aunt Tillie. "Tillie is on a rampage," she announced.

I purposely kept my face neutral. "I'm going to need more information than that."

"She's haunting my store."

My lips quirked but I held it together. Evan had already explained what Aunt Tillie was doing. Of course, Mrs. Little would take it to another level. "She's haunting your store? How is she managing that when she's not a ghost?"

"You'll have to ask her."

"How is she haunting your store?" Thistle demanded. "What sort of proof do you have?"

"Well, *Thistle*, I should think the fact that she's standing on the sidewalk across the road and laughing like a maniac is proof enough," Mrs. Little hissed. "She's not even sly about it."

Aunt Tillie was never sly about anything, especially torturing Mrs. Little. She wanted full credit for her shenanigans. "We still don't know what's happening." We knew, but she hadn't told us. We had to play this smart. "How is Aunt Tillie haunting your store?"

"She makes the door open and close even though there's nobody there."

"Maybe it's the wind," I suggested.

"Oh, right." Mrs. Little was thirty seconds away from going nuclear. "That's why Tillie is standing on the sidewalk doing that dance she does. You know I hate that dance."

I did indeed. That's what made it so enjoyable. "I don't know what to tell you. If you're suggesting that Aunt Tillie is somehow making your door open and close when she's standing across the road, I suggest that you perhaps file a report with Chief Terry."

"Because he'll do what?" Mrs. Little was beside herself. "You guys are here. She's your responsibility. You need to deal with her or ... ." She didn't finish.

"Or what?" Thistle prodded.

"You know."

"We don't."

"You know," Mrs. Little insisted. "You know darned well what she's capable of and I'm sick of you guys doing nothing. You let her run roughshod over anyone who disagrees with her, and I've had it. That's why I brought in a real witch. I'm going to end this."

Thistle's face was blank. "You brought in a real witch?"

"Kristen Donaldson," I volunteered. "I interviewed her the day of the shooting at the high school. She owns the new store."

"She's from Salem," Mrs. Little added.

Thistle's expression remained blasé. "So?" she asked.

"So, real witches live in Salem."

"Yes, I believe I saw that on a shirt somewhere," Thistle said. "I'm not sure what you're implying. Are you threatening to unleash this real witch on us to do ... something magical?" Thistle was clearly having fun at Mrs. Little's expense. It was hardly the first time. Aunt Tillie had taught us well on that front. Mrs. Little was having none of it, however.

"I'm done putting up with your crap," she growled. "I've been the butt of your family's jokes for decades. Well, no more." She pulled herself up to her full height, which wasn't saying much. "I'm done. I will not be the butt of your jokes ... or your punching bag ... or whatever else your family thinks is funny on any given day. No sirree. It's done."

"Got it," Thistle said on a head bob. "No more Mrs. Little butt jokes. That's going to severely limit our dinner conversation, but we live to serve."

I bit the inside of my cheek to keep from laughing. Scout didn't bother hiding her smile. Evan, however, was too invested in the conversation to remain quiet.

"Do you actually make a living selling those ugly unicorns?" he asked.

"Does she?" Scout asked. "Those things are works of art. I bought one for twenty-five percent off the other day and I'm going to mount it on the front of my motorcycle and use it as a weapon. It's pink and sparkly and glorious."

Evan's grin widened. For the first time since I'd met him there seemed to be legitimate joy in his eyes. "I can't wait to see that."

"Who are you again?" Mrs. Little demanded. "I know you don't belong here. I would know if you lived in this town."

"I work with your niece Marissa," Scout reminded her. "We've met several times."

"Oh, right." Mrs. Little's expression was so dark I had to wonder if even the sun could burn through the hate she radiated. "Marissa doesn't like you."

"I'm fine with that." Scout was breezy. "As for Tillie haunting your store, good luck proving that. I can't wait to see you swear out a complaint to the police chief stating than an older woman is haunting your store and your proof is that she stood on the other side of the road laughing. That should go over well."

"It's the truth," Mrs. Little snapped. "I know it and so do you." Her eyes were back on me. "Don't make me tap my secret weapon."

Even I was grinning now. "You mean Kristen? I hope you realize that just because she grew up in Salem doesn't mean she's a real witch. Her mother owns a store there. She's not Sabrina ... or Samantha ... or those witches from *Charmed*. She's just a woman."

"Oh, that shows what you know." Mrs. Little was back to being haughty. "Kristen knows exactly what she's doing. She told me so. On top of that, she's in a foul mood today, says that you guys have been up to no good. She's poised and ready to take you on ... and she's going to mop the floor with you."

The vehemence behind her statement caught me off guard. "She told you she's going to mop the floor with us?"

It was only then that Mrs. Little recognized her mistake. "I won't put up with any more nonsense." She extended a finger, momentary worry clouding her eyes. "I've reached my limit. You've been warned."

I remained in my seat as I watched her go.

"She's delightful," Evan noted. "Back when I was a full-fledged vampire, I would've enjoyed torturing her for sport."

Thistle snickered. "Awesome. Is that still a possibility?"

He shrugged. "Never say never."

Scout cleared her throat, but it was to get my attention, not admonish Evan. "What is it? You know something."

"Not *know*," I corrected on a headshake. "I'm ... intrigued."

"About the Salem witch?" Evan let loose a snort. "Very few real witches live in Salem. They think it's gauche to be part of that scene."

"It's not the Salem part. It's her insinuation that Kristen knew she was here to fight us ... and that she'd been in a bad mood all day. What would put her in a bad mood?"

"Maybe losing her power source," Scout mused, catching on. "Do you think she's our culprit?"

"She's new to town. I've only met her once. It's possible. Maybe Mrs. Little lured her here with a promise of more than cheap rent."

"If so, she must realize she doesn't have enough power to stop us now," Scout said. "Is there any way we can verify this?"

There was only one way I could think of.

"Oh, you're going to break into her store," Thistle whined. "That never goes well. We always get caught."

"I was actually thinking of breaking into her house, not her store," I admitted. "She wouldn't keep anything incriminating in the open."

"She's living above the store," Thistle replied. "We've seen her out and about once the store closes. She always goes back when she's done walking around, and the lights on the second floor are on until we go to bed."

Well, that was interesting. "I guess we are breaking into the store." I smiled. "We just need to find a way to distract her."

Scout pointed at Evan. "We have a vampire who has access to superpowers. He can do it."

"What if I don't want to?" Evan complained.

"Then you need to suck it up. This is important." Scout beamed at me. "We might actually be getting somewhere."

CHAPTER
Twenty-Six

We hashed out a plan — one that couldn't be tackled until after dark for myriad reasons — and then headed back to the inn. Gunner and Landon were already there when we arrived, beers cracked as they loafed around the library with Landon's family. I would have to sell him on breaking the law if this was going to work.

"There's my future wife." He beamed at me as I hovered in the doorway. "Do you realize we're going to be married forty-eight hours from now?"

I hadn't done the math, but the wedding clock had been steadily ticking away in the back of my over-taxed brain. "I know." I greeted his family with the best smile in my arsenal and lowered myself next to him on the couch. "It's exciting."

"It's so exciting," Connie agreed. She had a cocktail, and her cheeks were flushed with color. "Landon hasn't said much about your honeymoon, only that you're going to an island. Did you pick the location?"

"I think I mentioned it," I acknowledged. "It's called Moonstone Bay, off the coast of Florida." It was a paranormal stronghold I'd always wanted to visit. "We're looking forward to it."

"Yes, nothing but sun, sand and relaxing with my wife," Landon said. "Sounds like heaven."

"It's going to be fun," I agreed as I watched Landon link his fingers with mine. He was relaxed enough that I had to wonder how many beers he'd had. I needed to cut him off so he could sober up before dark.

"Where's Scout?" Gunner asked. He looked as relaxed as Landon.

"She's in the greenhouse with Evan," I replied, speaking before thinking.

"Evan?" Gunner sat straighter. "He's here ... with her?"

Crap. I didn't want to get into a conversation about Evan in front of Landon's family. "He's feeling social," I explained. "He seems all right."

"Who is Evan?" Connie asked.

"He's ... a friend." I flashed a smile and did my best to act as if I wasn't plotting something that could get me in a load of trouble. "He's been going through a hard time, but he's coming back to his old self."

"Drugs?"

I could see why she would jump to that conclusion. It somehow seemed unfair, though. "Not drugs. Well, not like you're thinking." I searched for the best way to explain but came up empty.

"It's a witch thing," Landon volunteered. "You're better off not knowing."

"Oh, but I love the witch stuff," Connie complained. "In fact, I love it so much we're thinking about making regular visits to Hemlock Cove. Your father isn't retired yet, but he gets six weeks off a year."

Horror washed across Landon's features before he could blank them. "You're coming here six weeks a year?"

Connie drew back her head. "I guess I don't have to ask your opinion on that."

"It's not that I don't want to see you," Landon said hurriedly. "It's just ... the guesthouse is small."

"Who says we want to stay with you?" Earl countered, gripping his own beer bottle tightly. "We can rent a room. Here, or at another inn."

"It's not just you two we want to see," Connie assured us. "We want to hike and antique. This area has a lot to offer. Plus, well, when you have children, we'll want to spend time with them. As much as I love Winnie, I don't want to cede the spot as favorite grandmother without a fight."

"Oh, don't worry about that," I said. "My mom is too strict to be the favorite grandmother. You've got this in the bag." I gave her an enthusiastic thumbs-up.

Landon nodded. "You're definitely going to be the favorite grandmother." He shot a guilty look toward the library door to see if anybody was eavesdropping. "Don't ever tell your mother I said that," he whispered.

"Your secret is safe with me," I promised. "You're welcome to visit here anytime," I continued, focusing on Landon's mother. "We don't see nearly enough of you. It's just ... we always have something going on."

"Yes, and from what Landon's been telling us, it's usually something magical," Connie said. "We had fun last time when we got to see you in action. A few more adventures like that would be fun."

"Then we're telling the stories wrong," I grumbled.

Landon shot me a quelling look. He didn't want his parents to feel unwelcome, but we couldn't explain everything. "Things have changed a bit since last time you were here," he hedged. "Bay has changed."

"Meaning what?" Connie's eyes were piercing when they landed on me. "What aren't you telling us?"

Oh, so very much. Thankfully, I didn't have to respond because footsteps on the hardwood floors drew my attention to the hallway. There I found Thistle, dressed in head-to-toe black, taking in the scene. "I need a drink," she announced. "I was going to be polite and not intrude, but I want whiskey more."

"Have at it." I gestured to the drink cart. "Don't get too drunk," I warned. "You need your faculties tonight."

"What's tonight?" Landon asked.

"We'll talk about it later."

Rather than let it go as I hoped, he straightened. His gaze was suspicious as he studied my face before he moved on to Thistle. "You guys are planning something," he whined, shaking his head. "I should've known we wouldn't have a quiet night after what happened earlier."

"You definitely should've known," Thistle agreed. She carried her drink to the couch and wedged herself between the arm and me. "Scoot down, Landon."

Landon did as she instructed. "What do you have planned?"

I forced myself to remain calm. "We can talk about it after we have drinks with your parents."

"You don't have a drink," he pointed out. "I should've known you were up to something when you didn't immediately pour yourself one after what went down this afternoon."

That FBI thing he had going, the one in which he was the most observant person in the world, was annoying sometimes. "Landon, it's fine," I reassured him. "We can talk about it later."

"I want to talk about it now." He was adamant. "My parents are well aware of what you are. They might not understand everything you can do — even I don't understand that — but they can hear."

"You might feel differently when she tells you the plan," Thistle offered. "By the way, have you filled in Aunt Tillie on what we're doing tonight, Bay? She's going to need a different outfit. She can't wear those red leggings I saw her in earlier."

"Why don't you go and fill her in now?" I suggested pointedly. "That would be best for everybody."

"Yes, and while you're doing that, Bay can fill me in," Landon insisted.

I didn't see that I had a choice. "Landon ... ."

"Tell me," he insisted.

I slid my eyes to Thistle. "I'm going to make you eat so much dirt that you're going to mistake yourself for an earthworm."

"I don't think earthworms eat dirt," she replied. "They simply live in it."

"Is that the hill you want to die on?"

She shrugged. "Maybe."

"Tell me," Landon growled. "The longer you drag it out, the worse I'm going to think the idea is."

"Fine." I exhaled heavily, channeling my teenage self for a moment so I could remember my 'You're going to like what I have to say no matter what' approach. "Mrs. Little stopped in Hypnotic this afternoon."

"What else is new?" Landon muttered. "She's a horrible woman. Why does that require a change of clothes for Aunt Tillie? Wait, you're not going to sneak around and torture her tonight. That can wait until after the honeymoon."

"Believe it or not, torturing her is low on my to-do list," I replied. "We're not going torture her. We are, however, going to break into Kristen Donaldson's store because we think she might be the evil witch we're looking for."

Landon blinked several times and then slowly moved his beer bottle to the end table. "I think I'm going to need more than that."

"Sure." I filled him in. When I finished, he shook his head but didn't immediately speak. I was nervous enough that I had to fill the silence or scream. "It could be a long shot."

"It could be something," he surmised.

"It could."

To buy himself time, he focused on the window, tapping his bottom lip with his index finger. The entire room was silent, other than the sound of Thistle messing with her ice cubes.

"I know you don't like when I break the law," I said when I could no longer take the silence. "But it feels as if it needs to be done. I mean ... she could be a legitimate enemy."

"And, if she is an enemy, we'll be able to take her out tonight," Thistle added. "That will leave all day tomorrow — and all night — for you and Bay to hide away in the guesthouse and prepare for the wedding."

"I thought you guys were taking over the guesthouse for a night of woman stuff," Landon replied.

"Woman stuff?" Earl asked, confused.

"Facial masks and cocktails," Thistle volunteered. "That was the plan ... until Clove refused to give birth. She can't really participate."

"No, but Scout could," Landon said. "Stormy could. I know you wanted it to be the three of you, but there's no reason Bay can't still have the night she's always wanted."

He was so hung up on that it was starting to grate. "Landon, you need to let that go." I was deadly serious. "I'm getting the husband I always wanted. Everything else, the details, are just that. We can't always control what's happening."

"I know that. I can't help that I want everything to be perfect for you."

"I already got the perfect husband." I squeezed his knee, forcing him to look at me. "Everything else pales in comparison."

He smiled, which had some of the worry constricting my heart lessening. "That was very smooth. I appreciate it. As for the other thing ... do we really think she's a potential suspect?"

"She's new to town," I replied. "She seemed ... odd ... the day I talked to her."

"Odd how?"

"She seemed to know who I was before I introduced myself. I thought it was strange but didn't have time to focus on it because the thing at the high school happened directly on the heels of that interview."

"Do you think she's the *she* Granger Montgomery wanted?"

"I don't know." I opted for honesty. "In a weird way, it makes sense. Mrs. Little brought her in to mess with us. It turns out she might've meant for Kristen to mess with us in more ways than one."

"Yeah, it's not just retail warfare now," Thistle agreed. "Mrs. Little seemed off her rocker this afternoon. I'm starting to think we might've been better served by stopping Aunt Tillie from torturing her a few times the past year. Monitoring Aunt Tillie has turned it into a full-time job and Mrs. Little is clearly cracking under our lackadaisical work ethic."

"Do you think Mrs. Little knows what she's doing?" Landon's forehead was creased in concentration. "She's a terrible woman. I've known that since the first time I met her, but she's afraid of magic. She can't really think what this woman is doing is right."

"We don't know that it's Kristen," I warned. "She makes an enticing investigation target, but we can't jump to conclusions. Mrs. Little has no concept of magic. She doesn't understand the truth of it, the scope. All she knows is that Aunt Tillie makes her life miserable."

"That's not all she knows," Thistle countered. "She's been around when other things have happened. She kind of knew what was going down with the Floyd situation. Then there was that whole thing with her ghosts of the past coming back to haunt us ... with a gun. Let's not forget what happened out at the lake house. She's well aware that we're the real deal."

"Which should make her fear you," Landon said. "But she's not smart enough to fear you. In fact, as far as I can tell, she's a freaking idiot. She gets tunnel vision and can't see beyond herself."

"Which means she could've brought a real witch in to go after us," I said. "I didn't sense any real magic when I was in Kristen's store, but I remember thinking that she had a lot of authentic items for sale — antique books — and I'm convinced the scrying set I saw on the table was the real deal."

"So ... she could have knowledge," Landon mused.

"When I interviewed her, she said she'd been in town a month. She was waiting for the store to become available after some quick renovations. Maybe she decided to tour the area during that time and wandered upon Hollow Creek."

"And once she was down there, she absorbed the magic," Thistle added. She was working this out in tandem with me. "Her mother was a well-known Salem witch. She told you that. Maybe there's real knowledge there and being exposed to magic — our magic — was enough to trigger some latent ability."

"What does that mean?" Connie interjected. "Is she more powerful than you?"

"Not by a long shot," I said. "If it is her, we can easily take her down. We just need to prove it's her."

"And the only way you can do that is to break into her home?" Earl didn't look thrilled at the prospect.

"It's the path of least resistance," Landon said, taking me by surprise. "I assume you have a plan to make sure she doesn't catch us."

"Us?"

"You're not going without me." He gripped my hand. "We're a team. When you break the law, I'm going along for the ride."

"My how the tables have turned."

"Don't get cute." He extended a warning finger and then leaned in to kiss me. "You have a plan."

I bobbed my head. "We're eating dinner here and waiting until dark. Then we're heading downtown. We're taking a small team ... that's just grown bigger by one."

"Who are we taking?" Landon was already plotting it out in his head.

"Thistle. Me. Scout. Gunner. Aunt Tillie. You."

"That's it?"

"We figure the smaller the team, the better."

"What about me?" Connie was petulant. "I want to go. I love the witch stuff."

I shook my head. "Not this time. I'm sorry. The stakes are too great."

"But ... ."

"No." Landon was firm. "You're better off here."

"Fine." Connie was morose. "I want to participate in something witchy before we leave. You've been warned."

"We'll figure out something," I promised. "You have my word." My eyes drifted to the door, and when I found my mother standing there my heart skipped. "How much did you hear?"

She shot me a dirty look. "I heard it all. I figured you guys were up to something when Scout and Aunt Tillie snuck out back with Evan. I'm not so old I didn't recognize him. It's only been a few weeks since I saw him last."

"We need him." I refused to apologize. "We thought it was best for him to remain outside of the inn, just in case."

"I don't care about that." She waved a hand and then grinned. "I thought you should know I was just upstairs checking on Clove."

"Is something wrong?" I was instantly alert. "I thought for sure that she would go into labor when the magical problem was solved in Hollow Creek."

"That's just it." Mom's eyes sparkled. "Her water broke. She is in labor. They're upstairs getting the room ready."

"Seriously? How soon?" I was already doing the math in my head.

"It's a first baby so there's no way to know for sure. But you have time. You can have dinner and carry out your plan. By the time you come back, if everything works out, we should have a victory to celebrate and a baby to welcome."

I didn't know what to say. "It's going to be quite the night."

"And a clear shot to the wedding," Mom added. "This is it, guys. Clove is going to have her baby and you're going to get the wedding you wanted. Everything is going to work out."

She didn't add that her assessment was contingent upon solving this final mystery.

"Dinner first." Mom insisted to the assembly. "I made a full turkey dinner because that's one of Landon's favorites." She hesitated and then continued. "And then I thought we would do prime rib tomorrow because that's one of your favorites."

Tears pricked the back of my eyes. "Thanks, Mom."

"Come on." She held out her arm. "We'll eat and then you can save the world. Again."

I laughed. "That sounds a little dramatic."

"We're Winchesters. That's what we do."

CHAPTER
Twenty-Seven

I stopped in to say goodbye to Clove, wishing her well and promising that we would be back to see the baby as soon as possible. She looked torn and I knew she wanted us to stay.

We took Landon's Explorer into town, Scout and Gunner taking their motorcycles. Evan said he would find his own way and handle the distraction when it was time. It was odd, but he almost seemed excited to be part of something. Scout noticed as well because she was grinning when we left.

Once parked, we headed into the police station to wait it out. We needed to be sure that Kristen wasn't inside before entering. That meant watching Evan work his magic.

It didn't take long. He appeared on the sidewalk and began to talk to himself. I couldn't hear what he was saying, but he looked animated. After a few minutes, Kristen appeared. She locked her store door as she left and approached him.

Landon's hands were on my back, and he rubbed, his eyes on the scene playing out through the window. After a few minutes, Kristen and Evan started down the sidewalk. The second they were out of view we left the police station.

Aunt Tillie used her magic to bring in a sudden storm. She could control the weather when she wanted — something I'd yet to master despite numerous attempts — and Thistle magically popped the lock on the door.

We were inside.

"Split up," I ordered, glancing around. "I doubt she's keeping anything good down here, but you know the best places to search. Then we'll head upstairs."

"What do you think Evan told Kristen to get her to go with him?" Landon asked as he followed me to the storage room behind the cash register.

"I don't know." The storage room was locked, and I had to use my magic to open it. Inside, the front shelves were full of trinkets and candles, items that would appeal to tourists. Farther back, she'd set up a small altar with a bevy of items spread upon it. This was clearly meant for her and not shoppers. "Bingo."

"In here," Landon called to the others. "What am I looking at?"

"Dark magic." I picked up the athame on the altar and studied the hilt, my lip inadvertently curling. "Bone." I handed it to Aunt Tillie as she joined us. Normally full of snark, she was quiet tonight. Perhaps news that Clove was officially in labor had her focusing more than usual.

Landon recoiled as Aunt Tillie studied the knife. "Animal bone?"

I shrugged. "I'm not a doctor."

"I think that's human bone," Gunner said. I hadn't realized he'd joined us. "May I?" He accepted the knife from Aunt Tillie and held it under the light. "I think this is a tibia."

"Meaning that's a human bone?" Landon had gone unusually pale. "Well, that's just great."

"It's gross is what it is," Thistle countered. "Only a truly dark witch would have that."

"Unless she doesn't know what it is," Scout said. "Isn't it possible she picked up the athame someplace not knowing what it was?"

I shrugged. "Anything is possible. If she's the one doing this, though, I have to think she knows what that thing is made of."

"Totally," Aunt Tillie agreed. She was busy perusing the other items on the altar. "These runes are bone, too." She pointed. "Not animal bone."

"Ugh." Landon made a disgusted sound deep in his throat. "Is it possible she didn't kill people to make these things? Could someone else have dug up a body and gotten the bone that way?"

I arched an eyebrow as I regarded him. "Does that make it better?"

"Slightly better than murder. What do we do?"

Something caught my eye on the shelf in the corner and I moved in that direction. The book I grabbed seemed to pulse in my hands and I wanted to drop it. Instead, I flipped it open. "Look at this."

Aunt Tillie popped up beside me. "That's bound in skin."

"If you tell me that's human skin, I'm out of here," Landon warned.

I knew that wasn't true. Nothing would drag him from my side until this was finished.

"I'm not sure what type of skin it is." Aunt Tillie held it up under the light, her eyes narrowed. "I don't think it's animal."

"Well, this is all kinds of disgusting." Landon refused to touch anything else in the room. "She's the one we're looking for, right?"

I hesitated and then nodded. "It would be a heckuva coincidence if she wasn't. We still don't know how she's controlling these shadow things."

"We also don't know how many she can call," Scout pointed out. "If she has an army at her disposal ... ." She didn't finish the statement.

"What do we know?" I prodded, changing course. "She has dark arts books. She has bone tools. She's from Salem. She has to be the 'she' Granger and Will were referring to. What's the end game here?"

"She's the only one who can tell us," Scout replied. She was grim as she regarded me. "Let me text Evan. He can lead her back around this way. We need to question her."

She was right, no matter how uncomfortable the idea of forcing Kristen into her storage room so we could interrogate her made me. I glanced at Landon to see what he thought.

"This is your show, Bay," he said. "You're the power here."

The words jolted me, reminding me of what the shadow woman had said in my dream days ago. "Maybe that's the problem." I was working it out in my head in real time as I spoke. "She made it sound as if she loved her mother, but there was a hint of bitterness when she was talking. She said that she came to the realization that her mother was never going to retire and that forced her move.

"What if she came here assuming there were no real witches?" I continued. "What if she thought she could be the lone real witch in a town full of fake witches? That would give her a level of power that might appeal to somebody who thrives on being in control."

Landon shook his head. "Mrs. Little brought her in. She knows that you guys have real magic. She doesn't want to acknowledge it, but she knows. She would've told Kristen, especially because she thinks Kristen will be able to take you down."

"Let's look up her mother," Thistle suggested, retrieving her phone from her pocket. Her forehead creased when she pulled up a search window. "Wait ... there's no service in here." She glanced around.

"Is it a dead zone?" Landon pulled out his phone. "It's not even reading dead networks." The color drained from his face. "It's like when we were trapped in the newspaper office earlier."

"It's a spell of some kind," I surmised. "She knew how to cast it because that's how she protected her altar room."

"If we're not getting service, Kristen could be on her way back," Scout noted, striding toward the front of the store. "Evan could be texting to warn us." She made it to the door before a figure appeared in the opening in front of her. Taken aback, Scout stopped walking. It was already too late.

"I believe you're in my space." Kristen, her eyes black, planted her hands on Scout's chest and jolted her with a bolt of magic powerful enough the Spells Angels witch was thrown across the room.

Gunner was faster than a normal human thanks to his shifter blood and his reflexes were topnotch. He flew to the left and used his body to cushion the blow for Scout, his shoulders hitting one of the other shelves hard enough that the metal contraption rocked backward. He managed to keep Scout from absorbing the blow, even though he looked as if he was rocked with pain.

"What are you doing in my shop?" Kristen demanded, her eyes bouncing around the room. "I could have you all arrested for this." When she focused on Landon, hatred kindled. "Of course, since there's an FBI agent involved, that seems unlikely."

Landon was calm as he faced off with her. "I have a few questions."

Her laughter was high-pitched and deranged. "Of course, you do. But I don't have to share answers." She slammed her hand into a shelf. "This is my space!"

I had to wonder if I'd spent more time with her that first day, would I have figured out what she was sooner. All I remembered from that initial interview was that she didn't feel magical. There was only one explanation.

"You shrouded yourself," I said, drawing her attention. Aunt Tillie, behind me, remained silent. "That day I interviewed you, you shrouded yourself so I couldn't see what you really were."

Kristen nodded, amused. "Yes, and it was quite the magic suck. I don't think you realize how powerful you are. Margaret told me there were real witches in town, but the way she described you was ... lacking."

"Mrs. Little doesn't understand real magic. She's incapable of telling the truth on top of everything else. It's really your fault for falling for what she was offering."

"I didn't fall for it," Kristen clarified. "I was intrigued by what she had to offer, but no witch worth anything would move into an area without checking out the competition. I've been watching you for weeks."

"What have you found?" I was simply buying time.

"This one thinks she's the power." She pointed at Aunt Tillie. "Unfortunately, she uses her skills to play pranks on Margaret instead of building a power base. So disappointing."

She turned her attention to Thistle. "This one cares more about creating pretty paintings and statues. She's only tangentially interested in magic. She wants to serve as a second to you, but her heart lies elsewhere."

She turned to Scout. "That one I can't get a read on. She's different. She's been in town several times since I arrived. I can sense her when she gets close ... and there's a tremor in her power, but there's ... something ... standing in my way. She's the reason I knew you were in here. The vampire you sent to distract me has the same tremor. He got it from her."

Kristen's eyes glowed when they flicked back to me. "Did you really think I wouldn't recognize the vampire?"

Fear for Evan reared up and punched me in the heart. "What did you do to him?"

"I caught him by surprise and knocked him out. I couldn't waste time — or energy — doing anything more permanent. I knew I had to get back here before you found my inner sanctum. Apparently, you worked faster than I anticipated."

"We enjoy surpassing expectations," I said. "You haven't finished," I prodded. "You said you've been watching us. What did you find?"

"Your mother and her sisters have magic but rarely use it," she replied. "They're happiest serving food and working in their gardens. They're not a threat."

"Take them on and you'll find out exactly how wrong you are."

She snorted. "You all talk big. Very few of you can actually follow through."

"Try me," Aunt Tillie snapped, speaking for the first time. She was agitated ... even more than normal, which left me with a dull worry in my stomach.

Kristen never moved her gaze from me. "You, however, control the flow of magic from your family. You're not well trained — I blame those who came before you — and everything you do is on an instinctive level. While you're powerful, you're not skilled."

"I guess we'll have to see." I stepped closer to her, increasing the distance between Landon and me but not getting so close that she could unleash the same magic on me that she had on Scout. "What's the plan?" I demanded. "Why have you done this? What did you hope to accomplish?"

Kristen turned the picture of innocence. "I'm just a woman trying to make a living in a tourist town. You're the ones who invaded my space. I'm well within my rights to kill you all. I'll start with you, Bay."

"Don't threaten her," Landon growled. "Don't you even think of raising your hands to her."

It was only then that I realized he'd leveled his gun on her.

"You can't shoot an unarmed woman," Kristen said. She didn't look worried. There was something we were missing. "You'll lose your badge if you do, perhaps even go to prison. Is that what you want?"

"I'll do whatever it takes to protect this family," Landon responded. "When you love something with your whole heart, you'll find you're willing to make certain sacrifices."

I did not want him making that sacrifice. I had to change the conversation again.

"Tell me," I insisted. "Why did you go after Granger Montgomery?"

"Why not?" A small smile curved the corners of Kristen's mouth. "I had to test you. I met the boy the day before. He helped me drop brochures at businesses around town for fifty bucks. It wasn't difficult to plant the idea in his head.

"You were outside my shop the day before. I felt the power radiating off you," she continued. "Up close you were even more interesting. I wanted to know how you would react ... so I tested you."

I felt sick to my stomach. I was the reason for all of this. "How did the spell jump from Granger to Will Compton?" I had to know everything before I ended her. I would never be able to sleep otherwise.

"That's just a little something I added to the mix." She looked far too pleased with herself. "I wanted to make sure that you felt my presence ... even if you didn't realize what it was."

"What did you get from it? Did you get some sort of perverse thrill from forcing a man to take his life?"

"A weak man," she corrected. "Only the weak can fall for that spell. That's why Granger was susceptible ... and Will ... and Marlon on the highway. All it took was one suggestion after he'd been in my store five minutes. The weak don't deserve to survive."

I wanted to kill her. "And the shadows? What was behind them?"

She let loose a haphazard wave. "They were simply tests. I wanted to see how you would react. Unfortunately, they were nowhere near as effective as I'd hoped. I've done a great deal of thinking since you so easily dispatched the one in your office. Sending lone shadows was the mistake. That's why I've built an army."

"Well, you're not going to get to use it." I was done with her. "This ends here."

"You're not in control." Kristen's voice ratcheted up a notch. "In fact, you're nothing. You don't get a say in how this plays out."

"Yes, I do." I squared my shoulders. "You said I was the power here. I think Scout, had you not sucker punched her, might have a little something to say about that. This is done."

"Oh, it's just the beginning."

"No." I shook my head. "We're not letting you unleash that army. Whatever your motivations, it doesn't matter. Whatever you hope to accomplish, it's not going to happen. You are finished."

She laughed so hard I thought she might choke. "You still don't get it, do you?" Her eyes were glassy when she recovered. "You don't understand what's happening. That magical potluck you served up at Hollow Creek was a delight. You managed to create a magical nexus with remnants of leftover power. Do you know how rare that is?"

"The problem at Hollow Creek has been rectified. That power is gone."

"Yes," Kristen agreed. "I was counting on that magic to recharge myself after building my army. When I went out there this afternoon it was gone. All of it."

"Bummer for you."

"Maybe, but if you managed to do it once, you can do it again." Her eyes narrowed. "I need that nexus, Bay. You're going to give it to me or you're going to die."

"Yeah, I think you should count again. You're woefully outnumbered."

"I still have enough magic to end all of you."

I didn't believe her. "No, this is finished. You don't have a move to make here."

"Perhaps I would believe that if I was alone." Her smile grew wider as my heart began to thud.

I gripped my hands into fists at my sides. "What do you mean?"

"Just this." She leaned close her eyes lit with mayhem. "Only an idiot would come into a situation like this without backup. Even now, my backup is maneuvering your family into giving us everything we'll ever want or need to rule this town.

"You've been so focused on your petty family problems — babies, weddings, personal crap that nobody cares about — that you haven't seen what's happening under your very roof," she continued. "There is no stopping this."

I opened my mouth to argue with her, perhaps threaten her, but it was already too late.

"We'll just see about that," Scout gritted out. She was back on her feet, pale but determined when she slapped her hands to either side of Kristen's head. "Show me what you've got, you horrible witch."

Kristen slapped at Scout's hands, but she didn't have the power to fight her off. "How ... ? You were down. That blast would've leveled any other witch."

"I'm not just a witch." Scout's eyes were serial killer black as she pushed her face an inch from Kristen's desperate stare. "Show me."

The room pulsed with magic, and I rocked back on my heels. Kristen's eyes went wide as Scout dug inside her brain. It only took seconds — although they seemed to drag on for years — and then Kristen's skin went black. Scout flooded her with so much magic that she turned the color of death before she began flaking away. By the time Scout dropped her hands, there was nothing but a pile of ash on the ground. The witch who had been here only seconds before was gone.

"We have a problem," Scout announced as she turned.

"You just solved the problem ... and in terrifying fashion," Landon said. "That was frightening."

"She pissed me off." Scout was grim as she snagged my gaze. "She's working with someone. I saw inside her head. There's an army of shadows surrounding the inn."

My stomach threatened to revolt. "Clove."

"They want her baby to feed on. They think they can create another nexus with it."

"Who is they?" Thistle snapped. "Who else is involved with this?"

"The midwife," Scout replied. "She's not what she appears."

Aunt Tillie pumped her fist and let loose a triumphant howl. "I knew it! I told you she was the devil."

I pinned her with a dark look. "Yes, you know all and see all. That doesn't change the fact that she's with Clove and there's an army of magical shadows standing between us and our family."

Aunt Tillie sobered. "Yes, but I was right. That's the most important thing."

"We have to get back to the inn." Landon was grave. "We'll hash out a plan on the way."

That was easier said than done, but he was right. The fight was here.

CHAPTER
Twenty-Eight

The drive back to The Overlook was tense, and when Landon pulled to the side of the road before reaching the parking lot I was frustrated.

"What are you doing?"

"Look, Bay." His voice was soft.

I pushed through my agitation and focused on the inn, my breath clogging in my throat when I realized what had caused him to pull over before we'd reached the finish line.

"Holy ... ." Thistle was breathless in the back seat and her eyes were wide when she leaned between Landon and me. "Is that ...?"

I nodded, swallowing hard. It was an army of shadow creatures. There had to be at least a hundred of them. They'd formed a wall around the inn, trapping us outside, and the rest of our family inside.

"What do we do?" Landon was beside himself.

I pressed the heel of my hand to my forehead, my heart hammering so hard I thought it might pound through my ribcage.

Landon must've read the panic on my face because he started rummaging in his pocket. "Let's call inside, make sure they're okay."

"They're fine," Aunt Tillie replied, determination in her eyes. "We need to get past those shadows. The wards on the inn won't let them cross over."

"Even if somebody is hurt inside?" Landon's question had my heart pinging.

"Even if," Aunt Tillie confirmed, her eyes gliding to me. "Maybe we should call Stormy."

"We don't have time to wait." A plan had started forming. "The shadows might not be able to get into the inn, but Minerva is there. We have no idea what's happening, or if anyone even realizes that Minerva is evil."

"That's why we call," Landon insisted.

"And then what? My mom and aunts have magic, but if Minerva is super-charged thanks to Hollow Creek, they won't stand a chance."

"And that won't stop them from sacrificing their lives to protect Clove," Thistle said gravely. "Bay's right. We need to get into that house."

"How?" Landon threw open the door of the Explorer and climbed out, his face red with frustration.

I followed him, forcing myself to remain calm. "I have an idea."

"Of course, you do." His eyes were searching when they found mine over the hood of the vehicle. "You're not going to die doing this?"

"That's not the plan."

"Make sure you don't die on me, Bay." He looked pained, as if tears were close. "I can take a lot in this world, but losing you isn't on that list."

"I have no interest in dying," I reassured him. "I want to save my family."

"How do we do that?" Scout asked. She and Gunner had pulled over behind us. "I can kill them but only one at a time ... maybe a handful at once if I get lucky. I'll be swarmed before I can get near the building."

"I might be able to fight them too," Gunner offered. "I can shift and hope for the best. I just don't know what I can do against them." His expression was almost apologetic. "We can call for backup from Hawthorne Hollow but ... ." He held up his hands, helpless.

"They might not get here in time," I finished for him. "Even if they do, we still might not have enough firepower. That won't work."

"You have a plan, though," Thistle insisted. "I can see it."

I flicked my eyes back to the shadows. "I have a big freaking plan."

"Well, don't keep us in suspense." Landon planted his hands on his narrow hips. "Tell us what it is so we can help."

"They have an army. We need one."

"Where are you going to get an army?"

"She's going to summon one," Aunt Tillie replied, her eyes on me. She knew. "She's a necromancer. She's powerful enough to call every ghost in the state here if she needs to."

Hope flared in Landon's eyes. "Will that work?"

"I certainly hope so," I said. "It's our only option."

Landon flexed his hands and glanced over his shoulder. I could almost read his intent.

"You can't shoot them," I reminded him. "You can't challenge them to a fistfight. We need a magical solution."

He nodded in understanding. "Then do your worst, Bay." Blue eyes, the color of the sky after the sun pokes out between turbulent storm clouds, searched my face. "Kick that witch's ass."

That was enough to earn a legitimate smile. "And then, when we're done, we'll have a baby to spoil and a wedding to look forward to."

He strode the two steps to me, capturing my chin with his hands. "I want you to be my wife more than anything." The kiss he gave me was hot. When he pulled back, he was fierce. "Do it, baby."

I could feel their eyes around me as I strolled away from the Explorer. The shadows registered my presence as I walked along the driveway, shifting in unison. They didn't speak. They simple rippled with energy ... and waited.

"I don't know if you can hear me, Minerva," I said. "Kristen is dead. We know what you're doing, what you have planned. We're coming for you."

There was no response, but I was almost positive the shadows briefly glowed brighter, as if Minerva was somewhere inside laughing at us.

"*Venio.*" My voice was low and yet it somehow reverberated through the air around me, magic coalescing.

If the shadows could talk, I had no doubt they would be whispering now. Instead, they simply waited for me to make a move.

"What's going on?" Viola demanded as she popped into existence at my side. She looked annoyed. "I thought we talked about you asking when you need help."

"There's no time." I was grim as I focused on the shadows. At least twenty ghosts had appeared, most I didn't know. They floated across the lawn, waiting for me to issue orders. "We need to get through that wall."

Viola followed my gaze. If ghosts could gulp, that would've been her response. Instead, her eyes went wide. "Oh, that's not good."

"Definitely not," I agreed, raising my hands in the air. I felt something sparking at the tips. "*Venio*," I intoned, grim satisfaction rolling through me when I felt more ghosts pop into existence.

I pulled on my magic harder, the wind beginning to whip around me. Something felt hot, as if the sun had decided to peek out from behind a cloud on a steaming summer day. When I glanced up at my hands, I realized the heat was coming from me. I was glowing.

"Bay," Landon whispered behind me. "Oh, geez."

I didn't look away from the shadows. This time when I let loose my magic, it felt like a tidal wave being released. "*Venio*." I didn't scream it and yet the single word boomed across the property. The echo was met with hundreds of glittery souls arriving to do my bidding.

"You did it, Bay," a familiar voice said.

Uncle Calvin, Aunt Tillie's late husband, glowed bright blue as he smiled at me. I'd never met him in life, but he'd visited me several times in death. Now, he was here, a fierce fighter from the other side. It seemed fitting that he would be present.

"Give the order, Bay," a female ghost said. I found my grandmother taking in the scene with a trained eye. She didn't question why she'd been called, instead preparing for battle. She looked fierce. "You can't wait."

"*Destructo*," I ordered, power rolling through me as the ghosts took off on a tear toward the shadows. It reminded me of a movie, I realized in a detached way. It was like the scene in *Return of the King* when

Aragorn arrived with the army of the dead. Just like in the movie, my army shredded the shadows within seconds. They were strong. They knew their mission. And they'd opened a path to the inn.

I didn't call to the others. I put my head down and began to run. Their footsteps echoed behind me, but I didn't look back. We had to get to Clove.

The front door was locked, magic holding it in place, but I wouldn't be denied.

"*Fragor.*" The door blew off the hinges and I strode into the inn. I wasn't afraid to flex my magic. Not this day.

Inside, my mother and aunts sat on the floor, their backs to the front desk. They were magically tethered, fighting their restraints. The look of relief on my mother's face turned to wonder as she took in my wild appearance.

"You really do look like a superhero," she said breathlessly.

"Or a magical serial killer," Twila offered.

"Untie them," I ordered Thistle as I headed for the stairs. Clove was on the second floor. I had to get to her.

"No way." Thistle was determined as she gave chase. "Just because you look like you're about to go nuclear doesn't mean I'm not going to help."

I didn't argue.

The door to Clove's bedroom was open. I heard her panting — and crying. I swaggered through the open door.

"Bay," Sam cried out in relief when he saw me. He was sweaty, his cheeks wet with tears, but he was holding strong as he perched at Clove's side. "Thank the Goddess."

I didn't acknowledge him, my eyes landing on Minerva. She pressed the knife in her hand to Chief Terry's throat as she cowered in the corner like the coward I knew she was.

"Do something," Clove demanded. Her face was so red I thought she might pass out. "The baby is almost here."

"I've got her," Thistle said, hurrying to our cousin's side. "You ... do whatever that glowing magic wants you to do. I'm thinking killing her is our best bet, but I don't want to be presumptuous."

Under different circumstances, I would've laughed. I took an ominous step in Minerva's direction. "Let him go," I ordered.

"No." Defiant, Minerva shook her head. "I didn't plan for this as long as I did, work to position myself exactly, for things to end before I get my prize." She sounded deranged.

"That baby isn't your prize. That baby is our prize. You're not part of this."

"I've earned this," Minerva hissed. "I've spent years doing the bidding of others, having my position in the coven questioned because I had so little magic at my fingertips. This place changed things for me. I knew it would."

"Hollow Creek has been cleansed," I replied. "Kristen is dead. Your shadows are gone. There's no well to replenish your stolen magic. There's nothing here for you."

"That baby will replenish it," Minerva insisted. "That baby will elevate me to the next level."

"That baby is already out of your reach." I held out my hands to either side and wasn't surprised when Uncle Calvin and Grandma, the ghosts most strongly tethered to me, appeared.

"Kill her, Bay," Chief Terry ordered. He looked more annoyed than anything, as if he was furious to have been caught off guard. "She's been torturing Clove for the past hour, telling her what she's going to do with her baby."

"She said she was going to kill me after," Clove said through tears. "Why are you glowing, by the way? It's freaky. If you're going to glow like that, you should at least be wearing a superhero outfit. Like … don't you want to dress like Wonder Woman?"

I couldn't think of anything worse. "Minerva, I'm tired." I meant it. "You've been playing games for days. Kristen has been watching us for weeks, plotting. None of that is coming to fruition. Do you want to know why?"

"No," Minerva barked.

"We're better than you." I waved my hands, releasing Uncle Calvin and Grandma from their magical restraints. They moved fast, descending on Minerva as if they were predators and she was their evening meal. "Our family is more powerful than you could ever imagine. Enjoy your fate."

I moved in fast as Uncle Calvin grabbed Minerva around the throat, causing the midwife to gasp and jerk back the knife. I used my magic to force her hand out wide and waited for Chief Terry to scramble away.

"I'm sick of people trying to take what isn't theirs," I said as I pressed my hand to Minerva's chest. Uncle Calvin and Grandma were on either side of her, holding her. "It's time to send a message." I leaned close. "Go with the Goddess ... and don't come back."

I sent a bolt of magic through her, watching with grim satisfaction as her eyes rolled back in her head. She went limp almost immediately, her knees buckling. Then she hit the ground so hard her head bounced.

The glow extinguished the second she was no longer a threat, and when I turned to Clove, I had to suck in a breath before absorbing the scene. She was red-faced, tearful ... and pushing. "Oh, man." The power from seconds before was long gone. "Now?"

"I can't help it." Clove was crying so hard she couldn't catch her breath. "It has to be now."

"Minerva gave her something to hurry the labor," Sam explained as he crawled on the bed to hold Clove's hand. He looked desperate. "She knew you would figure it out but thought she could get away before you did."

"That's so Minerva," I muttered as I crawled onto the bed behind Clove and positioned myself behind her shoulders. "Okay. Go ahead and push."

"I am pushing!" Clove was so sweaty it felt like she'd just gotten out of the bath. "Somebody help me."

I offered a blank stare.

"Down there!" Clove gestured to the spot between her legs.

She had to be joking. I looked to Thistle. She was also on the bed but nowhere close to a helpful position.

As if reading my mind, Thistle started shaking her head. "That is not happening!"

"I'm already up here." I used my most pragmatic tone. "It's easier for you to help down there."

"What did I just say!"

"Get down there, Thistle," I barked. "That baby is coming and you need to catch it."

"Why can't you catch it? Why does it have to be me?"

"You don't catch the baby," Clove wailed. "You have to gently help her out."

I ignored her. "I called hundreds of dead ghosts to my side and waged war on our enemy," I reminded her. "You just followed behind offering snarky comments. It's your turn to do something."

"I'm not doing this. I'll do whatever you're doing — which looks like nothing, by the way — and you catch the baby."

"No. I've been through enough for one day." I paused, something insidious taking over. "Consider it my wedding present."

"Oh, I hate you." Thistle kneeled between Clove's legs. Her mouth dropped open. "Is that the head?"

"Yes." Grandma's ghost was still present. She didn't look bothered in the least by what was about to happen. "Get in there, Thistle. Put your hands right under the head and help. Then we just need one more big push, Clove."

"Why can I see you?" Clove demanded.

"It's a long story," I growled. "As for why you can see her, have you forgotten that you can hear ghosts when you're near me? It's part of our bond."

"This is different," Clove snapped. "This is my dead grandmother looking at my ... you know."

"We all know," Chef Terry complained. He was still in the room but refused to look. His eyes were trained on the ceiling. "Clove, you're stronger than you think. You're about to be a mother. This is your moment."

It was the perfect thing to say and reminded me of one unassailable truth: I had a father, but Chief Terry was my dad. He'd been my dad for so long I took him for granted sometimes. Even now, when he would rather be anywhere else, he was here with us.

Tears flooded my eyes. "Push, Clove," I ordered. "End our torment."

The growl Clove let loose was unearthly. She sounded like a horror movie monster, screaming as she gave in and did the only thing she could do.

"I've got it," Thistle said, slowly pulling her hands from between Clove's legs. "I've got it." She looked to me, a tiny baby covered in ... things best left not mentioned in her hands, bewildered disbelief clouding her eyes. "Now what do I do?"

"Clear the airway." Mom appeared in the room, her eyes fierce. She took one look at Minerva's unconscious form on the floor and stepped over her to join us. "Is she dead?"

"No." I shook my head. "I figured we'd deal with that later."

"Oh, we're going to deal with it. And it's going to be ugly." Mom took the baby from Thistle and grinned at the small form, her smile faltering as she looked the infant over from the tip of her dark head to her toes. "Is that ...?"

"Willy Wonka?" Thistle asked. "Yeah, I thought I was seeing things too."

I was confused. "What's wrong?" We couldn't have gone through all of this for something to be wrong with the baby.

"Nothing." Mom said briskly as she shifted the baby toward Clove. "It's just ... we have a boy." She beamed at Clove, who looked dumbfounded.

"What?" Clove rested the baby on her chest, her hand cupping the shock of dark hair on the baby's head. Sure enough, when I got a better look, there was definitely a little something between the baby's legs that none of us were expecting.

"But ... how?" I turned my questioning gaze to my mother.

She shrugged. "Nothing in this world is set in stone. The witch in Sam's blood probably had a little something to do with it. It doesn't matter." She grinned at Clove. "He's a boy ... and he's healthy." She leaned in and kissed Clove's forehead. "Good job, mom."

Clove worked her jaw, glancing between Sam, Mom and Thistle. Finally, she focused on me. "Is this some sort of punishment? I wanted a girl. Nothing ever goes right for me. I mean ... nothing."

I stared at her and then burst out laughing. "Never change, Clove." I sagged against the pillows and met Landon's curious gaze as he appeared in the doorway. He looked a little rough around the edges, but he was whole and on his feet. "Well, this has been a busy day, huh?"

Landon grinned and inclined his head toward the baby. "Do you want to take some cake home and hide away until the wedding with me?"

That was the best offer I'd had all day.

CHAPTER
Twenty-Nine

I was nervous.

Studying myself in the full-length mirror in the upstairs bedroom Clove had given birth in, taking in my strapless wedding gown with the simple lines, I thought I might pass out.

"Oh, don't even." Thistle strode into the room, her lavender hair matching the straps of her bridesmaid dress. She looked the purple picture of innocence. Anyone who knew her would realize how funny that was. "You can't melt down now. You've held it together for weeks. If you fall apart now, I'll never let you forget it."

Her words had the desired effect. "Thanks for that. I guess."

She grinned. "Are you ready?"

Was I? "Is everybody here?" I moved to the window and looked down. The backyard had been turned into a wedding wonderland. Decorated folding chairs littered the lawn and somebody had erected a beautiful lily arch. "Where did that come from?" I was dumbfounded.

Thistle, who had joined me at the window, shrugged. "You can't get married without an arch. It's illegal."

Of course, it was her. She was the most creative of all of us. I thought back to what Kristen had said. It was true. Thistle didn't mind using her magic. At her core, though, she liked creating things. "You're next, right?" I shot her a grin when she scowled. "You can't be the only one of us not married. People will laugh and point."

She didn't bother to hide her eye roll. "Let's get you married and worry about me later. If we don't get you through this day without some sort of major catastrophe, Landon will turn into a huge baby."

"He just wants me to be the center of attention. I think he's afraid that Clove and the baby will overshadow me."

"That's not going to happen," Clove countered as she walked into the room, her son — we still didn't know how a family that only offered up female heirs had managed to break the cycle — clutched in her arms. "Sam will stay inside with him. He wants to see the wedding but if the ceremony is interrupted by a screaming baby Landon will melt down."

I made a face. "Stop giving Landon grief. He can't help himself." I ran my hand over the baby's soft head. His hair felt like strands of silk. Calvin Samuel Cornell, named after the great-uncle who crossed over despite the bonds of death, and his very brave father. The name seemed fitting. "How are you feeling?" I asked Clove.

"I'm sore." Clove smiled despite the admission. "Babies hurt. They totally lied about that bat thing, and I'll never get over it."

"At least you didn't crap in front of everyone," Thistle noted. "That's something."

Clove nodded. "Right? Between being threatened by a crazy midwife and Chief Terry seeing my hoo-ha, that would've been the final straw."

"The Goddess never gives more than we can take," I teased as she moved the baby to his bassinet.

"Are you ready?" Thistle asked. "The guys are down in front of the arch." She gestured through the window. "Landon doesn't look half bad in his monkey suit."

"I'm ready." And saying it in the midst of my cousins, it was true. The nerves were still there, right below the surface, but I'd never wanted anything more.

Thistle had to help me with my dress train because Clove couldn't bend over. I expected that to become a thing at the reception, but they were determined not to fight before the ceremony. When we arrived at the back door, my father was waiting for me. My heart stopped when I saw his expectant face.

"What ...?" I stopped myself. I could not make a big deal over this. It would ruin the ceremony for everybody.

"I'm here to walk you halfway down the aisle," Dad said, his grin as wide as ever. "I thought this was the plan."

I was beyond confused. "But ... halfway?"

"Yeah, then I hand you over to Terry." He didn't look bothered by the thought of doing that.

"But ... ." Tears pricked the back of my eyes as I darted a look down the aisle. Sure enough, Chief Terry stood halfway down waiting for me, his hands clasped. He looked happy. I glanced at Thistle, unsure.

"I believe Landon did some last-second arranging this morning," she whispered, grinning. "He said you were getting everything you wanted no matter what."

I nodded, tucking my arm through my father's waiting crook. I knew if I said anything I would cry.

"We should get going." Thistle craned her neck and looked around. "Where is Aunt Tillie? She's the flower witch."

Clove pointed to the start of the walkway, where Aunt Tillie appeared. We'd bought her a lovely, matronly lavender dress. She'd ... modified it, for lack of a better term. The staid skirt had been replaced with shiny silver leggings. A light purple tutu was bunched at her waist. I didn't even know what to say about the top, which was cut so low it was obvious she wasn't wearing a bra.

"They're cracking open the wine on the bluff tonight," Thistle volunteered. "I guess she's getting ready early."

I sighed. There really was no point in fighting the outfit. "Let's go." I shot Aunt Tillie an enthusiastic thumbs-up.

The music started; Aunt Tillie used magic as she tossed out the flower petals. She whipped the wind so much that the petals started making noise when slapping people in the face. It was hardly a serene environment.

"I've got this," a soft voice said from my left. Grandma Ginger, who had somehow found a lovely dress on the other side, dampened Aunt Tillie's magic with raised hands and a soft smile. Dad didn't look at her, so I knew only the witches I was closest with could see her.

"Thank you," I whispered.

"You're welcome."

"Did you say something?" Dad asked, glancing around.

I shook my head. "I'm ready."

Clove was first down the aisle. It took her longer than it would've under normal circumstances — she really was sore — and Thistle went next. I held my breath as Dad marched me down the aisle, briefly wondering if there would be trouble during the handoff. Instead, he shook hands with Chief Terry and kissed me on my cheek before taking his seat in the audience.

My hand shook as it landed on Chief Terry's forearm.

"I don't think there's ever been a prettier bride," he said as we started down the aisle.

I burst into tears. I'd promised myself I wouldn't cry — Thistle would never let me hear the end of it — but I couldn't stop myself. Monsters I could take. Evil witches I could overcome. Everything coming together exactly as I wanted it was somehow too much to bear.

"Oh, sweetheart, don't cry," he whispered as he helped me down the aisle. "Everything is going to be okay."

"Everything is perfect," I wheezed.

He smirked. "You've earned it." He flicked his eyes to Landon, who looked concerned. "You've even earned that pain in the ass you're hitching your wagon to. He loves you more than anything."

"I love him too." I was a blubbering mess.

"I know. I can't imagine ever wanting to give you away, Bay, but the fact that you're going to him ... well ... it makes it okay. I won't ever doubt how much he loves you."

The coven priestess leading the ceremony smiled as I reached my final destination. She seemed amused when she instructed Landon and me to join hands. We'd gone for a hybrid ceremony, something to placate both of our families. The fact that I couldn't stop crying when the unification rope was woven around our joined hands left Landon looking pained.

"You are killing me," he muttered.

"You gave me Chief Terry as a wedding gift," I sobbed.

"Your wedding gift is back at the guesthouse. We'll exchange those later. I gave you Terry because if I can't give you a happy day now, I don't deserve you."

That was the most ludicrous thing I'd ever heard. "Maybe I don't deserve you."

"Oh, geez." He swiped at my tears, his gaze earnest. "I love you, Bay. More than anything. But if you don't stop crying, you'll give me a complex."

I did my best. The priestess talked about magical bonds, souls colliding, and I felt to my core she was talking about us. When it came time to recite our vows, I went first. For a moment, I couldn't find my voice. Then I looked into Landon's eyes, and everything came into focus.

"Sometimes in life things work out exactly how they're supposed to," I started. I'd written vows but I no longer needed them. I knew exactly what I wanted to say. "When I first met you, I felt this pull I couldn't explain. Sure, you were undercover and giving me grief, but I felt something so deep in my soul that it caused my entire being to shift.

"I never believed that one person could complete another until I met you," I continued. "It's not about arranging my life around you. It's about coming home ... and you are my home. Every breath I take, I think of you. Every night when I go to sleep, I thank the Goddess for bringing you into my life.

"I can't imagine going a single day without seeing you. You are my heart ... and soul ... and my forever." I took the wedding band Thistle handed me and slid it onto his finger. "With this ring, I thee wed."

He was silent so long I thought something must've happened. When I found the courage to look up, he was blinking back tears.

"You can't cry," I said. My tears had mostly dried. "They'll give you grief about it forever. Aunt Tillie will make fun of you."

"I will," Aunt Tillie agreed, making a big show of throwing a handful of flower petals in his face. "Don't embarrass me in front of all these witches. I'll make you pay until the end times."

Landon managed a wobbly laugh. After a deep breath, he focused on me. "I don't know where to start," he said. "I thought I knew what I was going to say today, but nothing feels good enough. You're the best person I know, and I want everything to be perfect for you, but there are no perfect words. So, here goes."

He exhaled slowly. "We've talked about hearts connecting a few times, usually when we're alone and there's cake."

I laughed, as I'm sure he intended.

"I feel that to my very bones," he said. "You're part of me. When I breathe, I'm with you. When I sleep, I'm with you. When I cry, I'm with you. When I laugh, I'm definitely with you. You're the last thing I think about before I fall asleep and the first thing I think about when I wake. I'm going to love you like you deserve to be loved, every single day, and beyond.

"I used to think love was limited," he continued. "I thought it was finite ... but I love you more than I loved you yesterday and that shouldn't be possible. I'll love you more tomorrow." He lifted the hand that wasn't joined to mine and brushed my cheek. "My love is forever. When we take our last breaths on this earth, we'll go to another place and love each other just as much there. You, Bay Winchester, are my reason for being.

"There is no me without you any longer. We're going to be together in this life and the next. I want to be a better man for you. I want to be the strongest person I can be, and that's only because I have the strongest woman in the world beside me.

"I want to hear you laugh. I want to see your smile every morning. I'm even willing to put up with Aunt Tillie to make sure that you're never unhappy."

"You're on my list," Aunt Tillie warned, earning an appreciative laugh from the crowd. She bowed to her audience upon realizing she was a hit, which earned her more laughs.

"This is just the beginning," Landon said as he accepted my ring from his brother. "With this ring, I thee wed."

The priestess talked about unbreakable unions as she blessed the rope. She talked about family and strength. I didn't hear any of it. All I could hear was the beating of Landon's heart as my fingers rested on his chest.

Then we were at the end, and she gave him the all clear to kiss me. He wrapped his arms around me, more bravado than was necessary on display as he dipped me low. "Here comes forever," he whispered right before kissing me.

"I now pronounce you forever bound," the priestess declared. "What love has united, no man, woman, witch, warlock or monster will be able to tear asunder."

We'd made it. We got the wedding of our dreams. Now it was time to embrace forever.

Printed in Great Britain
by Amazon